SOULFUL

Return

FIDELIS O. MKPARU

DX VAROS PUBLISHING

Published by:
D. X. Varos, Ltd
7665 E. Eastman Ave. #B101
Denver, CO 80231

Book cover design and layout by Ellie Bockert Augsburger, Creative Digital Studios
www.creativedigitalstudios.com
using original cover art by Rosie Smith

ISBN: 978-1-955065-60-3 (paperback)
ISBN: 978-1-955065-61-0 (ebook)

Soulful Return is a novel inspired by my experiences. It's partly a literary mystical journey made possible by my deep appreciation of my Igbo heritage. None of my wonderful life experiences would have been possible without my late parents, Dennis and Virginia Mkparu, diligence and nurturing during the early years of my life. To them I owe everything that I am.

When you realize that the attractions of a foreign
    land, however grand,
Are nothing compared to the homeliness of your
    own native land,
When you realize that in spite of all the problems
    here that we face,
Surprisingly, our motherland still never loses its
    charm and grace,
You can be sure you have returned to where you
    belong.

Sanath Kumar
from *Return to your Homeland*

CHAPTER 1

The hounding voice inside me would not let go. The sun gleamed overhead, my shadow barely noticeable as it followed me down a narrow concrete path carved into a manicured green lawn by the banks of the Charles River. I sat at the Boston edge, watching the boating events. That demanding voice ordered me to roll up my pants, take off my shoes and socks, and dip my naked feet into the water. Curious eyes on both sides of the river observed me as I removed my suit jacket and loosened my tie. My feet felt as heavy as lead blocks, and as hard as I tried I couldn't muster the strength to lift them from the water.

Ignoring all the eyes peering at me, I relished the sensation of the water cleansing my feet. I watched as waves cascaded up my ankles and bobbed to a rhythm like drumbeats, the ceremonial drumbeats of my ancestral home, the type that made dancing feet float in the air and twirling waists reach their breaking point. These drums raged inside my head for only me to hear, sounds I had missed in the four decades since leaving home for my university education.

As time passed along the river's edge, I lost all desire to refute what I was feeling and hearing. Accepting the wondrous, inexplicable presence of these drumbeats, I let my ears savor them as they tickled the tranquil air around me, intoxicating my body with their resounding tempo. Surrendering to their rhythm, I took off my shirt and waved my hands through the air, my head bobbing.

The intensity of the drumbeats increased, and the number of waves splashing onto my feet doubled. Snared by the wonderment of the drums, I turned around and was surprised to see an ice cream truck with mounted speakers moving against the downtown skyline. I shook my head to free myself of the illusion. This was Boston. Not the place that the hounding voice wanted me to believe I had crashed into: my ancestral home six thousand miles away.

Something always drew me to the banks of the Charles River. This was where I had fallen in love, gazing at the sparkling eyes of my wife, Elisha. When she accepted me unconditionally, I celebrated the end of my loneliness in a foreign land by throwing pebbles to bounce on the water's surface, the way I used to do as a child in my homeland, to impress her.

By the same riverbanks I had mourned the death of my parents. When the burden of losing them made me weak, the river washed away my tears.

Today, yearning for my homeland had brought me back to the river in search of relief, but the sights and sounds around me made me miss home even more. The river that had once brought solace to my life now pulled me in a new direction, leaving an empty longing for the grasslands of home and the rivers that glistened there in the tropical sun.

After an hour of cleansing, the river set my feet free, but it did not release my mind from the desire for my homeland. Without looking back, I returned to my office, feeling befuddled.

CHAPTER 2

When my eyes opened to a quiet bedroom the morning after my river visit, a beam of sunlight shot from an opening in the curtains to the bed. The single line of light painted an irony of loneliness as it crossed my torso and landed on the empty space left by Elisha. I reached across the mattress, lifting the rumpled comforter as I searched the shadows for a woman too tall to hide in small spaces.

It was not only Elisha's absence that I felt that morning. When I turned back to my side of the bed, I faced my own emptiness, as if it were peeking at me from the window. I had no other choice than to embrace the only source of light in my life at that moment: a lone streak of sunlight. As my sleepy eyes followed the light, it stopped at the gap between the two curtains.

Thinking about my marriage, I wondered why Elisha's absence from our bed bothered me so much. For many years I had woken with her head on my chest. At times I fondled her body, or she held my erect member. Other times we fondled each other. It was our morning routine, and on days when we had enough time, one of us, or both, got lucky.

My mind wandered back to the curtains in search of the answers to my problems. I thought that if a perfect union had formed between the two curtains, the morning sun couldn't meander into the bedroom.

Standing up, naked, I reached for my robe to cover the streak of sunlight between my legs. An act to hide my nakedness and vulnerability. I walked to the bedroom window and pulled the curtains tight, as if my body was still exposed. For a moment, I stood in the middle of the bedroom, reciting what to say to Elisha. After several sighs, the magnitude of it all was much clearer.

By the time I left the bedroom, I was eager to find her. I followed the sound of the television to the living room. She was sprawled on her back on our old creased black leather couch, staring at the barren white ceiling. The noises I made as I approached elicited no reaction from her. Standing close and looking down at her, I faced her blank stare. She didn't offer me a smile, or even a blink, as we gazed at each other.

"Good morning, babe," I said. She ignored me. Undeterred, I added, "I don't know when you left our bed." She blinked once while I spoke, her countenance impassive.

Searching for clues on her face, I noticed tears starting to roll down her cheeks. I knelt and wiped her weary eyes with my sleeve. Even without flowing tears, albeit temporarily, her face looked as vulnerable as it did the night she had miscarried, six months after our wedding.

"I feel lonely lying next to you," Elisha said, her voice quivering.

"I don't know why," I said. "I'm always here for you."

"You don't listen when I talk to you."

"I do, babe. When don't I listen? About yesterday, I'm sorry I fell asleep. I was tired."

"It's not only about yesterday, it's every day," she said. "How can I know you're listening when you don't say anything? You're preoccupied."

I watched as she wiped away tears with the back of her trembling hand. I'd seen her hands tremble before when I heard anger in her voice, but when she spoke now, the crack in her voice reminded me of her bouts of angst, not anger.

"I promise to do better."

"We'll see."

Lying down next to her on the couch, I placed my arm around her waist and pulled her body closer to mine. She didn't resist, so I hugged her tightly. I felt her fast heartbeat, her deep breathing resonating in my ears.

"I need you, babe," I said.

"Don't just say it. Show me that you do."

"I do. I rush home from work every day."

"Just to fuck me. No emotions. No passion. I'm just an object to you."

"That's not true," I insisted. "I love you."

"You have a funny way of showing it. When was the last time you kissed me? Not a stupid peck on my cheek. A real kiss."

"I always do," I said. My heart was racing. It was the fear of being a failure that gripped me. Fear of a failing marriage, of losing her.

"You don't even hold me anymore after you fuck me. I feel lonely when you turn your back on me."

I held her tighter, as if to compensate for all her complaints against me. "That's not true. I hold you every night."

"Only when you want something," she said.

"You're wrong, babe. I want you because I love you."

"How about my needs? What I want?" She sniffled. "Do you ever care about how I feel?" Her voice quavered, and she exhaled as if expelling her frustration. Looking at her frown, I knew she was keeping more from me.

My eyes welled with tears, but I held them back. The right thing to do or say eluded me.

The hounding voice inside me said, *Our men don't cry. Little girls wail, and men comfort them. Don't disgrace your culture for a woman.* I dreaded its taunting and chauvinism. The distracting drumbeats and metallic gongs returned. I moved my head closer to Elisha's and drifted to sleep.

I heard boisterous dancing steps, the earth-stomping sounds that young men's feet made after drinking palm wine, and the peculiar smell of raised African dust. The sounds of dancing feet intensified, and I saw barefooted villagers kicking up red dirt in my hometown of Obodo. Tall, bountiful palm trees swayed in the wind. Their flickering fronds caressed each other in the smoldering heat.

When I woke, I heard Elisha say, "I sacrificed everything for you." I wondered anxiously how long she'd been talking to me without knowing I was asleep. One word—*sacrificed*—worried me more than all the rest.

It was difficult for me to confront that word. It felt like a knife piercing my chest and cutting my heart into pieces.

"I'm sorry, babe," I answered. "You know I've been busy lately. We need to get out. Do something outdoors or check out the museum." She ignored me. "You hear me?"

"The way you're treating me, I need to shut down my feelings," Elisha said. She sounded callous as her nostrils flared with each breath.

"What do you mean, shut down?"

"I won't let you hurt me," she said, her voice lacking emotion.

My grip around her waist loosened, but it troubled me that I could let go of her so easily. She looked at me as if in protest.

"I'll never hurt you," I said, mostly for my own benefit as the conversation was going in a direction I didn't expect.

"But you are hurting me. That's what neglecting me does. It's always about you and the hospital."

"It's our responsibility to be successful," I said.

"Our responsibility? When did your obsession with work became our responsibility?"

"I want you to be proud of me."

"Really? I need my husband, emotionally and physically. You only reach for me when you want sex." She spoke with such emphasis that it annoyed me. I had hoped that I could mend things between us, but I appeared to have widened the gap.

CHAPTER 3

As I grew older, two things had come to worry me the most: professional failure and loneliness. Judging by my position at the medical center, I was successful. Patients and fellow physicians had told me many times how proud they were of what I'd accomplished. However, a feeling of failure gnawed at my core, troubled my sleep, and propelled me to work more hours than my colleagues. Nothing guaranteed me perpetual success, and I'd seen many people regarded as successful fail in their ventures.

Sitting in my office that morning, I remembered something my father had said many years ago, before I left home: "Success and failure live across from each other." He meant that failure could happen to anyone, depending on their resilience and the available opportunities. So I had embraced hardiness in every aspect of my life.

On my desk were photographs divided into two groups: my past and present lives. Looking at the photographs of my present—Elisha and our adult children, Ikenna and Obialu—opposite the photographs of my past—my parents—I realized the enormity of my dual responsibilities.

I accepted that my parents' deaths didn't extricate me from their muted expectations: to finish my education in America and return home to an exalted position as the family patriarch. But sorting my priorities wasn't as easy as I had initially expected. My wife had been with me for thirty-one years, but my parents had been with me at my conception. How to reconcile the two opposing family obligations challenged me.

# # #

The day before my sixtieth birthday, I walked the empty hallway to the executive conference room. It was 11:45 a.m. and the silence, both in my head and in the hallway, surprised me. It wasn't a holiday, but the deserted hallway indicated as much.

When I opened the conference room door, Brad Peters, the president of the hospital board, was the only attendee waiting for the clinical directors' noon meeting. A man who stood almost as tall as the wall behind him. He had been one year ahead of me in medical school and rose through the hospital's administrative ranks faster than his peers, all those seeking power in the multibillion-dollar Boston healthcare system. His smile welcomed me into the room, and when I felt his cordial handshake, I sensed the charm that had helped him reach his position.

"I expected you to be the first," Brad said, his smile lingering.

"That fear of being late hasn't left me," I replied.

"When were you ever late to anything? Never."

"I don't want to disappoint anyone. That's why I try to be on time."

"You've achieved too much compared with your colleagues to worry about such trivial things."

"I'm sure you worry more than I do about little things," I said.

He shook his head. "My worries are different. We're expanding around Boston, and I need your help."

"I'm not sure how, but I'll help any way I can."

"We're buying a hospital west of Boston, and we need an interim CEO."

"A young professional with promising ideas, I hope," I said. We both laughed.

"You're the young professional I recommended," Brad said.

I laughed again. "I'll be sixty tomorrow. My younger days are over."

"I need a hard-working physician with management experience like you," Brad said. I heard the conference room door open as he spoke.

Rachel Schulman, the director of surgery in our affiliate hospital, entered with Michael Kraus, the interim CEO. In her regular green scrubs and surgical cap, Rachel walked gracefully toward Brad and shook his hand.

As she shook mine, she said, "You're always the first to arrive for our meetings." I smiled. I liked Rachel and her poise. She had published more than most of her competitors in the surgical literature and was a good ambassador for female leadership in medicine. Most importantly, if judged by the amount of research funds secured by faculty members in her division, she was a competent leader.

"Afam wants the boys to praise him," Michael said, beginning to pace around the room. I wondered if his expression was a smile or a grimace.

"Brad came first," I replied. "I'm not like you, Michael. I don't need a pat on the back all the time." We laughed, though his unflattering comment about me seeking praise made me angry.

"Who're 'the boys,' Michael?" Brad asked.

"You and the rest of the board," Michael said.

"Afam's not the type," Rachel said. "Now, if you accuse him of being too competitive, I'll agree with you."

"I know," Michael said. "Sometimes he makes the rest of us look bad."

"I'm not sure what I do, but forgive me for it," I said.

"Here's how I look at it," said Brad. "If you're in a situation where winning, success, or whatever you call it is what you want, who would you choose if you needed a partner?"

"You choose the best person to help you succeed," Rachel said. She and Michael looked at me as if they knew what Brad was alluding to.

Michael was in his late fifties, but his scraggly hair and gray beard gave him the look of a much older man. Looking at him closely, I saw the deep age lines digging into his face, despite his smile. I didn't want loads of responsibilities as the interim CEO to age me like it had done him.

As more of the clinical division directors gathered, Brad assumed the role of the meeting chair. As hard as I tried, I couldn't focus on the meeting; my mind wandered to Brad's proposal. It was generous. A wonderful opportunity. But I knew that accepting his offer would keep me away from my homeland for additional years.

Would I die in Boston pursuing professional titles without setting foot again in Nigeria? What about my role as the family patriarch? Would I be recognized as such if I stayed away longer? What was more important to me: my professional success or my position among my people?

When Brad approached me at the end of the meeting, even his smile couldn't convince me to accept his offer. My homeland was more important than being the CEO of a Boston-area hospital, a position that grooves a man's face with deep wrinkles. I didn't even know what it would do to a man's heart, and I wasn't eager to find out.

"Let me think about it," I said.

"We have to know as soon as possible," Brad replied as he shook my hand again.

"I should talk to my wife about it, but I know how I'm leaning."

"It's the opportunity you deserve. You shouldn't hesitate when you have such a wonderful prospect," he said, looking at me as if he expected my answer then.

15

"I must be fair to my wife and at least tell her about it before I decide."

"Several of your colleagues are soliciting for it. I don't know how they found out, but I recommended you."

"I'm grateful for your trust in me, but I know my wife. She would feel slighted if I didn't tell her first."

"I understand. You need a happy home, but I bet she'll be thrilled," Brad said.

"You seem to know more about wives than I do," I said, and we laughed again.

# # #

My ambition was inherent. It had lived with me for as long as I could remember, and it was that yearning that had brought me to Boston. Unchecked, my professional aspirations had consumed me and relegated my responsibilities in my homeland to nothingness. When I walked into our bedroom that night, I was aware that accepting Brad's offer would destroy me.

Even in the dimly lit bedroom, Elisha's smile and beauty set my heart racing. When I reached out across the bed to touch her, she moved toward me and held me close. I needed that closeness between us.

"Brad offered—no, he suggested—well, he recommended me for a CEO position," I said.

"It's about time they recognized your talent," she replied.

"I didn't accept. Not yet. How could I?"

"But that's what we've worked for. All the sacrifices I made for us are finally paying off."

Why would Elisha use the word *us* when talking about a position offered to me? Her statement surprised me, but I couldn't find the right words or the courage to seek clarification. Her support mattered more to me than understanding what she meant.

"I thought we would travel," I said. "Go back home. Spend more time together."

"I want your happiness. That's all I want."

I felt relieved. "I'm happy to hear that. I don't need more stress in my life."

"But do you want that job?" she asked. "I hope you do." I wondered if this was the same Elisha who'd complained about my preoccupation with work.

I wished there was enough light in our bedroom to reveal her inner feelings to me. Her contradictory statements left me confused.

"I need some time away from Boston. To go back to my roots. Find what I lost in my life," I said.

"Think about the prestige you'd be giving up. It'll boost our status here."

"I've achieved more than I expected from your country."

"My country? It's your country too."

"You know where I came from," I said with a laugh.

"It's not funny. You're throwing away an opportunity."

"I find myself in a dire situation. If I turn down Brad's offer, I could lose my current job. If I accept it, I'll lose my soul."

"That's silly. You need that job—to be recognized for who you are and what you've done." By her tone of voice, I knew she was frustrated with me. It felt as if I was losing everything: my heritage, my wife's support, and my employment.

"All I want is you," I said. "To love you, be with you, make love to you." I waited for Elisha's reassurance, but she was silent. "If I accept Brad's offer, I may never have the time to visit my homeland. It would be a tragedy if I died in Boston without ever seeing the sunrise from home."

Elisha rolled away and left me sitting in silence. Even in her presence, I felt alone.

Looking at her, I remembered the special times we'd spent together. The times we'd gazed at each other until we giggled uncontrollably. The carefree rainy nights at an outdoor café in Boston. I couldn't stop smiling, thinking about the way Elisha had sipped hot tea in the rain, drinking slowly, the way we ended our goodbye kisses. Endless. That was what I wanted from our marriage, but I wanted to go home too.

CHAPTER 4

The following day, I walked into my office after a long medical faculty conference across the river in Cambridge to see my desk lamp illuminating a red envelope. Handwritten in black pen was *Dr. Afamefuna Onochie Nwaku, Director, CardioNeuroHormonal (CNH) Division*. I opened the envelope and took out a card with a one-line greeting: *Happy sixtieth birthday*.

The simplicity of it surprised me as much as my sixtieth birthday did. For a moment I felt as if the card must belong to someone else. Had I really been around that long?

I took a blank sheet of paper from my desk drawer and smoothed it gently. Sitting on my chair, I faced the framed photographs of my parents, my wife, my son, Ikenna, and my daughter, Obialu displayed on my desk. Their eyes appeared to scrutinize the one-line dance my pen twirled on the blank paper. Excluding my academic and professional achievements, I listed volunteering for a free clinic when I was thirty years old as the only important thing I had done without being paid. I felt disgusted. How about my contributions to my homeland? None.

Look at you. A wasted son of the land. Sixty darn years of forgetfulness, the voice in me said, mocking everything that I was. Frustrated, I sighed. It laughed at me, as if my life had no importance. I hung my head and let the pen slip from my hand. My hand began to shake, and no matter how hard I clenched it, it wouldn't stop. My eyes wandered, searching for something that I knew wasn't in the room: the source of that voice in my head.

The hounding voice didn't explain which land it meant, but I knew. The place I had left at the age of seventeen. The voice might ignore the heaps of forgetfulness that came with the passage of time, but how could it ignore the treachery of distance, six thousand miles of ocean and desert, to scold me?

I took my red birthday card out of the envelope again and wrote all my accomplishments on it. "I've done a lot, and all my patients would attest to that," I said aloud. In that, I found some relief from my guilt.

It's time to come home, the voice said. Its stern tone worried me. I looked around again and saw only an empty office. When I decided that there was no way to negotiate with this stupid voice, it became more audacious: *Don't expect to get more time. Your time has come.* I wanted to ask on whose authority it was setting timelines for me to follow but doing so would have terrified me all the more. My sanity was already questionable.

Judging by certificates and achievements alone, I had done a lot with my life, but the rules were different for the voice taunting me. I stared at a photograph taken during a hunting trip with my father when I was fifteen years old. In it, I held a rifle and stood next to him.

I had exuded confidence back then, but that was a product of his parenting. His daily instructions to always show poise helped me.

You're going home, the voice said again.

"Not before the downtown traffic clears," I said, wondering why I was speaking to myself again.

That was when the voice started to yell. The long tantrum that followed flew over my head with machine-gun rapidity. When it ended, I remembered only a few words. I just wanted the scolding to stop.

The only thing that would delay me from returning to my homeland was finding that elusive "best time" to begin my journey, and that would depend on when I could get enough vacation days.

A blaring fire alarm outside rocked me out of my chair. Walking to my window, I looked out at the streets of downtown Boston but didn't see any firetrucks. I approached my office door and opened it slowly. Peeking into the hallway, I looked in both directions but didn't see anyone.

When the alarm stopped, there was silence in my head and in the room, except for the ticking of the clock. The time was 4:15 p.m. and I felt like a prisoner. I decided to leave.

I found my way to the hospital's main lobby, an expansive space with a glass roof and walls, decorated with sturdy chairs and tables with a tropical theme.

The lobby gift shop was full of trinkets and plastic flowers. Across from it, a small noisy crowd had gathered around beautifully colored wool rugs displayed on tall wooden stands. A man wearing oversized black pants, a loose white shirt draped with a red velveteen vest, and a black ornamented hat stood by a sign on the wall that read *Kurdish Rugs*. With a puffed-out chest and arms whirling like a helicopter, he answered questions for the crowd. The spectacle interested me, but I couldn't find the courage to join.

I entered the gift shop to observe the show from a distance, but I had to pretend as if I were shopping for a present.

Below the cabinets of trinkets, simply worded get-well and sympathy cards abounded. None of the cards were truly intimate. There was nothing with which to express my love to my wife. My eyes wandered to the lobby.

Rose, the store manager, a white-haired, elderly woman wearing a bright yellow dress, watched me tap each card I liked. At times I touched an item twice, which was when she would smile as if knowing my interest. Her gaze prevented me from watching the event going on in the lobby.

When I approached the counter and smiled at her, her own smile broadened.

"Good morning, Sunshine," Rose said. I looked around as if searching for the person she'd addressed. She shook her head, laughed, and said, "That smile of yours has brightened my day. We need more smiles in this world."

"I agree, and we also need more people like you around here," I said.

"Where have you been, Doc? It's been a long time since I last saw you."

"Nowhere. I've been busy with work. Sometimes with family," I answered. "How about you, Rose? Look at you: weight loss and a fancy dress." I smiled again, but she frowned. I was confused. "Are you okay?"

"Not really," she said, glancing down.

"What's wrong?"

"Everything is wrong. I can't sleep. I have no appetite. Worries make me forget things."

"Have you seen a doctor?" I asked. She took a deep breath and exhaled.

"Doc, I'm dying. Lung cancer," Rose said. This time it was me who exhaled.

"Sometimes it's curable," I said.

"They gave me a fifty-fifty chance with radiation," she said, her eyes moist with tears. "They'll cook my lungs. I don't want it."

"You don't give up. You fight," I said. I looked into her eyes, which welled with tears as I spoke.

"Fight? I can't fight alone. I've got no one. My only child is in Afghanistan."

"You won't fight alone. I'm here for you," I said. She wiped away her tears.

"I want my baby home, Doc. What's my son doing in Afghanistan? In some country halfway around the world?"

"My parents asked me what I was doing in America. They're gone now, and I'm still here," I said. I shook my head as I watched Rose dab at her tears. I wondered how many times my parents had wiped away their tears during my long absence.

"Where's your home?" Rose asked.

"Nigeria. It's in Africa."

"I've seen you around here for years. Don't you miss Africa?"

"It's hard to find time to travel," I said.

"You make time for what you want."

"I agree. I hope your son comes home soon."

"He hates the war. He can't stand the killing and maiming over there. Is there a war in your country?" Rose asked.

"Not at this time."

"Too many wars in the world."

A couple walked into the gift shop. Rose left me to join them in the stuffed animal section. I went out to the crowd checking out the Kurdish rugs in the lobby.

"Mister, buy a rug to support Kurdistan," the man in the black hat said. I looked around and saw I was the only other man within his view.

"Where's Kurdistan?" a woman asked as she walked up to him. He ignored her and pointed his finger at me.

"I don't need a rug. I'll send money, if you've a donation site," I said.

"Imagine how your people felt when they were brought here for slavery. Men and women with no country. That's how my people feel," he said as he searched his pocket. Was he unhappy that I wasn't buying a rug?

"Slaves came from different countries. It's different from someone without a country," I said.

"Thank you for the lesson, sir, but I need to sell my rugs. Here's the website." He handed me a card and I walked away. Although I wondered about his honesty, his enthusiasm about Kurdistan impressed me. Here was a man without a country yearning for one, while I, the only son of my parents, had abandoned my country. I felt small as I walked away from the hospital lobby. What was more important to me: going back to Nigeria to assume the role of my family patriarch or staying in America to become the CEO of a hospital?

CHAPTER 5

The sun had set by the time I returned home. I parked my car in the circular driveway in front of my two-story colonial house. In the dark, I could still make out parts of our surrounding acre of wooded land.

"Elisha, I'm home," I said while standing in the foyer. The house sounded hollow as I walked to the kitchen. It reminded me of when I'd lived alone, before Elisha came into my life.

The voice inside me said, *What you feel is the emptiness you left in your homeland.*

"I don't feel anything. Leave me alone," I replied.

If you forget your homeland, you'll die alone.

"I'm not a child who's afraid of death."

You've forgotten who you are and where you come from.

"How could I possibly forget the grasslands of home and our ancient rivers?"

The voice followed me into my study, tugging at my racing heart. Its scornful words caused me to lower my head in shame as I looked at the photographs of my dead parents, the ones who had yearned the most for my return before death relieved them of their anguish. Looking at my past evoked an overwhelming vulnerability. I felt like I was covered by a wet blanket that couldn't provide warmth.

There was a saying where I came from: "Only the dead give up." I was still alive and had to regain my resolve. Determination came from within, and I was the only person who had control over mine. I had felt so sure and confident until I remembered the voice. There had to be a remedy for what afflicted me.

When I returned to the foyer, I found only darkness, the same that had greeted me when I'd entered the house. As I reached for the doorknob to lock the front door, my cell phone rang.

I hurried to retrieve it from my pocket, hoping to speak with Elisha. It was a call from Nigeria, though. From my only sister, Adaku. My heart continued to race, but now it was out of excitement. Hearing from my homeland always gave me pleasure.

"Hello, sis," I said, still standing by the front doorway. I felt my excitement growing, lifting me out of my doldrums.

"Happy sixtieth, baby brother," Adaku said.

"Thank you. You just made my day."

"I'm glad I did. Do you ever think of me? It's been a long time since you called."

"Every day I think of home. I miss you."

"You never call. You don't come home. How can I believe what you say?"

"I've been busy with work."

"Busy for twenty-five years?" she asked.

"I promise to do better, sis," I said.

"I've heard that before. You promised me a lot when Papa died. Remember how you said you'd come home every year?"

"I'll come home soon."

"They've threatened me for years, but it's worse now. That's why I want you home. Please come back. If you don't, they'll take our land or kill me. I'm tired of fighting them alone," Adaku said. I thought about Rose at the hospital gift shop, about my dead parents, about my wife, and about my sister's plea. Everyone wanted the same thing.

"Who's taking our land? So, I'm coming home to fight for land?" I could hear the anger in my voice.

"It's your inheritance. Papa left it for you," she said.

"It's your land too."

"You sound foolish. Women don't inherit land."

"Who said so?"

"Papa made a mistake sending you to America. Listening to you hurts."

"It's your comment that hurts."

"You don't even know our culture," Adaku said. "That's what hurts."

"I know enough. It's calling to yell at me on my birthday that hurts."

"When they kill me, I won't yell anymore." My phone went silent before I heard a dial tone.

There was sweat on my forehead and my feet wobbled. My breathing was deep. It wasn't anger that overwhelmed me but shame and fear. Fear of what could happen to my sister. I remembered what my mother had said once: "You can't go forward and backward at the same time. You have to decide the best direction for you." I had tough decisions to make, but I knew I wouldn't abandon my sister.

When I heard the garage door starting to raise, I walked down the long hallway leading to it. Once the interior garage door swung open, Elisha stepped forward and embraced me. Her hug lifted me from all the dreadful thoughts I had about my homeland.

She walked ahead of me, and I watched her tall, athletic body, no more than two inches below my six-foot height. Everything about her seduced me. When she turned around, as if she knew I was lusting after her body, her eyes teased a smile from me.

"Babe, you've never been this late," I said.

"It wasn't intentional. I should've called," she answered.

"Why didn't you? You would have if I were important to you."

"What difference would it have made? I thought you'd be at work as usual."

"Why would I stay at work late today? Did you forget? I turned sixty."

"You have an opportunity to become a CEO. A good birthday present. But you're screwing it up."

"You care more about that position than I do," I said.

"Sometimes you don't know what's good for you."

"Going back to Nigeria is what I want. That's good for me. My sister needs me too."

I watched Elisha walk away from me. Her stance on the CEO position added to my worries. If I turned down the new job offer, it would affect my marriage. It might even destroy it.

CHAPTER 6

I didn't wait for the garage door to close completely before I drove off. It was late on the night of my sixtieth birthday and I was as hurried as my aging.

On the highway, I glanced up at the sky as Elisha sat stewing beside me. There were no visible stars, and the moon was hidden. My mind wandered to Obodo, my hometown in Nigeria, where I hoped the stars lit the sky for my birthday. In Boston, it looked bleak.

For a Friday evening, the traffic on I-90 E traveling from Wellesley to Boston was light. We made it to Angelino Ristorante in thirty minutes. It was early fall, and the summer crowd had deserted the North End. The youth had gone back to school, and the playground belonged to the adults now.

As I opened and held the door for Elisha, the restaurant host, a middle-aged man in a black suit, met us. Framed family portraits emblazoned in bronze with the word *Angelino* hung prominently on mahogany-paneled walls. Dated photographs of the Angelino patriarch, his wife, and his two sons stared back at me, exhibiting family completeness.

"Welcome to Angelino. I'm Enrico," the host said, interrupting my thoughts. He motioned for us to follow him.

"Thank you," I said.

Enrico led us through a crowded dining room with subdued lights and whispers. Six busy chefs in white aprons stood by the open kitchen, their grills sizzling. The smell of cooked meat and the sight of plates stacked with food sent my empty stomach into a frenzy. It reminded me of the aroma in my mother's kitchen as she prepared our meals when I was young. I swallowed my saliva.

Close to a busy semicircular bar thronging with a younger group of diners, Enrico stopped. The bright spotlights from the bar illuminated the area better than the rest of the dining room. A nearby table for four had two occupants. It didn't take long for me to recognize Ikenna and Obialu watching us approach.

My son and daughter rose from their seats. Foolishly, I expected them to run to me, as if they were children. It had been three months since we'd spent time together as a family, and I couldn't fault myself for being impatient.

"Happy birthday, Daddy," Obialu said with a beaming smile and sparkling eyes, just like her mother's. I kissed the cheek of my twenty-seven-year-old baby before she buried her face in my neck as we hugged. My baby girl, who'd become a successful psychiatrist.

"You look beautiful," I said.

"Thank you, Daddy," Obialu said, blushing a little before she greeted her mother.

"Happy birthday, Pops. You still look good for an old man," Ikenna said.

I hugged him. As his arm found my shoulder, we stood together as if we were two teenagers, best friends who would face the world head on. Anyone who saw my smile would know that I was proud of him. A respectful son and a successful cardiologist at thirty. Obialu and Elisha joined us, and we had a group hug. We held on to each other and wouldn't let go.

I took a quick look at us, the happy Nwaku family, four graduates from Harvard Medical School, the epitome of a Boston medical family. My children and their professional achievements made me a proud father. I was sure that nothing could destroy the closeness we had.

# # #

A short while later, a young woman in a black skirt and a white top with an intricate hair bun approached our table. "I'm your server, Patricia." She smiled as she introduced herself and handed us menus.

"I'm sorry it took us so long to get seated," I said.

"You've got a beautiful family, sir."

"I'm a lucky man. They're good to me too."

My family watched the exchange with indifference. It was only when I praised them that they beamed in acknowledgment. Even Elisha, who usually guarded her emotions, gave a small smile. Patricia left us to contemplate the menu.

An air of contentment hung over us as we sat, my son across from me and my daughter across from her mother. The seating arrangement didn't stop Obialu from looking at me with an affectionate grin. To my surprise, Elisha kissed my cheek and briefly placed her arm around my shoulder. She rarely showed that type of affection to me publicly. I wondered if she did it to show our children that their parents still loved each other.

"I love you, Afam," Elisha said. With her head at an angle, she gazed at me tenderly, as if she was competing with Obialu for my attention.

"I know you do. I love you too, my beautiful babe," I said. My children looked at each other and grinned. I knew they liked seeing us happy.

"You guys are getting weird," Ikenna said before returning to flipping through his menu.

"It is weird, Daddy," Obialu said with a little smirk. "That 'babe' thing's got to go. It's 2018."

"Nothing's weird," Elisha responded. "I'm his baby."

"Mom, in this family, *I'm* the baby," Obialu said, laughing hard.

My stomach couldn't summon up any laughter; instead, it growled.

Returning with a tray of glasses and a carafe of spring water, Patricia asked, "Are you ready to order?"

"I was ready even before we came in," I said. My family laughed as if I was a comedian.

"I haven't decided what I want," Elisha said.

Ikenna and Obialu continued to flip through the extensive menu.

"Let's start with your drinks and appetizers," Patricia suggested.

Everyone's orders amounted to a sizable dinner. When Patricia returned, she brought a family-sized calamari plate.

"Daddy, are you taking Mommy on a vacation this year?" Obialu asked while sampling the appetizer.

"Do you mean, is he paying for it?" Ikenna asked. Even with a smile on his face, his voice was terse, that unmistakable sarcasm dripping from his tongue.

The sound made by Obialu's deep breathing surpassed the background noise.

"Leave me alone," Obialu said.

"I'm sorry, baby sister," Ikenna replied, his smirk more taunting than ever.

"Stop bickering. It's your father's birthday," Elisha said.

"Sorry, Mom," Ikenna said with earnest this time.

I moved my chair closer to Elisha. She looked in my eyes and smiled, but the weariness dragging down her face remained. I touched her hair, her ear, her neck. My hand finally rested on her shoulder. She reached for it and squeezed each finger.

"We need to spend more time as a family," Elisha said, adding, "With no fights."

"I agree, babe," I said. Everyone laughed.

"There's no redemption for Pops," Ikenna said. "It's babe all the way."

The cordiality we had always shared and cherished returned, but my stomach continued its rebellion, growling louder each time. As I reached for my water glass, my hands started to tremble so I stopped. Elisha caught this struggle and leaned her head toward me.

"Are you okay, babe?" she whispered.

"Just have an overwhelming stomach pain. I bet I've got low sugar," I said. My hands trembled more as I spoke.

"Is something wrong?" Ikenna asked. I could see the concern on his face.

"I know what's wrong. Two problems I can think of. Low sugar and ... I've been waiting to ask for your support," I said. Obialu took a deep breath. I stopped speaking to watch her reaction.

"Are you sick, Daddy?" Obialu asked.

"No, baby. My sister called. She wants me to come home."

"Boston is our home," Elisha countered forcefully.

"We have a home in Nigeria too. Our forever home in Obodo," I said with emphatic enunciation of every word. Not only did I feel angry, but I heard it rise up in my voice.

"You're giving up everything we've worked for," Elisha said.

"I'm not giving up anything. I want to see my homeland."

"When I stopped working, as if adolescent psychiatry was not important to me, yes it was, I supported you emotionally and measured my success by yours. If you aren't sure of the CEO job, it's a failure for me. You can't be a CEO in Nigeria."

Elisha pushed her plate away, lifted her napkin, and dropped it on top of her calamari. When I reached for her hand, she slapped it away. I withdrew my hand under the table and with a fake smile glanced at Ikenna and Obialu to see if they were watching us; inside, I was seething. Elisha avoided looking at me and focused on our children, but neither of them spoke.

Patricia returned with our food, and when she looked around our table, our eyes met. I feigned another smile that I fashioned out of guilt and desperation.

"Enjoy your meals," Patricia said and quickly left. She seemed aware of the tension at our table.

"You're inconsiderate," Elisha said. "Think of my feelings and the kids before you make crazy decisions."

"Your feelings? How about what I want? My happiness?" I asked.

"Let it go, Pops," Ikenna said. "Let's eat. Save your discussions for home."

"I'm starving," Obialu added.

"Your father ruined my appetite. I should've stayed home," Elisha said as she moved her chair farther away from me.

"I must go home to Nigeria. My sister needs me. It'll make me happy if you go with me," I said.

"It's your home, not mine," Elisha said, her voice louder than necessary, face unmistakably angry. I looked around us for curious eyes and ears. No one in the restaurant seemed interested in our conversation.

"I'm in, Daddy," Obialu said with unwavering enthusiasm, reaching across the table to nudge her mother's arm as if wanting her to say something. Elisha's face retained the same expression of disgust. After a second nudge, she turned to her daughter and opened her mouth to speak but held back. Elisha stood, pulled her chair back, and rolled her eyes at me. I stood, fearing that she would walk out of the restaurant.

"I need to use the restroom," she said as if she knew what was on my mind.

"Hurry back, we've got a lot to discuss," I replied. When Elisha looked at me, I grinned. She walked away quietly.

"Why now?" Ikenna asked, placing his knife and fork on his plate.

"I'm not sure what you mean," I said.

Ikenna shifted in his chair. "Haven't heard you talk about Nigeria in a long time." He looked at Obialu as if hoping for a consensus. I heard Obialu kick his foot. I smiled at my children as they rolled their eyes at each other.

"Keep me out of it," Obialu said.

"I've been away from home for so long. Now's the right time to go," I said.

"Explain it to Mom. She'll understand," Ikenna said. I watched him pull his plate closer. The bloody juices dripping from his ribeye steak almost shocked me. That's where we were different. I loved my meat well done. Well, his tongue was sharper than mine.

Elisha returned to our table after a long absence. She stood behind her chair for a while before sitting down. I resisted the temptation to speak. When she repositioned her chair, I stood and tried to help her.

"I don't need your help," she said while looking away.

"I've held chairs for you since we met," I said. It was then that she met my eyes.

"Mom, why can't you go with Pops?" Ikenna asked as he pushed his empty plate to the side.

"I don't give a crap about Nigeria," Elisha said.

"It's our home, Elisha," I said with a raised voice.

"I gave up my family and friends for you. That's enough sacrifice," she replied. Looking at her flushed face and quivering lips, I wished she would just scream and expel the demon growing inside her. I understood her restraint, though, in a public place.

"I didn't know you gave up your family," I said. "How is that possible? They visited often."

"It's not important," Elisha said.

"It is to me. I thought your parents loved me."

Riddled with concern, Ikenna and Obialu watched us silently, unwilling to intervene.

After a moment, Elisha said, "I'm tired. We should leave."

"I don't understand your anger. What's wrong with going home, taking care of our properties, and then coming back?"

"It's what you're giving up. You are abandoning your only opportunity to be a CEO. You want me to

41

tell you more? You're filled with the guilt of not being home for your parents. Once you leave Boston, I know you won't come back." Her voice was rising.

"I haven't been home for a long time," I replied. "All the while I've been chasing after accolades. What about my civic responsibility to my country?" All the things I'd wanted to say about my responsibilities as the family patriarch were beginning to spill out. I didn't want to scald the other diners with the steaming bubbles brewing inside me.

"Imagine it for just one second," Elisha said. "You'll be invited to join choice country clubs in Boston if you become a CEO."

"I don't need them. Take the damn job and the country clubs yourself."

"I could have, but *you* didn't want a live-in babysitter. I gave up my career to raise your kids. I deserve this. If you leave for Africa, it's over between us."

What she said felt like a punch to my belly. It sounded as if our relationship was a subjugation of her desire for mine, not a blissful marital union of two medical professionals. Sadness overpowered me, traveling through my body like the brutal air of a chilly winter day. It was the chill from thirty-one years of commitment to each other unraveling before me.

CHAPTER 7

There were things I couldn't understand even after many years of formal education; there were things I wouldn't accept after many years of exposure to them; and there were things that surprised me after many years of living. Those were the things that confused me.

When I reached the hospital that morning, I didn't go to my office. I went to the medical staff conference room to meet with the cardio-neuro team. The room was full when I arrived, and no one looked at me as I sat down. That, however, wasn't different from the other meetings we had that year.

"I invited our director, Dr. Nwaku, to this round with us," said Dr. Craig Olson, my associate director.

"It's always an honor for me," I replied.

Dr. Olson tapped the side of his coffee mug before closing his laptop. He took a sip from his coffee and resumed the tapping. I tried hard to ignore his annoying obsession with his mug. I wondered if Elisha felt the same way about my obsession with going back home.

Scanning the room, I saw physicians engrossed in their own worlds, looking at their cell phones or typing on their laptops. Dr. Shah, the chief resident, flipped through the papers on his clipboard, but he was the only one who sometimes glanced my way.

"We have an interesting fifty-year-old Jamaican immigrant. The rest are routine," Dr. Shah said, continuing to flip through his papers.

"Being an immigrant isn't an illness," I said. I watched Dr. Shah halt his paper-flipping for a moment as I spoke.

"You're right, Dr. Nwaku," said Dr. David. I wasn't surprised that Dr. David, a young Israeli research fellow, would agree with me first. He looked at everyone after he spoke. I wondered if he was searching for approval. Who needed approval when you were right?

"Who's the medical resident assigned to this case? Someone with patience, I hope?" I asked. No one answered. I looked around the room. I saw Dr. Shah close his eyes. I thought he would be the one to speak up. His silence began to change my opinion of him as an advocate for powerless immigrant patients. In the past, he had written petitions to me advocating for unbiased patient care.

"I'll assign a student to her. It's a psych case," Dr. Shah said.

"Take us to her room," I said. Everyone stood from their chairs, except for two physicians who took their time to join us at the conference room door as we waited.

We walked the long hallway from the conference room to the general medicine ward chitchatting about mandated decrease in resident physicians work hours and its potential impact on clinical competency of younger physicians.

As we approached the patient's room, everyone stopped.

"Katy Cliff is a fifty-year-old Jamaican woman who has been confused for two days. A friend brought her in. She has no family in Boston. Her head CT scan and MRI are normal. She speaks Patois and laughs to herself," Dr. Shah said. Some of the doctors snickered.

"My knowledge of Patois is limited," I said. "It's been years since I had a close Jamaican friend."

"They're taking over our country," someone whispered behind me. When I turned around, Dr. Benjamin looked at me, guilt written across his face.

I grinned at him like a dog barring its teeth. "Speak up if you have an opinion."

"These poor people come to this country. They abuse our system and use up our resources," Dr. Benjamin said.

"How do you know she's not entitled to the resources she's using?" I asked.

"A crazy immigrant isn't entitled to crap," Dr. Benjamin said. Most of the team members chortled. I found their reactions offensive but didn't say anything.

"I'm sorry, Director. Dr. Benjamin should respect your presence," said Dr. Alfred.

"He's entitled to his opinion as long as it doesn't affect his patient care," I answered.

"I don't mind immigrants coming to our country, but not ignorant ones," said Dr. Benjamin.

"Let's see the patient first before we label her," I said.

"I'll stand outside," said Dr. Benjamin.

"Dr. Benjamin, aren't you Jewish?" I asked.

"What does that have to do with anything?" Frowning, he took a deep breath.

"Race and racism are getting too complicated for me in this country," I said. "I feel confused at times."

"Me too," Dr. Shah said.

Inside the patient's room, a woman in a kente dress sat by the bedside. She caressed her braided hair and focused her eyes on a television game show.

I walked closer to Katy with my hand stretched out. She ignored me.

"You're a Jamaican?" I asked. Katy looked up and smiled.

"Yes, *baas*," Katy said.

"I'm Dr. Nwaku, the director. Not a *baas*," I said.

"*Tank yuh, sah*," Kati said. Her smile warmed my heart.

"You don't have to thank me. We haven't done anything for you yet," I said. I turned to my group. "Get a neuro consult and a social worker involved."

"I'm a social worker," Katy said. My group looked at one another as if they doubted her qualifications.

"Where do you work?" I asked.

"City of Boston," Katy answered, adding in a mumble, "*Di baas a yah.*"

"I'm not your boss. I'm a doctor. We're here to help you," I said.

"I won't talk to you if you're not the boss," Katy said. Everyone laughed. She picked up the clipboard hanging off the end of her bed and threw it at me. It hit my side as I tried to duck.

"It's wrong to laugh at your patients," I said, scanning the faces of my team as my breathing quickened. I was furious at them for their conduct and scared that I could have been injured.

"Katy, do you have a family?" I asked.

"Yes, sir," Katy said. Dr. Shah pulled a pen out of his pocket and handed it to her. I took two steps away from her after she received this sharp object. I wanted to rebuke Dr. Shah, but it wouldn't change what he'd done.

"Write their names and phone numbers for us," Dr. Shah said. I motioned for him to step away from Katy as she held the pen with a clenched fist.

"My husband married a new wife. He said I'm dead," Katy said. She lowered her head, eyes closed.

"Write his number for us," I said.

"No, sir. His wife said they'll deport me." Katy looked around the room, beckoned to me, and whispered, "She hates black women."

"We're here to help you. No one will deport you," I said. My group looked at one another as I wondered when I'd become an immigration officer. "Mrs. Cliff, do you mind if I examine you?"

"No sir, Doctor," Katy said.

"Do you know where you are?" I asked.

"Boston airport."

I smiled. "You're in a hospital."

"Okay, sir."

"Place the pen on the table," I said. She dropped it on the floor.

With my foot resting on the pen, I completed my physical examination, surprised that she cooperated.

"We'll do more tests to find out what's causing your problem, Mrs. Cliff," I said. She nodded. "I'll be back to see how you're doing." Her attention returned to her television show.

"Thank you, Dr. Nwaku. You were the only one she would respond to," Dr. Alfred said. "I'm glad she gave more information," I replied. "Find the person who brought her to the hospital. We'll need their assistance."

"We'll ask the social worker to help us," Dr. Shah said.

Once we stepped out of the patient's room, I spoke to the group. "Understanding and respecting your patients are as important as prescribing the best drugs. Respect is universal, and it promotes trust." Everyone looked at me blankly. Exasperated, I left them for my meeting with the hospital board to discuss the interim CEO offer.

Walking through the lobby, I stopped to look at framed photographs of the hospital's executive team on the wall. The CEO's photograph was at the top by itself, and the rest were below it. I thought about my CEO picture on the wall of the new hospital.

I stepped away from the wall and looked at it from a distance. For a moment, I wanted my photograph displayed that way, but when I thought about the sacrifice I would have to make, I felt sad. Staring at the wall for a long time, I became more confused about what I wanted.

CHAPTER 8

The dean's office for the school of medicine was a short distance from the hospital. As a young medical faculty member, I had visited the quadrangular complex regularly to present my academic progress, mostly my publications and the grant awards for my research. Those were not voluntary meetings, nor were they much fun; the medical school required them in order to advance faculty members.

During my visits, I would tremble when getting out of my car. Who could blame me? My professional future had depended on the administrators, mostly aging men, who held expansive offices on the marble-walled upper floors of the medical school complex. Watching those old men swagger through the beautiful hallways had been entertaining and yet terrifying. It was the center of power in medicine and healthcare delivery in Boston.

My trip that morning would be my first to the massive building in more than a decade. During my earlier visits, I had needed to convince those powerful people that I was worthy of associating with their prestigious institution. Decades had passed since they'd taken a chance on a young African immigrant, and I wasn't sure that things would be different for me now. As a professor at the university, one would think that my anxiety had dissipated, that my fear of rejection would've subsided, but I felt my heart race.

Getting out of the car, I remembered the name that some of the younger medical faculty had given to the building: "the Tomb," where old and dying men regain academic importance. Unfortunately, some young academicians' futures died in the same building. Where I now fit in the scheme of power, I wasn't sure.

It dawned on me that the allure of Boston academic medicine was partly responsible for my staying so long in America. The prestige I had gained by my mere association with an Ivy League institution was clear.

Entering the building, an intimidating edifice even from the inside, I made a sharp left turn down a long hallway. Admiring the marbled walls as if it was my first time, I greeted everyone I passed with a "Good morning" and a smile. Reading the names on the doors to various offices, I realized that several women now occupied positions of power.

After a sharp right turn, I arrived at the dean's office. I had been here before, but the mahogany entrance with glass sidelights still stood out.

Although there was glitter surrounding the entrance to the office, the main door wore a fading brass nameplate emblazoned with *Mark Edelson, MD. Dean, School of Medicine.*

When I entered the dean's office, I became worried about the potential outcome of my request.

Nothing appeared to have changed inside the waiting area, where subdued amber lights barely offered adequate illumination. Strategically placed windows created entrances for sunlight. The natural light offered what the honey-colored light could not; it brightened the room enough to reveal mahogany-paneled walls and multiple photographs of serious-looking bearded men. My eyes couldn't stop looking at the framed photographs of former deans, which revealed that only men had held that position of authority at the institution.

A part of me thought about walking out of the office. Maybe Africa could wait. It was another excuse to relegate my homeland and responsibilities to the backburner, but it could save my marriage. As I stood feeling flustered and with crazy thoughts swirling in my head, a middle-aged woman sitting in a corner of the office rose from her chair. She beamed with a consoling smile, as if knowing my struggles.

"Good morning, Doc," she said with a cordial tone, one that sounded familiar, but I couldn't recognize her face. Many years had passed since I'd visited the office. It troubled me that all that time had taken my memories with it. If ten years could rob me of the secretary's identity, what would it do to Africa?

"Good morning," I said as I approached her desk for a closer look.

"It's been long," she said. Again, her sweet voice had that tone of familiarity that made me feel welcomed. As she sat down, she added, "Miss seeing you around."

Closer up, her smile and grace could cheer up even the crabby old men hanging from the walls. Wondering where the trees for the walls had come from, I chuckled at the ironic thought that maybe the former deans were hanging on African trees. The secretary looked at me with her mouth agape.

"Not laughing at you. Just a joke I heard earlier," I said.

"You don't remember me?" she asked with slanted eyes.

"I'm sorry. I don't." I tried to feign a smile, though I felt small standing before her.

"I sang at your wedding," she said.

"Forgive my poor memory. It was a long time ago, but I still remember your beautiful voice," I said. I quickly realized that I'd made it sound as if the wedding wasn't important. But it was. So much so.

"Thank you," she said, grinning as wide as her face could accommodate.

"Don't ever change. Watching you smile brightened my morning," I said.

The outside door to the office creaked as it opened.

An elderly man in a gray suit walked in. He shuffled as he walked, but he appeared balanced with his stoop. Watching his determination reminded me of the bent coconut trees at home that had survived tropical storm winds capable of lifting iron roofs from houses. It was true, as my father said: "Resilience depends on one's substance and how one adapts to adverse situations."

Two steps away from me, the man halted and stroked his silver beard as he caught my stare. I tried to trade a smile, but his face remained still.

He opened his mouth to speak but hesitated at the sound of a squeaky chair. Our eyes moved to the source of the sound.

"Good morning, Doctor Edelson," the secretary said as she pushed her chair to the side. Her face had become serious. I wondered if she was going to salute him as she stood with her feet together. If I were a stranger in their presence, it would be obvious to me that he commanded immense power. I took two steps to the side, out of his path, as he ambled toward his secretary.

"Morning, Teresa," Dr. Edelson said.

"Hello, Mark. Sorry to invade your office," I said while extending my hand, which held an envelope.

When I looked at the dean again, I couldn't remember him having that stoop. A long time had passed since we last met. There was nothing I could do but accept that he'd aged. It was only my absence from his office that was odd.

He walked closer to me, looking at my face and the clutched envelope in my hand with curiosity. He watched attentively as I switched the envelope to my left hand and my right hand found his to shake. I consciously abandoned my customary firm grip. Contrary to his apparent frailty, he surprised me with a firm grip of his own. We looked at each other, and he smiled as if he'd won an undeclared contest between us.

"You're an early morning surprise. Things okay?" he asked as he led the way to his inner office.

"No problems, dean," I said.

"To come here this early must be important."

"I'm going home," I said.

He turned around to look at me with a frown, then a smile, before he spoke. "Where's home?" he asked. He reached out and held the side of his desk.

"Eastern Nigeria. I thought you knew," I said.

"Now I remember. You're leaving for good?" he asked and sighed. It sounded as if he had to remove a burden from his body.

"Just a sabbatical," I said.

"All I needed was a written request, not your presence."

"Well, I have a written request," I said as I handed the envelope to him.

After an unnerving silence between us while he sorted things out on his desk, he said, "I turned in my retirement last week."

"You deserve the rest," I said. I hesitated for a moment before adding, "I was just wondering what to do with my sabbatical request."

"Let me see."

"I'm sorry," I said, then wondered what I was sorry for.

Watching him read the letter with a crinkled face, my heart rate increased and my hands felt moist.

"I'm not sure if I can approve your request. To grant you a year of absence would take a longer time to approve."

"Well, I'm going home, even if I have to quit my job."

He leaned back in his chair, shook his head, and scratched his beard as deep lines formed on his face. He glanced at the envelope again and teased the sealing flap. He hesitated before he looked back up to me.

"I didn't expect you to say such a thing. We've been fair to you, haven't we? When you came here, we took a chance on you. Why not have faith in us?"

"So, I'm a charity case?" I asked. "I guess I was wrong to think that all the research money I brought to the institution mattered. I'm going home."

"It's not my decision to make, which is good for you."

"I don't know who it's good for, but it doesn't matter to me at this stage of my life. I've made up my mind." I left the dean's office angry, without giving him the chance to annoy me more. I'd done my part.

My cell phone rang before I reached my car. My hands shook as I held the phone.

"Hello, sis. I'm sorry I haven't called," I said.

"That's you. My no-promises-kept brother," Adaku said, sounding indifferent.

"I've been working on coming home. It's taking more time than I expected."

"Keep taking your time. They now watch me from the road."

"I don't believe that. Watch you for what?"

"Don't go there. It won't help your case. I see reflections from their binoculars. Afam, I'm afraid to leave the house." Adaku's voice quavered.

"Who are these people? I'll deal with them when I get home," I said, raising my voice. People walking by looked at me.

"I hope I'm still alive when you get home."

"Stop saying crazy things like that." My heart pounded as if a drummer had gone into a rage inside my chest.

"I'm facing reality over here. You won't know anything about that."

"You're not being fair to me."

"I guess abandoning me here is fair?" Adaku asked. I glanced around to see if anyone else was looking at me. I felt as if a guilty verdict was written across my face.

"Sis, I'll be home soon, I promise."

"I hope so. I'd like to see you before they kill me."

When I felt pain in my knuckles and in my chest, I realized that my fingers had tightened around my cell phone as if I was choking the last breath out of it.

Adaku hung up before I could say anything else. I got into my car feeling small and sat for several minutes before I could find the energy to drive away.

CHAPTER 9

Noon came faster than I expected, rushing in as quickly as the onset of dawn when my body needed more sleep. From my office, I heard its arrival announced by a loud church bell. Those twelve bell tolls signaled a daily ritual for me: as always, I checked my watch. One would think that after a few days of checking the bell's accuracy I would stop, but it had lasted for years. I wondered if the obsession would ever end.

One minute had passed since the bell when I reached inside my pocket, pulled out my cell phone, and found no missed calls.

The daily noon phone call from Elisha didn't happen. It was the first time after many years of marriage that she had forgotten to—or had chosen not to—call me at noon. Around me, everything else stayed the same; only my marriage appeared to have changed. I paced around my office feeling mentally wounded. When I gave up on hearing from her, I returned to my desk.

Instead of lunch, I focused on her photograph and the ramifications of a failed marriage. The two things that pervaded my thoughts were loneliness and the absence of love in my life. The only thing left would be my profession.

Death had taken away my mother in my absence, depriving me of her unconditional love, and when it came for my father, his death saddled me with burdens I couldn't handle properly from six thousand miles away.

On my office walls, I found things that would be with me even in my solitude: my certificates and commendations. For years I had collected accolades in Boston while relegating Africa to nothingness. Elisha's telephone silence at noon had taught me how neglect felt. The abandoned—my hometown of Obodo, my sister, and Africa—must have felt the same way I did. Luckily, there were no tears to wipe away from my inner conflict and yearning for solace. That thing in me, the African, had forbidden it.

After an hour of this mental torment, I lifted my cell phone and called Elisha. It rang five times without an answer. As I was about to hang up, I heard, "Yes." Her voice sounded subdued.

"What happened to hello, babe? I really miss your sweetness," I said. My question and plea received a long silence. It felt like she'd hung up the phone. "Can you hear me, love?" I added.

"What do you want?" she asked harshly.

"Just missing you, babe."

"What happened to Africa? That's what you're missing, not me." Her voice lacked every emotion that I had taken for granted over the years.

"Let's go out tonight. Have fun like we used to," I said.

"I don't need that type of fun. It comes with heartbreak."

"I turned in my request for a sabbatical," I said. I felt there was nothing left to lose by telling her. I took a deep breath in anticipation. After a few minutes of holding the phone, I asked, "Are you there?" but it was the end of the conversation. She had hung up without letting me know. It was a first in our relationship.

Everything inside me was boiling as I paced around my office. I couldn't sit or stand still for more than a second. My hands trembled, and my tongue uttered many curse words I couldn't remember later except for "Fuck her." I said them with no remorse. Opening the door, I let myself and the devil in me out of my office.

CHAPTER 10

The day after I received approval for my one-year sabbatical after a long one month wait, I scheduled a meeting with my division management team. I walked into the conference room with a feeling of contentment, I thought. My confidence wavered, however, when I looked around the room and felt a flutter in my chest, that overwhelming thud from the fear of uncertainty.

"We've been waiting for you," said Craig Olson, my associate director. He lowered his voice to a whisper but conjured a magnificent smile.

"Sorry I'm late," I replied. "Hopefully I'm not too late."

As I looked beyond Craig at the well-lit conference room, I found all the administrative members of my division sitting around the large oblong table. Their expressions were indifferent, and their interactions with one another appeared minimal. There was no visible sign of cordiality. They sat at the spots they'd adopted many meetings before, but they acted like strangers.

When I scanned the rest of the room, I found nothing uplifting. There was no one to blame for the bland walls but me, the director of the division. I wanted a distraction-free environment and had even prevented a clock from being mounted on the wall.

"Good morning, all," I said as I approached the chair I had chosen at our inaugural meeting many years before, an adjustable one that elevated or lowered my stature depending on the topic and position I took. Looking back, I regretted many of the things I had said or not said over the years. I noticed the eyes and frowns of the others following me as I sat down. No one spoke, as usual, until I declared the meeting open.

It felt good, embracing the power of division director. The fact that I had been chosen for the position over ten other candidates made me proud. I needed the reassurance at that moment.

"I told everyone. Some even volunteered to travel with you," Craig said, preempting my speech. He pushed a brown folder lying in front of him to the side. Watching my face while he spoke, he appeared delighted, but I wasn't sure why. Was he already assuming the role of acting director?

"I have no choice. They need me back home," I said. After looking around the room, I added, "I know we have new projects, but I need this time."

"We understand. Everyone here supports you," Craig said. The executives all nodded in agreement.

"Thinking about home gives me joy. For the first time in years I feel excited about being there." I stood and paced around the room. Something inside me was taking over. I could feel it. Remembering that the meeting was not about Africa but about my division and our research project, I returned to my chair.

"The summary I gave you came from Japan. They've made advances," Craig said while pointing at the folders.

"We're recruiting more patients. We need ten more to reach our goal," added Ralph, who'd been a mostly silent member of the department for years. He had an excellent analytical mind but preferred to communicate through writing.

I read the page as several discussions erupted among the executives in the room. Some instructed, while others argued.

"If our patient recruitment improves, I'll feel better," I said. I watched as Ralph smiled and shifted in his chair. I wondered why he appeared so restless.

"I'm sure they need you," Ralph said. "Too many problems in Africa. Poverty and diseases." It was a surprising assertion from a silent man and a diversion from the topic of the meeting.

That day, Ralph found his voice, both to my delight and anguish. When he raised his eyebrows, it unveiled eyes as bright as flames, his penetrating gaze like a searchlight scanning my soul. That vulnerable part of me hidden from strangers.

My body felt warm, and my hand traced the dampness on my face. I adjusted my chair to a higher level and inserted my fingers inside my shirt collar to loosen it. I leaned back for support.

Ralph watched me squirm, a nervous smile lifting his lips. Looking at him, a third-year faculty member with balding hair at thirty-two and a scrawny physique, I wondered how he fared better than the Africans whom he didn't know yet was trying to describe. Still, I smiled back at him. That was when something inside me turned on all the acid pumps in my stomach. The sour burn and concealed anger whittled away at any happiness left in me, slowly and painfully.

"Africa isn't different from other continents. There is good and bad," I said. I watched as Ralph rolled his chair back. It didn't matter how far he rolled; he was still within the reach of my tongue. Pulling my chair closer to him, I said, "People like you judge. You've never been to Africa, but you judge Africans. I wish you could be more objective with your comments." What I said and how I said it was revealing to me. My tongue was as sharp as my son's.

"It's your fault, Director. You've never talked about your homeland. All you talk about are grants, publishing, promotion, and patients. Nothing personal. We don't know you, and you don't know us," Ralph said. I looked at him, but he looked away.

"I'm judged differently than you," I said. "Always, I've needed to achieve so much more than most to be recognized."

"You don't have to prove anything anymore," Ralph said.

"Look at me, Ralph. Do you know the challenges I face every day?" I asked. He lifted his face up. I saw determination, not fear.

"Given what you demand from us, I'd say you created your problems," he said.

"Ralph, that's enough," Craig said. The smile on Craig's face had faded.

"Let him speak," I said. "It's better that he tells me how he feels. You too, Craig—tell me how you feel about me. I thought I was helping your careers by demanding that you all work hard."

"I'm grateful, Dr. Nwaku, for all you've done for me, but it wouldn't hurt to let us in on your life," Ralph said. His eyes remained still, and the horizontal lines on his forehead became more prominent.

"Let's finish our meeting. We're not here to cry on each other's shoulders," I said.

Ralph rolled his eyes. "I don't see anyone crying. The only thing I feel is tension. You sound as if you don't want to go. Instead of taking it out on me, stay."

"I appreciate your criticism, Ralph, but you're wrong. I'm not taking anything out on you. All I want is an objective approach to everything we do. Let facts support what you do or say."

"You know what? I'll keep my mouth shut. It's dangerous to upset my director."

"I prefer to know how everyone feels. There's no retribution for expressing your opinions." I lowered the height of my chair as I spoke.

Craig rolled around in his chair. Most of the other attendees played with their phones, except for

Ralph, who could hardly stay seated. He sat, stood, and at times tried to sit again but couldn't.

"Let's talk about patients. We have ten recruits. All women," Craig said. He opened a brown folder, removed a stack of papers from it, and distributed a copy to everyone.

The room fell silent, the stale air thick. Reading the summary of "broken heart syndrome," I wondered what was left to discuss.

Craig had a good analytical mind, and it showed in his review article. "Good job. Best review I've read so far," I said. Craig's smile lit up the room again. He blushed then, I'm sure, but against the white walls everyone's skin color stood out.

Ralph remained seated and rarely looked around. With a blank stare aimed at his laptop, he let his arms hang still by his sides, like suspended dead weights. I thought about our exchange. I was still angry with him and had no regrets.

"Good review for us, but how do I explain it to our patients?" Angela asked. Although she avoided eye contact as she spoke, her question made me happy. As a first-year fellow in our division, I considered it refreshing for her to ask a question in a meeting where her training supervisors sat around her. The seriousness on her face and her steady hands said so much about her confidence. I couldn't stop looking at Angela, and my smile betrayed my emotions.

"I've thought about broken heart syndrome for a long time," I said. "Forget the anatomy and physiology. Imagine you're a regular person with trauma and stress in your life. A dead spouse or parent. It broke your heart. As you mourn, your body spills an abundance of chemical compounds into your bloodstream, and your brain receives a chemical signal and releases its own chemical compounds to alleviate your pain. In stopping the flow of tears, your brain's action has caused a decrease of blood flow to your heart muscles. The heart muscles go into hibernation to protect themselves. So, tell your patient the heart muscles went to sleep from exhaustion. A deep sleep to protect themselves."

"Dr. Nwaku, I love your explanation," Dr. Flores said. I looked at him twice because for the first time ever he was actually awake during a meeting. He took his eyeglasses off to rub his eyes.

"Thank you, Dr. Flores. The challenge we face is understanding the message that the heart sends to the brain and how the brain responds. Our goal is to elucidate the method they use to interact. That is the core of our research. We need to decipher the communication language of the heart, then that of a broken heart," I said. No chairs moved. Everyone focused on me except for Ralph. The attention I received from my division made me sad, though. How could I leave them for Africa?

The voice inside me said, *We sent messages to you. Drums and gongs daily for more than twenty-five seasons. You ignored our messages. I'm here to appeal to your heart to hurry home.* I glanced around the room to see if anyone else had heard the whispers in my head. To my great relief, they had all returned their focus to Craig's summary paper, discussing various points among themselves.

"If you exist, identify yourself," I whispered. Asking a voice in my head to identify itself was as stupid as asking the wind to show me a physical form. You can hear it, feel it, and see its effect, but you can never see the wind.

The voice was silent for the rest of the meeting, leaving me to wonder about when it would return and if I needed to talk to someone about it.

It was my last day at work. When I left the hospital that day, I did not look back.

CHAPTER 11

A beeping sound woke me. For a moment I thought it was a wooden African flute played by an exhausted musician trying to wake me for a journey across an ocean and desert. It was dark outside, and the only light in the bedroom came from the digital clock on the nightstand: 4:33 a.m.

Defying the early morning brain fog, I realized that I was lying on my back, in the same position I'd fallen asleep in. When I thought about those hours of deep slumber, I remembered a dream of escape to my hometown and the rousing reception I received.

After a few minutes of lying still, I contemplated going back to sleep. When I stretched my hands, one of them hit an object. Maybe I'd forgotten to remove my suitcase from the bed before I fell asleep. I moved my hands to my sides. My mind wandered again to my dreams, wanting another escape to bliss.

"So, I don't deserve an apology? Hit me again and I'll hit back," a voice said in what I thought was a dream. It wasn't what I'd wanted. In my grogginess, I heard a deep sigh. Was I still asleep? Such was my mental state that I thought the sigh came from me. With all the confusing things happening to me, going back to sleep did not appeal anymore.

I sat by the bedside and yawned while stretching. It was the type of yawn I could only do when I was alone—a loud, embarrassing sound that made me laugh.

"Stop that crap. You're not in a zoo," a voice said. I was now awake enough to realize what I was doing and who was speaking.

"I'm sorry, Elisha."

"You better be."

I moved closer to her side and held her out of guilt. She didn't push me away as I expected. Instead, she turned around and held me too. In the darkness, relishing the surprising embrace, I felt her warm tears on my neck. Using the corner bedsheet, I wiped them away.

"Your hug means the world to me," I said, holding Elisha tighter. Her only reply was heavy breathing, her chest pushing into mine.

Our bodies' crevices found their perfect fit as we merged into one. When her lips met mine, her caged passion escaped. Her kiss aroused the yearning I'd tried to tame for weeks, and our mouths drew from each other, as if thirsty for the nectar of life. My tongue surrendered to her probing as she moaned to the verge of orgasm.

I tore her housecoat off to feel her naked body. She moved her hands all over me until she settled on my erection. As if in a hurry, she lifted herself up and straddled me. She rode me like a bucking horse while moaning to a rhythmic ecstasy; as time passed, she sobbed to exhaustion. Getting off me, she plunked herself onto the bed and broke the brief silence that followed with her loud, rapid breathing. As I reached for her, I felt her warm body drenched in sweat, and my ears heeded to her unabated panting.

"I needed you badly," she whimpered.

"You needed a good fuck," I blurted out. Her crying had stopped, her breathing back to normal. Expecting her to rebuke me for my vulgarity, I laughed haughtily. How could I not be vulgar after the way she'd just fucked me?

"You're right, babe. I gave it to you, but I didn't hear you complain," Elisha said.

"Babe, I'm sorry. I loved it," I said. I felt bad about my insensitivity, but she'd surprised me with her aggression.

"Your insult tells me how you feel. Keep loving that ride. That's all you get from me," Elisha said. I thought I heard her mutter, "You prick," but I wasn't certain. Well, I guess I was one.

Elisha got out of bed and left the room, trailed by a mumbling sound like a fading train's rumble after leaving a station. She continued to spit out inaudible words until a door in the hallway shut out her babbling.

Temper tantrums were not in Elisha's character. It troubled me to see her go through so much for me. However, my pride held me back from following her.

Ignoring our spat, I returned to my somber state and waited. As I watched the seconds pass on the digital clock next to me, I coveted the passage of time that propelled me closer to my foretold destiny, a journey to my homeland and a confrontation with my jilted past.

# # #

I felt a tug on my toe, and a voice said, "Daddy, wake up."

Opening my eyes, I found the bedroom invaded by morning streaks of sun and my daughter standing at the foot of the bed. Her red sweater and black pants reminded me of what Elisha had worn when she was younger.

Obialu grinned when I sat up in bed. The nightstand clock registered 8:17 a.m. Putting on my glasses, I had a better appreciation of the subtle things around me.

"You're early," I said.

"Mommy asked me to come early. Ikenna just got here. He's late as always," Obialu said. As she spoke, Ikenna walked into the bedroom. His gold-buttoned blue blazer and bowtie did not surprise me. Standing next to Obialu, he wore an affable grin and hid his left hand in his pants pocket.

"Good morning, old man. You're still in bed," Ikenna said.

"I was up early."

Elisha walked into the bedroom as I spoke. I smiled at her for making me a happy man. Her red sweater and a short blue skirt gave me naughty ideas, but the only thing I could do was smile.

"Breakfast is ready," Elisha said. She didn't address anyone directly and left the bedroom after she spoke. I wondered if she had regrets about our early morning sex.

"I'll serve you breakfast, Daddy," Obialu said as she left the room.

"I need to shower first," I said.

"Just brush your teeth, Pops. We're not waiting for you," Ikenna said as he followed Obialu out.

Alone in the bedroom, I wiped tears of joy from my face. All the tears of gratitude for the special treatment by my family, tears for the loss of my parents, and tears for neglecting Africa. The tears were not for me; they were for all the wrongs I had done.

After the tears, I accepted my failings, vowed to be a better man with boundless fairness to everyone, and pledged to compensate my family with abundant love. The loneliness I had felt for days left me, and the optimism that was bringing me to Africa returned.

I sighed in relief that I was going back home. It was a sigh to expel the doubt I had, which would be gone forever now, I hoped.

When the drumbeats of home reached my ears, my feet shuffled to the beat along the way to the dining room.

# # #

The four of us dined together for breakfast. Pancakes, oatmeal, omelets, fruits, and juices galore. The quantity of food prepared by Elisha worried me. It appeared as if it was a goodbye feast, a permanent one.

We steered clear of any discussion of my trip and instead talked about what was going on in our kids' lives and how proud we were of their chosen careers which were excellent extensions of our own legacies. Sitting in the dining room after breakfast, I couldn't keep my eyes away from Elisha. At times she blushed while looking at me. When I stood and collected the dishes, she followed me to the kitchen.

"We need to get ready for the airport, it's getting late. I'll miss my flight if we don't. I'll do the dishes," I said. Elisha looked at me and shook her head.

"I'll do the dishes in my kitchen," she said.

"So, I'm not allowed to do dishes in my house?"

"You'll have native women do your dishes in Africa," she said, her voice raised. Looking at her bare feet and her choice of words for African women, I smiled.

"So, you call African women 'native'?" I asked.

Obialu joined us in the kitchen.

"I'm sure you'll have a lot of them waiting on you," Elisha said.

Shaking her head, Obialu said, "I'm out of here. You're impossible."

Both Obialu and Elisha left the kitchen. Elisha walked hurriedly toward the foyer, as if she was urgently needed somewhere else. I rolled up the sleeves of my unbuttoned shirt and got to work on the dirty dishes in the sink.

Turning the faucet on and listening to running water took me back to my mother's kitchen when I was a teenager. We had washed dishes together, my mother and me. The nostalgia made me feel all the lonelier. Remembering my mother's smile made me sad and remembering what she'd said to me in her kitchen— "You'd make a good husband to a lucky woman someday"—hurt. Was I a good husband to Elisha?

# # #

Basking in the love and devotion of my children over breakfast, I'd pushed aside the reality of my trip home. When I focused only on Elisha's goodwill that morning, my life felt as balanced as the four-legged chairs we sat on. But I knew that my marriage was wobbling on the edge of dissolution—and that my trip home would likely push it over that edge. At noon, with the temperature warming up to near seventy degrees, we loaded my two suitcases into the trunk of Obialu's car. Elisha stood next to me, watching everything I did but not speaking. When I turned away from her, I could see her beautiful smile from the corner of my eye. I wondered if she was happy that I was leaving.

When I went back inside to find my house keys, she followed me. Obialu and Ikenna sat in the car. Elisha trailed behind me around the house until I found my keys.

"Have a safe trip," she said before I opened the front door.

"Save that for the airport," I said jokingly.

"I'm staying home," Elisha replied, walking closer to me and kissing my cheek. I saw her wipe tears from her eyes. Everything she'd done since I'd expressed an interest in going to Africa had confused me. Her conflicting behavior made me wonder if she'd become mentally unstable and if I'd caused it somehow.

"Babe, come with me. Think about all the fun we'd have together," I said. I held her hand and pulled her along. She resisted. When it felt as if I was dragging her against her will, I let go. She almost fell. When she regained her balance, she bowed her head, as if she wanted to hide her eyes from me.

When she lifted her head and closed her eyes, tears rolled down her beautiful face. Taking a step toward her, I hugged her tightly and kissed her. She held on to me and didn't resist.

"The kids are waiting for you," she said as she turned and walked away from me.

"I'm grateful for you and our love," I said. "Nothing will ever stop me from loving you. I'll miss you as if I'm missing my own life. Babe, it'll always be you that I need." I was confused and alarmed about what I was saying. I hadn't known that I was so sensitive. The words came out of me as if they'd been written for me to say. Even the warm feeling I felt inside worried me.

Although I was disappointed, my mind backtracked to our early morning lovemaking and the send-off breakfast feast she'd prepared. So many things went through my mind, but the fear of losing Elisha lingered.

The African pride in me, however, stopped me from going after her to proclaim my undying love. Had my words earlier not been enough? It would amount to begging if I continued to plead with her.

When I'd accepted the reality that I'd be traveling alone to Africa, I thought about the emotional toll that the loss of my parents had taken on me and the damage a failed marriage would do to my psyche. What Elisha would do about our marriage I couldn't tell.

When I closed the front door, I said to myself, "She fucked me, fed me, and dumped me, all on the same day." I laughed while walking to the car. My children looked at me and then looked at each other with puzzled expressions. If they'd known what I'd said, I wondered what they would've said to me.

"Where's Mom?" Obialu asked.

"She's staying home," I said. Instead of looking at Obialu, I turned to look at the front door, hoping that Elisha would come out to join us.

"I'm sure Mom is upset about Pops leaving. Wouldn't you be, if it was you?" Ikenna asked. "Tell me, old man, what did you do to my mom?"

"It's not funny," Obialu snapped. She opened her car door. "I'll go get her."

"Close the door and drive. She isn't happy with me," I said. I heard Ikenna sigh. I looked at him but didn't know what to say.

Obialu drove away, yet I kept looking back, hoping to see Elisha come out. When we turned onto another street, I not only lost sight of the house I shared with her but I also lost the hope of the two of us traveling together. I wondered if I'd said a proper goodbye to my wife.

My heart raced and my stomach felt queasy when it dawned on me that I couldn't go back to Elisha. I knew that my pride wouldn't let me change my mind, and now, with my fervent desire to be home in Africa, I couldn't delay this trip. To be home was an obligation assigned to me at the time of my birth, one anchored to the African soil for eternity. No matter where I went and how long I was gone, that moor would always pull me to it.

"Pops, where the heck is your mind?" Ikenna asked, smiling.

"I wish your mother was going with me. I need her terribly."

"Call her. She'll love to hear you say it," Obialu said.

"I did. Many times."

"She's afraid of Africa," Obialu said.

"Afraid of what?" I asked.

"All the bad stuff in the news about Africa."

"As if Africa is different from every other continent. Even America has crime and racial strife," I said.

"You're right, Pops," Ikenna said.

"Once I'm settled, I expect you to visit," I said. Ikenna smiled without replying, and Obialu focused on the road.

Reaching for my cell phone to call Elisha, I felt my hand shake. I held on to the phone, afraid to reveal my unsteadiness. The uncomfortable feeling made me reposition myself with one hand in my pocket. My body felt as if it was sitting on a tilted chair with a missing leg. It was the same feeling of imbalance that I'd felt throughout my life. Obialu glanced at me, smiling, as if she knew what was on my mind. I had a sense of loss without any death, leaving me with an emptiness I bemoaned.

# # #

Obialu stopped her car at the curbside designated for passenger drop-offs in front of the Delta Airlines departure terminal at the Boston Logan International Airport. Since it was midday, I expected a deserted departure area, but many vehicles lined up along the limited space.

When I opened the car door and walked out into the fall sunshine, it didn't feel as warm as the car's temperature gauge had indicated. At the back of the car, retrieving my suitcases, I felt a gentle breeze; it was as appealing as an escape to a tropical paradise during a harsh winter. A mesmerizing feeling transported me to the best windy day I could remember in my hometown of Obodo. I knew that things sometimes felt better imagined than when experienced, but still I cherished the moment.

A car pulled up so close to where I stood before slamming on the brakes that it made me jump out of the way. I frowned at the driver. I knew that I should be more careful—stop daydreaming and think about what was right in front of me.

Ikenna and Obialu joined me as I lifted the suitcases from the trunk.

"Let me help, old man," Ikenna said.

"I'll carry my own bags," I replied with a smile.

"We're here to help," Ikenna said.

"Who will help me in Nigeria?"

"Pops, you're on your own in Africa."

"Tell me something I don't already know." We laughed.

I saw a frown on Obialu's face and wondered if she was okay. She retrieved her cell phone and dialed a number. I carried my suitcases to the curb as Ikenna closed the trunk.

"Hi, Mom, we just got to the airport," Obialu said. She looked at me. "He's standing next to me." She handed her phone to me.

"Hello, babe," I said. I watched Ikenna and Obialu whisper to each other, frowning.

"I feel sick to my stomach," Elisha said. She paused before adding, "Maybe I caught the flu."

"Get some rest. I'll check on you before I board," I said.

"I still can't believe you left me." Her voice sounded solemn enough for a memorial.

"My sister needs me," I said.

"Really?"

"She has always needed me, but now she's in danger."

"How about my needs? Do they matter to you?" Elisha asked.

Ikenna and Obialu were listening to everything I said. I walked a short distance away from them. The voice inside me whispered in my ear, *Speak up*.

"It does matter, babe," I said.

"It's always about you and Africa. Now it's your sister. I've had enough of your neglect. Go back to your village and leave me alone," Elisha said. I heard her sob. However, her use of the word *village* stung me hard. I held my breath, trying to control my anger, before I replied to her. When I exhaled, it didn't change how I felt.

"I need you, babe," I said. "Please, never stop loving me. Well, even if you stop, don't forget about me." I became worried about what I was saying. I wished I'd expressed my true feeling of anger from her denigration.

"My love for you blinded me. Look where it's gotten me. You have no idea the pain I feel inside," Elisha said.

"Is Mom okay, Dad?" Obialu asked. When she reached for the phone, I handed it to her. I needed to be stopped from saying what I felt.

"What's wrong, Mom?" Obialu asked. She listened for a moment. "Okay, I'll be there soon."

"What's wrong now?" Ikenna asked.

"Mom's crying. She's distraught," Obialu said. I saw tears in her eyes as she spoke to Ikenna.

"What a crazy day," Ikenna said.

"A fucked-up day," I said. By the time I realized that I'd cursed, it was too late. I couldn't take it back. Luckily, my children were too preoccupied with their mother's plight to worry about what I'd just said.

"Let's go," Obialu said to Ikenna. She walked toward the car. Ikenna hopped in with her.

"That's it? No hugs? No goodbyes?" I asked before they closed their car doors and sped away. I stood at the curbside, angry at everyone. I kicked my suitcases before picking them up.

CHAPTER 12

I slept through most of the eleven hours of flight time across the Atlantic Ocean before the airplane landed in Lagos, Nigeria, at 2:45 p.m. local time. I picked up my cell phone, dialed Elisha's number, and listened to her greeting, the song "We Belong Together." She didn't answer her phone, and I didn't want to leave a message.

I was alone when I exited the airplane and set foot in Lagos, a coastal city, the former capital of Nigeria. Even with the burning African spirit inside me, Lagos welcomed me with innumerable challenges.

Carrying my bags off the airplane, a metal-encased passenger walkway enfolded me with hot, humid air. I quickened my pace to escape from the suffocating tunnel. My breath pumped in and out, faster and faster, forcing more stifling air through my nostrils. The air felt like it was roasting my throat. I imagined that the oxygen I needed to survive was warming up my blood cells to heat up the core of my body. There was nothing I could do but continue at my quickened pace.

In the arrivals lounge, women attired in beautiful African prints and men in bright short-sleeved shirts watched my hurried steps with amusement. When I thought about the spectacle I was presenting, I laughed. I wondered how long it would take my body to adjust to the heat and humidity.

Upon reaching the customs and immigration counter, I handed over my passports, American and Nigerian, to the agents. It was the first time I'd taken advantage of the privilege of dual citizenship. I considered myself a "real" African, not a hybrid, so the ploy didn't bother me, although I did wonder why a "real" African was sweating as if he'd poured water on his clothes and body.

An immigration officer who'd left his smile at home that day beckoned to me. Dressed in a khaki uniform, he looked as if he was in his fifties. After inspecting my documents, his eyes scanned me. The way he looked at me from head to toe left only one impression: he was wondering why I'd taken a bath inflight with my clothes on.

When he handed my documents to a plump immigration supervisor wearing a nametag that read Eunice, I became concerned. I had limited time left to make it to the local airport.

"Which one you be, *oga*? *Oya* Americana, we need money to eat," Eunice said. I wondered if she

86

was questioning my dual nationality using pidgin English to see if I understood it enough to claim my Nigerian citizenship. What troubled me the most was her request for a bribe.

"You called me *oga*? *No be me*. I'm just an employed worker, *I no be one of the rich Nigerians*," I replied with a smile.

"Cheap Americana," Eunice said. Her labored smile was as fake as mine. After she stamped my Nigerian passport, she added, "Pass."

At the curbside, many idling vehicles were lined up, spewing black toxic fumes from their exhaust pipes. The humid heat persisted, but my body ignored the discomfort and welcomed its first nibble of African sun. The longer I stayed in the sun, undecided about the right taxi to hail, the more I felt that burning sensation on my exposed skin. Prickly sun bites and profuse sweating reminded me of the consequences of being away from home for so long.

In my many years away from Africa, my body had adapted from tropical weather to the temperate climate of Boston. This was evident by the way it reacted to the humid air. Nigerians walking by me, their fellow citizen Afamefuna Onochie Nwaku, turned around to look at my soaked shirt. Or so I thought—maybe their stares were my imagination.

I gazed at people's elaborate garments and opulent necklaces. Many young women wore fitted fancy clothes with revealing necklines. Below their waists, their clothes hugged their bodies tightly, outlining and drawing attention to their generous buttocks. What I saw was an African bum show. Most of the younger men appeared slender and wore less attractive clothing. A sizable number of them wore faded shirts. It was almost as if Nigeria had achieved the status of an egalitarian society just based on the looser restrictions on women's clothing since I'd left home. Gone were the conservative African George wrappers, long skirts and dresses that I remembered.

As I looked around for the right taxi, three young men approached me. One wore an Adidas shirt while the other two were in Manchester United jerseys.

"*Oga*, you need taxi?" the Adidas man asked.

"I'm okay, but thank you for asking," I said.

"We can carry your bags for you," one of the Manchester United men said.

"They're not heavy, I can manage." They lifted my bags anyway.

"*Oga*, your brothers have to eat. We carry your bags, you give us money."

"Please, drop my bags before I call the police."

"Go ahead, call the police. They'll collect their own money from you," the Adidas man said. They all laughed.

"Their own money? I don't owe them."

"*Oga*, in Nigeria, you pay. Nothing is free. To drive your car, you pay; take a taxi, you pay," the Adidas man said.

"Well, I need to find a taxi."

A car stopped next to me as I was speaking to the men. The driver, a young man in his twenties, rolled down his window. The car behind him blew its horn. Even with his windows rolled up, I heard the second car's driver yelling as he laid on the horn and tried to get around. The young driver with the rolled-down window ignored the chaos. Watching it all like it was free entertainment, I said under my breath, "Welcome home, Afam."

"Where to, *oga*?" the driver asked, ignoring the blaring horn behind him. I couldn't help but frown. The *oga* obsession in Nigeria and the young man's callous attitude toward the other driver made me shake my head. The Nigerian in me remembered that anyone seeking something of value from a man would use the word *oga*, as Americans would use the word *boss*. However, the disrespect to other drivers baffled me.

The three men and the driver watched my reactions as if there was something strange about me. We looked at one another with suspicion. When I remembered that I looked the part of a crazy man after a long flight, I stopped shaking my head at the troubling things I saw. The driver rolled up his car window to drive away.

"Take me to the local wing of the airport," I shouted. He rolled his window down again.

"Which airline?" the taxi driver asked.

"Air Peace," I said. I wanted to ask the driver about the airlines, which ones were good, but I didn't. My flight would leave in an hour, and I had no time to inquire about the decisions I'd already made.

Two armed police officers approached the taxi driver and banged on his vehicle. He rolled down his window and said something I couldn't hear. One of the officers reached into the taxi, shook the driver's hand, and then walked away.

As the taxi driver stepped out of his car, the three young men left. I waved at them.

"Thank you, boys," I said. I thought about my use of the word *boys* and then remembered where I was. They smiled and waved back. It appeared as if they didn't mind me calling them such. I was back home in Africa, not in America, where the term could be offensive.

When the driver opened his trunk to load my suitcases, I pulled out my cell phone, took a picture of his license plate, and sent it to my sister by text message with the caption: *Arrived in Lagos, attached is the car's license plate taking me to the local airport. I'll be home soon.*

I can't wait to see you, Adaku replied.

She was the only direct connection I had with my hometown, Obodo, and to Nigeria itself. I dialed her number as the taxi driver watched me.

"*Oga*, get in, let's go," he said.

"Hello," Adaku said as I entered the taxi.

"Hello, sis, I'm home, finally."

"Not yet. You're in Lagos, not Obodo. Hurry home, please. They're still watching me. I need you here," she said. I could hear the tension in her voice.

"Lagos is home too. Don't worry, I'll be there soon to kick their asses," I said. I didn't know what triggered my laughter. Maybe I was trying to dispel her fear.

"*Oga, tell am*," the taxi driver said loudly in pidgin English. He joined me in laughing as if he knew what I didn't know: the cause of my laughter. His mannerism entertained me and reassured my judgment in hiring him.

"What's going on?" Adaku asked.

"Nothing, just heading to the local airport. I'll call you when we land in Asaba," I said as I hung up and watched my surroundings: the narrow roads, clusters of buildings in disrepair, and hurried pedestrians. It appeared as if things had changed for the worse.

On reaching the local airport, the taxi driver parked his car close to the entrance of the departure hall. Several young men hung around the entrance in small groups, as if there was nothing urgent in their lives. Some joked and laughed, while others appeared serious. It didn't take long for porters with carts to surround our vehicle. The word *oga* resonated from their mouths. When I opened the door, the youngest of the porters tugged on my shirt.

"American *oga,* I'll carry your bags for free," the porter said. The rest of the porters laughed. The taxi driver approached the young porter who'd made the outrageous offer.

"Carry his bag to Air Peace. I beg, no funny things," the taxi driver said.

"*Na you be the oga?*" another porter asked the taxi driver. It was a mockery that Nigerian touts were known for.

"*I go protect my oga,*" the taxi driver said. I wondered why I needed protection from the porters.

After the taxi driver pulled my suitcases out from his car trunk, I handed him a twenty-dollar bill. He looked at me without accepting the money. I worried that it was not enough since we hadn't negotiated a fare.

"How much is your fare?" I asked. He looked at me with a crinkled face and squinted.

"*Wetin be fare?*" the taxi driver asked.

"How much do you charge?" the young porter said to the taxi driver. I was impressed with his knowledge.

"Are you a student?" I asked the young porter. His eyes sparkled, and his face loosened with a smile.

"*Oga*, remember your flight," the taxi driver said.

"How about your money?" I asked the taxi driver.

"*Oga*, change your money to naira. Paying with dollars is dangerous in Nigeria. I go do it for you," the taxi driver said. I wanted to ask why it was dangerous to use dollars but didn't. He looked at the porters and said, "Watch my car." I gave him a one-hundred-dollar bill for exchange as the young porter carried my bags into the departure hall.

I joined a short check-in queue in a crowded departure hall louder than a stadium packed full of fans. The young porter stood by me with his eyes locked on my suitcases. As time passed, he was steadfast in his task, watching out for me and my suitcases. His dedication and patience impressed me. I wondered, though, if the taxi driver would ever return with my money.

The taxi driver returned when I was about to check in. He took out a bundle of Nigerian currency from an envelope. I watched him count thirty-eight thousand naira of dirty and worn bank notes. As he handed the money to me, I hesitated in taking custody of what I considered undesirable currency. He laughed at me.

"*Oga think say Nigeria money is dirty*," the taxi driver said.

"You're very astute," I said. The taxi driver and the porter chuckled.

"*Oga, you're in Nigeria now, speak English wey we go understand*," the taxi driver said as he continued in his pidgin.

"*Oga say you're smart*," the porter said.

"Thank you, sir," the taxi driver said.

"*This one be shakara*," said a passenger standing in line, a short man in his fifties.

"*Oga*, ignore him," the taxi driver said.

"Was he talking to me?" I asked.

"I am talking to you," said the passenger. "You're too good for our money. Is your American money better than Nigerian?"

I ignored him. He walked closer to me and when I turned to look down at him, we stood staring at each other. After we'd sized each other up, the man walked away shaking his head.

From the money the taxi driver had exchanged for me, I gave him five one-thousand dirty naira notes. The young porter received a clean one-thousand naira note.

As they were leaving, I said, "Driver, thank you for helping me. As for you, young man, go back to school."

"Okay, sir," the young porter said as he left.

"Thank you, *oga*. Safe journey," the taxi driver said.

The two young men walked away. I turned around to face the challenges before me: checking in and boarding the airplane for a journey to meet with my past.

The boarding was uneventful, and as I sat in the airplane for my trip to Asaba, my sister's plight worried me. When I thought about people watching our house with binoculars, I became afraid of what I would confront when I got home.

CHAPTER 13

Fifty minutes after we took off from Lagos, the airplane landed on a desolate runway at Asaba Airport. Instead of hotels, bountiful grasslands and a prominent gulley formed by erosion welcomed us. One exciting thing about getting off at Asaba was the twenty-mile journey it would take to get to Obodo. Compared with where I'd started my journey and where I'd been, I was now a short distance from the soil that had nurtured my childhood, a mere stride away from where my ancestors had trodden since the beginning of time.

Stepping outside the airport, I set foot on the western enclave across the Niger River. The air was fresh, and the sun was partially subdued by dark clouds. Studying the sky, I saw how the clouds resembled those I remembered before rainfall. A hint of the cool breeze coming from the Niger traveled through my lungs, a relief compared with the humid concoction in Lagos.

The next phase in my journey was crossing the mighty Niger. Eager to get home, I hailed a taxi to take me to Obodo. It was easier making that decision compared with Lagos. I was more trusting of the people here than in Lagos, a prejudice I had to accept.

As the taxi approached the Niger Bridge, the dark clouds I saw earlier descended to hang low over the river, limiting our visibility. The road traffic stalled, and the taxi driver joined a line of idling vehicles as long as the eye could see.

"Another crazy day," the taxi driver said after five minutes of silence.

"Is it common?" I asked. He turned around to look at me, a wry expression on his face. It appeared as if he didn't know what to feel about the stalled trip: anger or resignation.

"Every day, the same problem. No government solution," the taxi driver said.

"Very sad," I answered.

"*Oga, na the problem in this country.* Politicians steal. No money for a new bridge," the taxi driver said.

"Whatever happened to the second Niger Bridge? They had the drawing more than forty years ago."

"During each election, they promised to build it, claimed to have set the funds aside. After the election, they forgot about us."

"How about the local elected officials? Don't they travel through this bridge?"

"They're worse than the federal government. Some use helicopters to travel, but most are addicted to money. They'll even steal money from their own pockets," he said. I couldn't help but laugh.

Trapped in the middle of a traffic jam, we waited for another ten minutes before I became concerned. The thought of the sun setting troubled me. While waiting, I saw passengers disembarking from the vehicles in front of us. Most of them walked toward the bridge as if they were going to cross it on foot, while others walked in the opposite direction. As some of them walked by us, carrying heavy loads, I saw sweat and despair on their beleaguered faces.

"I must get home," I said.

"*Oga, you fit enough walk across the bridge?*" the taxi driver asked.

"I walk every day."

The taxi driver turned around again, looked me over, and smiled. "*Here no be America. Nigeria heat will quench you.*"

"How do you know I'm from America?" I asked. I'd wanted to ask that question since my arrival in Lagos.

"*Ha, oga! Na your fresh skin. Not like Nigeria skin,*" the taxi driver said. "We see you Americanas, always happy."

"I'm a Nigerian."

"On paper only, *oga*," he said. We laughed together.

"I need to cross the bridge and get home," I said.

"There's boat. Take a taxi after you cross the river," he replied.

"Sounds good to me."

"When you get to Onitsha, you'll face traffic problems too."

"We had traffic problems in Boston also," I said. When I realized what I'd said, it was too late. My desire was to avoid comparing Nigeria to America. Fortunately, the driver was focused on something else.

The driver opened his car door and I jumped out. We met at the trunk to retrieve my suitcases. He returned to his seat, turned off his engine, and locked his car. He lifted my suitcases.

"Let's go," he said as he carried my bags. I was too tired to protest his kindness and wasn't sure where we were going. "*Oga, na for boat. I want you pass Onitsha before dark,*" he added, as if he'd read my mind.

"My first boat ride in Nigeria," I said. Riding a boat sounded intriguing to me, though it wasn't a recreational event.

"You need to cross over quick. Armed robbers come out after dark in Onitsha," he said.

"Nothing has changed then," I said.

The taxi driver nearly dashed as we walked toward the riverbank under the low dark clouds. Apart from my worry about rainfall, now I was concerned about armed robbers. I looked across the river and saw vehicles on the street of Onitsha without any traffic stopping them. I exhaled. Amid the threatening clouds, I saw many boats tethered at the river's edge.

Close to the banks of the Niger, men in canoes beckoned with their hands in a frenzy at anyone who looked in their direction, including me and the taxi driver. Looking at the overly enthusiastic men in their boats, I thought they behaved in the same manner as wildly happy vultures hovering over a dying man. Judging them was unfair, but I did. Resolving not to engage in the services of the charlatans, I took one of the suitcases from the taxi driver and sat on it to stew. The taxi driver placed the remaining suitcase next to me.

"Good luck, *oga*," he said.

"Their canoes are small and their eagerness disturbing," I said. I looked at the swerving boats and their aggressive owners again. My stomach felt queasy.

"*Oga*, there's a saying around here. When you need to reach a destination urgently, don't look at the makes of the available vehicles. Hail the first one you can get."

"I don't agree with that saying. I'll call the vehicle that I feel is mechanically sound and would get me to my destination, not the first one."

"What happens if all the vehicles don't appeal to you?" he asked.

"I see your point," I said.

Two men hopped from their boats and joined us as the taxi driver continued his vigil over me. Turning to look at him, I realized that I hadn't settled his fare. I reached inside my pocket and retrieved some of the dirty naira currency I had left. I handed five thousand naira to him. The smile on his face made me smile too.

"Thank you," he said. I wondered who should be expressing appreciation, him or me.

"*Oga, make I take you across,*" one of the two men said after the taxi driver left. I looked at the dark clouds, then my watch with American time, and back at the approaching darkness. I sighed out of desperation and felt a knot tightening in my stomach when I remembered that I hadn't eaten in a long time.

"Okay," I said to the boat man. He was the first, and I did as the taxi driver suggested. I didn't even see his boat. My body was also spent; I felt like a wrung dish rag. He took my suitcases to his boat, and I followed him.

Sitting on a platform in the dingy, I crouched as the minutes passed. I watched as men, women, and children boarded small boats and canoes in large numbers. The spectacle of the operators taking on as many passengers as they could fit made me cringe when I thought about those vessels capsizing. Boats with more passengers than they could handle were easy to spot because their edges were close to the water's surface. When the departing boats passed, their waves splashed on tethered boats, often landing on seated passengers.

As more time passed, I reflected on the day I'd left home and how many years had passed. Memories of my parents overwhelmed me, and the fear of losing Elisha returned. I felt lonely, surrounded by strangers who weren't cognizant of what I was going through. As much as I tried to forget the enormity of my inherited responsibilities, it weighed heavily on me.

Sitting on the wrong side of the Niger and unsure when I would cross it, my worries sapped all the energy left in my hungry body. It was only a distance of twenty miles going east from the riverbank that separated me from my hometown, but it felt as if we were traveling to the moon. With every sunset, the crime rate in Onitsha increased, and it had been so for as long as anyone I knew could remember. My safety weighed on me too, and I was eager to get home.

When our overloaded dingy set out to slowly cross the river, it swerved and almost capsized. Women and young children screamed; even some grown men did. The screaming bunch, holding one another in one corner, almost tipped the boat until the skipper yelled, "Get back to your seat, idiots." They obeyed. I couldn't remember taking another breath until we reached the riverbanks in Onitsha. I hailed the first taxi that passed by.

# # #

A police officer, a young man in an olive uniform, stuck his head inside the taxi through a rolled-down rear window. He looked around the vehicle's interior without saying anything. As he pulled his head away, he plopped a kola nut inside his mouth. I sat and watched him ignore me. He walked to his partner, who was checking the registration papers he'd requested from the taxi driver.

Five minutes passed as other vehicles drove by without being stopped. When the police officer handed the registration papers to the driver, he came by the window to look me over. I wondered how many police officers it would take to decide

101

what to do about me, a passenger in the back seat of a taxi.

"*Oga*, what do you have for us?" the second police officer asked.

"I don't have anything for you. I'll have something for you next time," I said.

"We don't want your driver to be late. If you don't cooperate, we'll take him to the station," the police officer said. The driver looked at me, and I looked at him. He used a hand gesture, but I couldn't understand what he was trying to tell me.

"Driver, get out of the car," one of the police officers yelled. He removed his AK-47 from his shoulder and pointed it at the taxi driver.

The two police officers escorted the taxi driver to their parked truck. For about five minutes, they were out of my sight. I sat in the back seat, worried and afraid to get out of the vehicle. I wondered what would happen if the sun set and it became dark. When I saw the driver running back to his taxi, I was relieved. He even had a smile on his face.

"What happened?" I asked. The taxi driver looked at me and shook his head.

"They could tell you're not from around here," he said.

"I'm from Obodo, where we're going."

"You don't look like a villager, and your skin hasn't seen Nigerian sun for long. We can tell when you people return home from overseas. We call you American *bobos*." He laughed.

"How much did you give them?"

"Like everybody else, the police officers have to eat."

"Isn't that corruption?" I asked. He drove off without answering. "Didn't you hear my question?"

"*Oga*, you won't understand. The politicians and the big *ogas* in Abuja steal all the money. Government workers aren't paid. They beg for money to survive," he said.

"What I witnessed wasn't begging but intimidation," I said.

He shook his head. "At night, armed robbers won't intimidate. They kill. Which is better, *oga*?"

"Neither. We need better security and policing." I had no idea what Nigeria needed, but I wasn't proud of what I saw. "Welcome home," I muttered to myself.

The driver didn't tell me how much he'd given the police officers, but I decided to pay him more than he requested. I knew I was the cause of his problem, and it wouldn't be fair if I didn't pay back what he'd lost.

# # #

Before the sun set, I crossed two rivers, the Niger and the Iyiofolo, to reach my destination, a fertile land tucked away in the small village of Obodo. On seeing the magnificence of what laid before me, I was elated.

"Driver, drop me off at the gate," I said.

"It's a long walk to the house," he replied.

"I've been waiting for too long to take it." I paid the driver and exited his vehicle with my two suitcases.

I stood close to the gate of my father's estate to appreciate the splendor of what I'd forsaken for decades. The gentle wind fanned my tired body and traveled across the land, swaying tall grasses in a rhythmic dance.

It was my father who'd told me that the expansive land was my grandfather's goat-grazing field, that it had been so for decades before my life began. Standing alone there, it felt as if the immortal African spirit inside me was watching the natural beauty of my heritage with me.

My feet floated as if I was a dancer, easing along the path guarded by two anthills to my father's house. I stared at the fresh red soil dug up by the ants, claiming territories they didn't own. Fearless, they moved around on their earthen mounds as if they were the new owners of my land. I smiled. After taking a few steps, I turned around and returned to the red mounds.

"I know I've been gone for a long time, but I'm still the lord of this land. It's not for termites," I said. They ignored me, continuing to wander. What troubled me was my seriousness. I wasn't making fun of the termites; rather, I was making a claim to the land that belonged to me. I was either going mad or was far too hungry.

Halfway along the path to my father's house, birds congregated on several trees with ripe fruits. On one tree, red-feathered birds and buzzing bees shared their bounty. The birds' beaks and talons probed the abundant feast while the bees buzzed on oozing fruits. It was a mesmerizing splendor of African bounty.

At my father's house, standing at the entrance to a two-story building with fading white paint and a rusted corrugated-iron roof, I placed my suitcases on the ground. I turned around to look behind me. I didn't regret making the decision to walk the long path as a reintroduction to the land that had not felt my presence in many decades.

When I raised my hand to knock on the front door, rumbling sounds interrupted me. It was the sound that came before a tropical rain, and it didn't take long before drops began to fall on the dry soil. As the soil fizzed, a uniquely African earthen scent mixed with the still air around me. Anticipating a tropical deluge, I knocked hard on the front door as if I was a stranger.

The door opened. Adaku stood there. She was my height with a fit physique; short, curled gray hair; a red damask blouse; and a disarming smile—one fashioned and made by our mother.

Adaku hugged the life out of my body. As she held on to me, she wept. We stood outside, hugging and crying in each other's arms.

"You're really home," Adaku shouted. Her voice echoed into the house.

As the sound traveled, four cousins I had grown up with came from the living room. Their presence surprised me. Ejike was the first to reach me. Although he was my first cousin, he'd spent most of his life in my house when we were young. We were close before I left, but he had stopped answering my phone calls more than three decades ago. Anayo, Ofomata, and Unoma, my third cousins, were not as close to me. We only associated with each other at large family gatherings.

Ejike was not the same person I had once known. His broad nose stood on his face as prominent as the oversized doorknobs on my father's old house and his obese body waddled around the living room. His huge mass shocked me. I hadn't anticipated finding this type of obesity in Africa. But the emaciation of my other three cousins worried me more. They looked so thin that I considered them malnourished. No, none of my cousins looked healthy.

As Ejike walked by, I wondered about his sister, Ifeaku, but was afraid to ask him. Where was she? The four of us had grown up together: Adaku, Ejike, Ifeaku, and me. We were first cousins and close friends. The most ebullient among us was Ejike, the only son of my father's sister.

It was the 1960s Nigerian Civil War that had brought us together. The bonds of our friendship were as strong as the strings that held our shared genes. War children, they had called us, but we were not at war. Adults fought in, died for, and deliberated about the war. We, the children of the war, played, fished, and sometimes pushed one another around. That was the extent of the conflict between us. We were youthful but not youths. The war taught us about life and death. It exposed us to violence, but we were not violent. Not then.

As our cousins watched my sister and I hug, I worried that we were ignoring them. My sister held on to me and rendered my worry trivial.

"I missed you terribly," I said.

"I missed you too, my baby brother," Adaku said, her sadness mixed with laughter.

"Only African women can cry and laugh at the same time," I said.

"That's your problem, if you don't understand African women. This African woman wants to know something. Where's your family?" Adaku asked as we separated.

"They're in Boston," I said and turned to the other people around me, hoping to avoid my sister's inquisition.

"You're my welcoming party," I said to them.

"Welcome home, Afam," Ejike said as we shook hands and hugged. "No one invited me. I saw men clearing the compound this morning, and I knew something big was about to happen."

"I'm happy to see all of you," I said.

"We're happy to see you too, my American cousin," Anayo said.

"I plan to visit America someday," Ejike said. I looked at him with interest but didn't take the statement seriously.

"You'll visit America for food," Anayo said. The rest of the cousins laughed. Ejike frowned and walked away.

I walked over to where the sulking Ejike stood. He smiled as I came closer and moved his hands in and out of his pants pockets.

"We're cousins forever," I told him. "I know we've been cruel to each other since childhood, but we love each other too."

"Look at us," Ejike said, his voice quavering. "You have lands, properties, money, and other things I don't even know of, all of what your father left for you. I have nothing."

"Whatever you think I have, I worked for it. What my father had didn't matter to me."

"He sent you to America to study. Look at me. I stayed here to suffer." Ejike breathed heavily through his prominent nose. I couldn't decide if it was from anger or his obesity.

Anayo interrupted. "We're not here to judge our misfortunes. Welcome home, Afam. Please, forgive Ejike." She looked at the other cousins as they shook their heads.

Adaku leaned against the doorframe and placed her trembling hands behind her back. She seemed to be holding the doorframe to support her wobbling legs. Ejike looked at her and rolled his eyes. He paced around and avoided looking at me. I became confused.

"Sis, are you okay?" I asked. I placed the back of my hand on her forehead.

"Stop. I'm not your patient," she commanded. I removed my hand.

"Since you're assessing everyone's needs, I have a request. I want my share of our land," Ejike said.

"Which land?" I asked.

"All the lands that belong to us." He waved his hand to indicate the grasslands outside.

"You can't want what's not yours. Only criminals do that. Are you a crook, Ejike?" I asked.

"You and your fancy education can go to hell. Call me a crook again and see what happens. Here in Obodo, I'm known. I'll get what's mine." He stepped closer to me. His eyes were half shut, his face seething with anger. His nose flared. Perhaps he needed those big tunnels on his face to exhale all the evil thoughts he accumulated inside him.

"I didn't call you a crook, but you want what belongs to my family. What should I call a man who wants to take what doesn't belong to him? Ejike, tell me what I should call you."

"Call me your nightmare," he answered.

The rest of my cousins leaned their heads toward one another and whispered.

"My brother came home today," said Adaku. "Instead of palm wine, you brought anger to welcome him back. Instead of love for him, you have jealousy. Ejike, I want you to leave our house."

He pointed his finger at her. "You're a woman. You can't tell me what to do."

"She's my sister, and this house belongs to her. She has the right to ask you to leave," I said.

"It's an abomination in our land for her to ask me to leave my grandfather's property. The house belongs to us, not Adaku."

"The house belongs to me, not us. I want you to leave now," I said.

"I'll report you to our people," he replied. "You have come home to desecrate our culture."

"Our people don't steal, but you're asking for what doesn't belong to you. That's desecration to our people."

Adaku spoke: "Ejike, you came back from Lagos broke, came to me for loans, and when I refused to loan you more money, the threats started. Before Afam came back, you claimed the land belonged to you, and now you say some of the land belongs to you."

"I'll take what belongs to me," Ejike said.

"You come here trying to take my family's land. You think you can walk in here and tell us to leave?" I asked.

"You don't deserve anything in Obodo. Our women were not even good enough for you. Go back to your American wife," he said.

"This conversation is over. Leave my property," I demanded.

Ofomata spoke up. "The sacred bird said that only ignorant children aim their slingshots to kill it. Adults waved and revered it. We're cousins. We keep away hurtful words from one another. If we aim our arrows at one of us, we're aiming it at ourselves." Ofamata was the silent one, but his words were profound. No one spoke after him.

Ejike fidgeted as we stared at each other. If his eyes could kill, I would've been dead. I walked away from him. He remained in the house, but we ignored him.

All the things I wanted to do as soon as I got home had been affected by Ejike's belligerence, but I couldn't defer them any longer. After I removed my shoes and socks, I went outside barefoot. Even with thunder rumbling closer, and a few raindrops, the deluge I expected did not come. My sister and cousins, except for Ejike, followed me. With the first step I took with my naked feet, I felt my body quake, as if it had received an electric shock. It was like a mystical transformation. I knelt and kissed the

110

ground before walking back into my father's house. Had I been struck by lightning?

Although the curtains and chairs hadn't changed over the years, when I looked around the living room I felt the absence of my parents. Their favorite chairs sat empty. A gnawing sense of loss overtook me. A vivid image of the last time we had stood together as a family in that room, feasting and laughing, came back to me. I looked from one family photograph on the wall to another.

Adaku followed me around as if she was a guide in a museum, but unlike a museum guide, her face wore a serious look. When I came to an old family portrait resting on a small table, I picked it up. Two missing family members, my mother and my father, looked as fresh as the day the photograph was taken. Never could that image be taken away from my memory. I wished I had spent more time with them.

Looking at the portrait of my own family that I had sent to my parents, I saw me and Elisha sitting with our children standing by our sides. It brought back memories of the early years of my marriage.

There were several family members missing in my father's house, but I accepted that, until now, the most important thing missing here had been me, the new patriarch.

As the sun set on Obodo that day, I accepted my responsibility as lord and overseer of this land, this part of Africa. It was my birthright.

"Ofomata, the wise one, tell all our elders to convene in my house on the next *Afor* market day after their morning palm wine," I said.

"We use real time in Obodo since you left. I'll tell them to meet with you at 8 a.m.," he replied. We laughed.

"I won't come with them," Ejike said.

"I didn't ask you to. I'm the patriarch of the Nwaku family. You're a subordinate member of the family. Never forget that."

Ejike walked out the front door and slammed it behind him. He didn't return to the house that day.

# # #

Close to midnight, pulsating drumbeats from a short distance away traveled through my body in bursts like the rhythm of my heart. Sitting on my father's chair, as awake as the African sun, I bobbed to the drumbeats of Obodo. As the music grew louder, I felt everything African in me coming out of dormancy. Once liberated, they revived the essence of me, which was truly African. When I stood and danced to the rhythm of the distant drums, it filled my body with youthful exuberance. I shimmied and twirled as if I was possessed. For a change, I was dancing to real African music.

When the drumbeats stopped, it felt as if my life was ending. My body's sway diminished, the sense of elation in me drained. In the family room, without my parents, my emptiness only deepened. Reclining in my father's chair, I whistled to fill the void.

Inside me, time seemed to stand still, but I knew that it was a deception. Even the termites and birds knew that I had been gone. My excuses for not coming home had been an endless search for academic fame in America and the fear that I would lose it all if I didn't stay in Boston. Contemplating what would become of me, a stranger now in my own country, I resolved to be a patriarch that my father would be proud of.

I had a lot to accomplish, but I wasn't deterred by the responsibilities.

CHAPTER 14

Despite my internal turmoil, a surreal night in Obodo left me feeling calm. Waking up at sunrise, I stepped outside my father's house to embrace the early morning air, which was filled with the sweet smell of sunbaked red earth. Indulging my body in the essence of African purity, the sunshine and clean air, my mind was at peace, at least for that moment.

Wearing only a pair of shorts and walking barefoot, I inspected the grasslands surrounding my father's house. The feel of African earth on my feet, the interspersing sounds of mourning doves, and the gentle breeze caressing my bare chest sent me into nirvana.

While I was playing in the field like a child, dark clouds started to move in, blocking the beautiful African sun. As I walked back to the house, the wind picked up and the heavy clouds descended, barely hovering above the tall palm trees. The drastic change in the weather was unusual for an October morning in Obodo; *unusual*, which was what they had named climate change in other parts of the world. Whatever it was, I was dismayed.

I reached the gazebo, a construction of rusted metal pipes and a weathered corrugated-iron roof. Pieces of earthen pots littered the ground, a sign of many years of neglect. Standing inside the gazebo, I watched the wind whip the palm fronds into a frenzy. Distant clapping sounds of thunder followed. I sat on a bench in the gazebo for less than a minute before the anticipation of my first tropical storm in many years drove me back toward the house.

I was near to the house when I heard Adaku yell, "Afam, where are you?" It was the same way my mother used to yell at me growing up. I heard the urgency in her voice, a trait of overprotective African women, and quickened my pace. Maybe I had underestimated my exposure to danger, as broken tree branches and detached roofing materials could quickly turn into flying missiles that could maim or kill.

When I reached an old pine tree twisting in the wind, I closed my eyes the way I used to when I was a child, listening to the wind's mesmerizing whistling. At that moment, all the ambivalence I had felt about leaving my medical career in America dissipated.

When I opened my eyes, the hovering clouds had passed but the sun remained hidden. Looking beyond the grasslands on the eastern side of the property, I focused on a small forest with lush green vegetation. My father had once told me that my grandfather, a revered shaman, harvested medicinal herbs from that forest and used them to heal the sick. How I wanted to explore there. A major clinical discovery from the herbs could help my hometown. How wonderful it could be to have Obodo become a renowned town internationally.

I realized that fate had brought me back to Obodo, where my life had started. It had brought me back to where they'd buried my umbilical cord to tether me to the African earth for eternity. It had brought me back to where my soul had remained to roam in my physical absence. There was no doubt left in me that the land where I stood belonged to me and that I belonged to it.

Closer to my father's house, a strong wind blew across my face, lifting sands from the ground as it sped up, the tall grass swaying along its path. It swept through a cluster of my father's pine trees, whistling my name across the land. It wasn't my imagination. I heard my name, a protracted, high-pitched version that saturated the air around me and traveled to other homesteads all over Obodo. Afamefuna Onochie Nwaku had returned to his homeland to deliver on the dreams his father had had when he sent his only son to a faraway land to study Western medicine.

# # #

Adaku and I sat in the covered balcony overlooking the entrance to the house. It reminded me of the way

117

we used to eat breakfast with our parents when we were young.

Plates of assorted muffins, vegetable omelets, toasted wheat bread, and a pot of brewed tea covered the small round table in front of us. The sounds of rainfall hitting the iron roof accompanied the clatter of knives and forks on my mother's plates. We sat for a long time without exchanging words, but Adaku kept looking at me. I wondered if she even knew what to say to me. When I looked at her, she smiled, which lifted my spirit and untied my tongue.

"Thank you, sis, for taking care of our property while I was gone. I'll repay you someday."

Her smile became more electrifying than before. "Mama asked me to take care of you. Taking care of home was expected of me while you were away." She moved her chair closer so that she was less than a foot away from me.

"Mama should have known that Elisha would take care of me," I said.

"She wasn't happy with your foreign wife. Wondered how she treated you and worried about you to her grave," Adaku replied.

"I told them I was happy. Elisha was there for me, cared for me, loved me. She is a good wife." Adaku looked in my eyes for a long time and shook her head.

"If Elisha loves you, she should be here with you. Your children too."

I took a deep breath. "She's an American. I can't force her to come home with me," I said. That emptiness in me returned. The unsteadiness in my voice surprised me. I could have explained her

118

absence better. Being an American was a lame excuse.

"My little brother, I'll be blunt. If she loves you, she'll love Obodo too," Adaku said. She stood up and walked to the balcony railings.

"What's wrong? Forget about Elisha. I'm home."

Adaku looked at me and returned to her chair. "When Papa died, you came home, stood around, and then ran away after two days. That was twenty-five years ago. You left me to grieve alone and take care of Papa's estate. Well, your estate," Adaku said. Her voice cracked as she spoke, tears starting to roll down her cheeks.

"That's not what happened. Remember, Elisha's mom was sick. We flew back to Boston to be with her. You forgot about that."

Adaku turned to me, her eyes swollen and mouth agape. Several times she opened her mouth to speak but hesitated. Finally, she said, "You promised to come back as soon as you could. How many years did it take you?"

"My job and my family were my responsibilities too," I said.

"I had a husband who I neglected when I was caring for Mama and Papa," she replied. "When they died, I took care of their property."

"You can't imagine how much work I had to do to be recognized. As a foreigner in Boston, I had to work my butt off to receive accolades given to other doctors who had far fewer publications."

"You made the choice to remain there, chasing after whatever you said you wanted. Papa wanted his only son home."

"What about what I wanted?" I asked. "Did it matter?"

"You sound selfish. That's not the brother I know," Adaku said, shaking her head.

"My happiness comes first," I answered. "That's a natural process. It doesn't affect my love for you or my love for this land." Adaku stared at the grasslands. "Sis, I love you. Nothing will ever change that but understand that I have needs too. I made mistakes, but I'll make things better around here."

As time passed, we sat at the breakfast table with our guarded thoughts like two prizefighters afraid to throw hard punches. For a while, neither of us ate. We looked at the food as if we didn't know what to do with it. Finally, when Adaku lifted her fork, it fell on the table. She pushed her plate away.

"You should hear yourself. My job, my wife, my happiness, my recognition, it's all about you. What sacrifices did you make for your parents? Would you make any for me?"

I answered, "Our name, Nwaku, is known worldwide in medical research. That's something we should be proud of. Papa made it possible, and I'm grateful for it."

"What happened to you? You don't sound like my brother. I don't know whether to feel disappointed or betrayed by you."

"Nothing happened to me. I gave up everything to return home. Am I not home?"

"My own brother forgot his responsibilities," Adaku scolded. "The only son forgot where he belongs. I often wondered if you knew your role in this house. Listen to me, Afam. You're the father and patriarch of this house. It's you who owns everything." At times she sounded as if she were my mother.

"I know my place, but things were tough for me when Papa died. Elisha's Mom was sick. She was their only child. They needed her."

"The same way our parents needed me as if I was their only child."

"I'm sorry again, but it feels like you're sticking a dagger into an old wound and twisting it." Sitting next to my sister, her eyes on me, I felt like a small child sitting on a big chair.

"If you really know what your role is, bring your family home," Adaku said as she stood up. "I've been taking care of this place since you abandoned me. I risked my life chasing squatters away. Where were you? In Boston with your family. How about me? I'm your sister, Afam. Am I not family? You should have the same commitment to me." As she spoke, I could feel the anger building inside her. I could hear it in the way she pounded the floor of the balcony with her feet. My guilt swelled.

"I can't bring them home. They're adults," I said tersely.

A crosswind whipped rain across our faces and drenched our clothes as if quenching our heat. It brought back memories of our childhood, playing in the rain, splashing puddles at each other.

When we looked at each other and our rain-soaked clothes, something we shared, something that lived in us both, made us smile. There was no doubt in my mind that our thoughts were in sync. There was nothing either of us could do but smile. As angry as we were, the soaking rain reminded us about what we'd had as children. The silly side of us.

Picking up wet paper napkins from the table, we wiped each other's faces the way we used to do in grade school. At that moment, I felt closer to my sister.

The wind passed, my wet shirt cooled me down, but instead of changing my clothes I reached for my cup. When I took a sip, expecting hot tea, the bland, cold liquid taunted me. Regardless, I drank it. I realized that that was how I felt about my family in Boston. Sometimes I let unpalatable things happen if there was no other choice.

As my sister looked at me, I wondered what she was searching for in my face. It would have been easier if she asked me.

"I know a lot about being alone," she said. "I've been alone since Fred died. Loneliness lives with me. Things would have been better if I had children."

"I'm sorry I didn't make it to his funeral. I'm really sorry."

"The only brother-in-law you had died, and you didn't come home. I buried him alone."

"I did so many wrongs, but I'm here now," I said as I reached out to hold her hand.

"You're here now, but for how long?" Adaku asked.

"When I left Boston, I asked for a one-year sabbatical, but I have no intention of going back there." I looked at my sister and my surroundings as if I wanted to reassure myself of my honesty. In Obodo, it was said that a patriarch's statement was an oath between him and his ancestors. My heart raced thinking about what I was promising.

"I hope so. I don't want you to leave," Adaku said.

"I'm home. Let's not talk about me leaving."

"I kept the money Papa left for you at First Bank, but the rent from the Onitsha properties goes to UBA. I've spent some money renovating. I have documents for everything." From her purse she pulled out a brown envelope sealed with stamped red wax and handed it to me. "Here's Papa's will. I believe he willed everything to you."

Adaku did not sound angry, much to my surprise. She had gracefully managed everything our father had left for an absent son. It surprised me that my father had handled his financial affairs in the traditional African way. In my culture, men inherited properties and women were excluded, but I considered my father an enlightened man. That was the bane of my discontentment with his will.

"Sis, the money should go to you. You deserve it. It's not enough for all you've done for me."

"It's your money. I did what you'd have done for me if things were reversed," Adaku said.

"It's a gift from me."

"The only gift I want is for you to stay here. I need you home."

"I'm here," I said. I wondered if there was something I had said or not said that made her doubt the permanency of my return.

The rain had stopped but the dark clouds remained. On the eastern side of our property, a rainbow formed a wide arch, ascending before

123

descending into a grass field. Well, maybe it ascended from two flanks and met at the middle. I wasn't there when the rainbow started, so how could I tell how it had formed?

My sister stood up and walked to the edge of the balcony to look into the distance. She wasn't looking at the rainbow but far away, beyond the grasslands. I joined her, and we stood next to each other as if we were there for the same purpose. I could tell that she felt at peace standing next to me by the way she smiled, albeit briefly.

"I need to go," she said. "My neglected house first, then to the market for meat."

"I'll come with you," I said.

"Call your family. I'll manage." She picked up the dishes and walked into the house. I followed her, and as she placed the dishes in the sink, I picked them up and laid them on the countertop. After filling the sink with water, I washed all the dishes as Adaku watched.

"That's my job at home," I said with a smile.

"I'm proud of you. You're not like some of these African men. A disgraceful bunch."

"Mother trained me well."

Adaku rested her purse handle on her elbow before she picked up her keys. She walked to the front door, turned around, and asked, "Are you going to be okay while I'm gone?"

"I'll be okay, Mom," I said. We laughed as she left. I needed that laugh to expel the loneliness I felt even before she'd left.

Adaku drove away, leaving me to tend to Father's house, the way it was supposed to be.

Holding the door half closed, I watched as the misty rain morphed into a heavy downpour. Even with the limited visibility, I found beauty in the way the thirsty grasslands soaked up the rain.

# # #

Wind-whipped rain beat against the windowpanes as if it was trying to break into the house. When it stopped, it left a hollow silence. That pattern repeated until even the intervals kept a rhythm. After locking all the doors, I retreated to my parents' former bedroom, the place Adaku and I used to hide as children when there was lightning and thunder. This time I didn't go to the bedroom to hide but locking all the doors—as if I was locking out all the monsters—was reminiscent of my childhood. Was I afraid of something or someone?

Turning the lights on, I felt like my father still occupied the room. Nothing seemed to have changed, including their ornamented iron bed and the worn, heavy window drapes. Behind the drapes, colored windowpanes shielded the room. When I heard what I thought were whispers outside the house, I inhaled deeply with trepidation. Pulling the curtains apart to look outside, I saw no one. I closed the curtains to focus my eyes inside the bedroom, but I still listened to all the sounds outside the building.

In the left corner of the bedroom, my father's wooden locker, where he kept his documents, remained just as he'd left it. His two gun cases sat on the locker. I sat on a chair and opened the cases. In the one, I found the rifle that my father used to teach me how to shoot when I was eight years old; and in the other, I found a double-barreled shotgun. A fresh shine of cleaning oil glinted on the guns, which made me wonder if Adaku had been taking care of them. Inside the wooden locker, I found a hardcover notebook tied with a rope and boxes of ammunition. There were enough cartridges for the rifle and shotgun to start a small village war.

I stood to look around the bedroom again. It felt like something was missing. Stepping into the bathroom while holding the rifle, I looked in the mirror. What I saw was an aging man, not a gun-toting iconoclast. Even the thought of being a rebel made me chuckle.

Returning to the open locker, I inspected some of the gun cartridges. I also found a revolver loaded with bullets. I took the bullets out and returned them to an empty ammunition box, stashing the revolver in the rifle gun case.

When the drumbeats of the rainfall stopped, I realized that I was singing one of the local songs aloud. I left my father's chair and sat on my parents' bed with the notebook I'd found in the locker. The message written on the first page left me confused.

My dear son,

Welcome home. I have joined my ancestors as expected after a fulfilled life. No one takes earthly belongings with them at their death. For you, I'm leaving behind all my earthly belongings and my problems too. I'm also leaving for you what my

126

father left for me. Your authority among our people is predestined, and there is no one who would challenge it.

Before your birth, my father told me that you would become a shaman and, with benevolence, a patriarch of the family. On the first night of a full moon after you return home, take my machete and a rifle to the Iyiofolo River for a cleansing. Stand by the riverbank and face the moon in your nakedness. Sprinkle water from the river all over your body. Wipe off the water from your hair only and let the rest dry from the wind. You will return home anointed, a shaman.

The machete and the gun are witnesses to your cleansing. Hence, they will protect you and your family from any adversaries. When the sun rises, your eyes will see everything hidden from you before then.

That was where I stopped reading. My heart pounded. Was being a patriarch not demanding enough that my father wished to add another responsibility, that of a shaman? Was I not a doctor already? And a doctor of Western medicine at that. My hands trembled as I closed and tied the notebook. I placed it in the locker and left the bedroom.

It has always been you, the voice in me said as I left the room. *We've waited for so long for your return. Nothing will ever change what's destined.* So, the voice had followed me to Obodo. I wondered if I should continue to ignore it or seek some help this time.

I took out my phone and dialed Elisha. I needed something else to occupy my mind. Even my wife's antagonism would be better than the plan my father had for me. Becoming a shaman cleansed by the Iyiofolo River was more than I could handle alone. The phone rang without an answer. At the voicemail prompt, I left a simple message: "Call me, babe." Thinking about all the things I had experienced here, I sent a text message to my wife and children: *Doing well at home, don't forget about me.* I wondered if I needed to be rescued from my responsibilities.

I caught myself whistling and wondered why I did such a foolish thing when the birds could sing for me. It was as bad as crying for attention in the rain when the sky is already weeping. Who would notice tears in the rain?

Standing alone in the hallway outside my parents' bedroom, I yearned for the sun that had darkened the skins of my ancestors to come out. I wanted to roam free in the grass fields and feel the African sun. I had the foolish thought that if I was a shaman, I would have the power to direct the sun to shine. It was a shameful thought for an Ivy League medical director. But a foolish, childlike thought was a good way to cope with adult realities.

No matter what my American status was, I wanted to exalt my African heritage. After all, the wind whistled my name, and the rain cleansed me as I sat on my father's porch. My unusual assertion of being cleansed was from the folly of my assumed enthronement as the family patriarch and an anointed shaman. How could I assume such a position without an inauguration ceremony? It had been destined for me since my conception.

CHAPTER 15

My ringing phone woke me at 5:23 a.m. I thought I was in Boston until I looked around the room. I reached for the phone with enthusiasm, expecting to hear from Elisha.

"Good morning, my brother," a male voice said. The word *brother* confused me. I hesitated until the voice continued. "Afam, it's your brother Ejike." Then I remembered that in Africa everyone was either a brother or sister. Some even claimed the title of mother or father depending on the blood relationship. Ejike's enthusiasm surprised me after the encounter we'd had on the day I returned home. As much as I wanted to hang up, I decided against it. Maybe he wanted to apologize for his behavior.

"My own lost brother, where have you been?" I asked. I heard his laugh. I imagined his body waddling.

"I'm coming over with our cousins," Ejike said.

"It's too early." I rolled around in my bed and sighed.

"We're coming after breakfast," Ejike said. That worried me even more. He was using the old inefficient time scheme that Ofomata claimed had been abandoned after I left. I knew I had to wait until noon to accommodate his request of "after breakfast."

"Call me before you leave your house," I said.

I remembered the day I left Obodo for America. It had been a painful day for my parents and a bewildering one for me. I had been happy and sad: sad for leaving my parents and happy that I would be educated at one of the best institutions in the world. Ejike had come to my father's house early that morning. His muddied rubber shoes had caught my mother's attention. She had looked at Ejike with a silent rebuke, and to avoid soiling the house, we had stood in the veranda to say goodbye. I left Obodo for America, and Ejike left for Lagos. We promised to change the world for good. That was the last time I had seen Ejike until the other day.

I turned over in my bed and fell asleep.

# # #

The crash of thunder woke me. Looking at my phone, I saw that it was 6:45 a.m. I sat by the foot of the bed, wondering about Ejike's visit. I left the bedroom and entered a dark hallway to search for my sister. It surprised me that my father's house was so gloomy at almost seven in the morning in the middle of October. Instead of searching for Adaku, I walked to the front door, guided by lightning flashes that illuminated the house intermittently.

"Are you going out?" Adaku asked from a shadowy corner.

"No. Just wandering around."

"We'll leave for Onitsha when you're ready," she said.

"I'm sorry. I forgot the meeting."

"I can cancel it if you want." The way she said it made it hard for me to agree.

"I received a crazy call from Ejike. He's coming over."

"Ejike can wait. You need to meet your tenants," Adaku replied emphatically. I wondered which was more important: meeting our tenants or waiting for Ejike.

"Ejike said he's coming with our cousins," I said.

"We've no cousins, just leeches." Adaku stepped closer to me. "You make your choice." She walked away without giving me the chance to respond. I returned to the front door to assess the weather before we left for Onitsha.

Heavy clouds had covered Obodo since I had woken. Lightning took advantage of the sun's absence to unleash frightening flashes of light from all directions. As I watched the light display with worry, repetitive thunder drubbed my ears. Looking out across our property, I saw broken tree branches carried away by howling winds.

As the wind grew more forceful, I heard a crash. It sounded like my house had split open. My hands trembled as I tried to close the front door. From a distance and through flashing lightning strikes, I saw a big iroko tree, one of the mightiest trees in West Africa, cleaved in half. Hurriedly, I locked the front door as if doing so would prevent the wind from damaging my house. I left the rain, wind, and thunder behind in search of my sister.

I found Adaku sitting at the base of the steps that went up to the second floor. I sat next to her.

"Is your wife coming home soon?" Adaku asked.

"I couldn't reach her," I said. I wanted to tell her about my marital problems, but my pride wouldn't allow me.

"She's your wife. You should be able to reach her any time of the day. Only dead people can't be reached."

"She's not dead. I was with her when I left home." I laughed, but Adaku didn't.

"You left Boston, not home. Here's your home." The way she addressed me bothered me. She was not my mother.

"I understand what you're saying. I meant figuratively," I said.

"Don't confuse me. You need to forget America."

"Really? How can I forget America when my wife and children are there? Should I forget them too?"

"You know what I mean. Bring your family back home."

"I'll call Elisha after breakfast, Mom," I said.

"Was that supposed to be funny?"

"Sis, you need to lighten up. We're not at war with each other."

"You don't seem to take your role as the head of your family seriously."

"When you deal with adults, they tend to have their own opinions and preferences," I said. "I can't force them to travel to Obodo. It's a choice they have to make."

"Papa made decisions for the family. Why should yours be different?" Adaku's voice was rising.

I hesitated to say what was on my mind. That I was more progressive than Papa. "I'm hungry. You should feed me if you want to continue being my mom," I joked.

I shook her shoulder and laughed, but she didn't reply. It was those reactions that made me feel that Adaku harbored some resentment toward me.

# # #

We ate breakfast in the dining room for the first time, ignoring the lightning and thunder outside. At times I felt that Adaku had something more to say but didn't know how to say it.

We had just finished breakfast when a loud bang from the front door jolted me. It sounded like the wind had lobbed a broken tree branch against it. My body trembled, but after the sound came once more, I realized that someone was pounding on the door.

A voice thundered above the storm. "Open the door. It's me, Ejike."

"Don't knock the door down," I yelled from the dining room. With the storm raging, I wondered if he'd heard me.

"Let him stay out there," Adaku said.

"I want to hear what he has to stay. Maybe it's the apology that we deserve from him."

"It's your niceness that I'm worried about," she replied.

"I'm not being nice to him. I want an apology. That's the least he could do."

"Obodo is different now. People here have changed."

"I'll open the door for him. Hear what he has to stay." I left the dining room to welcome our guest.

When I opened the front door, I saw many men standing in the rain with Ejike. There were two groups: a group of ten older men, some in wet feathered caps, and another group of ten younger men. Greeting me, Ejike claimed they were my cousins, but I didn't recognize any of them.

"We're here for you," Ejike said, turning to the men with him.

"Welcome home, brother," the men said in unison. The words sounded rehearsed.

"Thank you," I said. "I thank all of you. I wanted to meet our elders on *Afor* day. You're two days early." Thinking about all the African brothers I had, I smiled. Their enthusiasm was contrary to what Adaku had said about the people of Obodo.

There were too many men to invite inside the house, so I stood at the door to welcome them in the rain. I thought of my mother and her feelings about men with muddy feet. I knew that I was doing the right thing.

"I brought our people to meet you. The young ones were not born when you left," Ejike said. The men were silent as he spoke.

136

One of the men cleared his throat. He was wearing a wet feathered cap and had darkened, leathery skin and a wrinkled face. He stepped closer to where I stood.

"I'm Chukwuma, the oldest. Our brother Ejike came to us. He wants his share of the land your father held for the family." The old man cleared his throat again and looked at the rest of the men. I stood silently, watching Ejike's chest pumping.

"What Chukwuma said is true. Your father didn't share our grandfather's land with my mother," Ejike said. I wanted to put my hands around his neck, but I resisted. My face became warm.

"I asked to meet our elders without Ejike," I said. "He's just a grandson to our people. As our culture stipulates, he has no rights to our land. Let him go and inherit his father's land."

"I'm Uzunta. We heard what you said, but a grandson can move in with his mother's people. Our culture accommodates it." He took off his wet red hat and wiped the rain dripping down his lips with his hand as he spoke.

"We accommodate grandchildren out of benevolence, not by their demands. Ejike demands land that he doesn't own. Tell me what we call his demand in Obodo. Uzunta, what do you call Ejike's type of demand?" I asked. I waited, but no one spoke. "We call it stealing. He hasn't earned any grace from me."

"I want what belongs to me," Ejike said. The men who came with him whispered to one another.

"Come and get it, if you're bold enough," I said. I was about to close the front door on Ejike when I

137

stopped and stared at him. "Why didn't your mother ask my father for her share of the land?"

"Your father refused to share," Ejike said.

"Your mother is gone and my father as well. The land belongs to me, by our tradition," I said. I stepped outside the house and looked around the grasslands before resting my eyes on the older men with Ejike. Their eyes locked on me. I continued, "I've returned home. My lineage heads this village. My ancestors founded this town. As the patriarch of the Nwaku family, I'm the head of the village. If you want to challenge my assertion, raise your hand." They looked at one another, but no one spoke.

What I wanted was a peaceful transition to my leadership, but there was a saying in Obodo that a weak man can't summon his ancestors for protection. This situation demanded forcefulness.

I entered my house and closed the heavy front door, although I could still hear Ejike yell, "You'll regret coming back here." From a window I watched him leave with his men—men whose interest in Ejike's ambition I did not know.

When I turned around, my sister was standing close to me. She had startled me, but I didn't show my uneasiness. In my culture, it was cowardly for a man to be openly afraid. I smiled to hide my petrified state. Luckily, she didn't look at my wobbling legs.

"Ejike is a troublemaker. He's a crook. Be careful in dealing with him," Adaku said, placing her hand on my shoulder.

"I have no business with him," I said angrily. I wasn't worried about the confrontation with Ejike but about the crowd that had come with him. Their roles were suspect.

"I said before that he's dangerous." Her statement concerned me even more now.

"Papa was the most honest man I know. He was kind and generous. I'm sure he was fair to his sister," I said.

"Ejike lied. Papa gave his sister some land. She sold it to land speculators. Papa bought the land back from them," Adaku said as we walked to the family room. We sat down across from each other.

"Why's Ejike angry? I haven't done anything to him," I asked.

Adaku shook her head, looking as if she expected me to answer my own question. Then she sighed in what sounded like disgust. I wondered if I was daft.

"My own brother, it's jealousy," she said with an unmistakable smile, one that was beaming and not sarcastic in the least. Her use of the African phrase *my own brother* was emblematic of true pride. If she were a man in Obodo, she would have walked around the family room with a swagger as she spoke.

"Jealous of what? He's our cousin," I asked, as if I didn't know what my sister was insinuating.

"Your academic success," she answered. It wasn't what I'd expected.

"I disagree with you, sis. He's upset about Papa's accomplishments."

"A lot of people were, but Papa is gone. You're their focus now."

Another loud knock at the front door interrupted our conversation. My sister stood, looking worried. I used my hand to signal to her to sit, but she moved toward the door.

"I'll get the door," I said. She looked at me as the knocking continued.

"Be careful," Adaku said. Her request made me sound like I was a dimwit who needed guidance.

On reaching the front door, I looked out from the side window and saw three men wearing local police uniforms. Two of them carried AK-47 rifles, the muzzles pointed at the ground, and the third had a black pistol attached to his belt. I tried to alleviate my fear by focusing on the fact that their guns were pointed away from me. I opened the front door halfway to peek my head out.

"Good morning, sir," said the police officer with the sidearm as he stood at attention. The other two officers slung their guns over their shoulders. I opened the front door fully. When I shook their hands, I read their names from the patches on their shirts.

"Sir, I'm the DPO, Dan Uka," the officer with the sidearm said. I wondered why a divisional police officer, the equivalent of a police chief in America, would visit my house.

"The big *oga* paying me a visit. Now I'm really home," I said.

"*Oga*, sir, we're here to pay *our* respects. We heard you came home."

"Come inside," I said. When I turned to take them to the living room, Adaku's presence startled me again. This time, she was as close to me as my shadow in the African noon sun.

"Adaku, meet Mr. Uka, our DPO," I said.

140

"We've met," Adaku snapped. Frowning in disdain, she stood in front of me and then next to me, trying to shield me from our guests. Her reaction astonished me.

"Hello, miss," Dan said with a smile.

"It's missus," Adaku shot back. In my part of Africa, acknowledgment of one's title was as important as remembering their last name. First names were relegated to the dustbin, except for young people.

"Sir, we're in a hurry," Dan said as I led them to the family room. I turned to face a man whose actions now seemed urgent. "We received two complaints about you."

"Really? I just came back home. Are you sure they're about me?"

"Your brother came to us and said he had twenty witnesses. Did you threaten him?" Dan asked. There was no smile on his face. I forgot the joke I had wanted to tell.

"No, I didn't," I said. I turned to my sister to solicit her support as my witness, but I didn't ask.

"I need to see your guns. I checked our files, and they're not registered," Dan said. He walked toward me. I took two, or maybe three, steps away from him.

"I don't own any guns. Just to correct your mistake, I have no brother," I said. I heard my voice quaver. "You've got the wrong guy."

"My brother has no guns," Adaku said emphatically.

"I'm her real brother, and she's right," I added.

"I'll search for your guns. If I find them, I'll arrest you," Dan said. He looked in all directions, as if trying to decide where to start his search. Looking at the DPO, I wondered how I would explain a false accusation to an African.

"Oh! I understand," Adaku said. She smiled for the first time since the police officers showed up. "Who complained?"

"Madam, your people did. I'm from Lokoja. I've never seen his guns," Dan said.

"My father owned guns," I replied. "He's been dead for years. By the way, he was granted a waiver to own hunting rifles by the British before independence." It was difficult to contain my anger.

"If they're not registered, it's a crime," Dan said.

"Sir, they don't need to be registered. The Nigerian government granted my father the same waiver after independence."

"Afam, I'll take care of the boys," Adaku said. Bribery, of course. It made me angry, but I wanted to avoid being arrested.

"You don't look like a violent man so I won't arrest you. Come to my office and I'll register your guns," Dan said.

"How much?" Adaku asked.

Their conversation was beyond me, so I walked away as they negotiated the price for gun registration. I rejoined them when they'd finished.

"Your brother Ejike came to us and said you threatened him," Dan said to me.

"I didn't. He lied."

"Register your guns at the station and then settle things with Ejike," Dan said as they were leaving the house.

"Fuck Ejike. There isn't anything I need to settle with that crook," I said.

"I warn you: If you cause any trouble, I'll arrest you."

"Welcome back to my country, where crooks have rights and I have none."

"Miss, tell your brother to cool down."

"Like I told you before, it's not miss," said Adaku. "I'll support my brother in defending his property."

"I'll arrest you both if you threaten my friend," Dan said.

"The truth has come out," I replied. "You're here as a friend of Ejike, not as a police officer paid by the government. Now I know who to be afraid of."

"I'll carry out my duties, even if Ejike isn't my friend. I'm warning you for the last time," Dan said. He left our house with his men, and I closed the door behind him.

Pacing around the family room, I wondered how Ejike had assembled all the men he needed to circumvent our culture and influence the national law. Adaku frowned, retreating to her room.

When she came out, her purse hung on her left arm and she held a small plastic bag. Her face looked strained, and I could sense her disappointment.

"We must follow them," Adaku said as she walked toward the front door. For a woman who barely rushed in any situation, she moved with urgency, and the sound her shoes made interrupted the silence that the police officers had left behind.

The sun had come out to brighten the cloudy day. It was my African sun, shining from a clear and

143

beautiful blue sky. The air was humid, even with the light breeze that barely moved the weakened tall grasses. Birds made short dashing flights and sang with excitement.

I noted that the wind was not forceful enough to make the pine trees whistle, and their stillness added to my apprehension. When I entered Adaku's white Toyota Camry, my heart was racing. I belted myself into the passenger seat and took a deep breath, trying to calm that fear. My mind wandered to the last time I rode in a car with my father. The memory was as vivid as that of the breakfast I'd had that morning.

"Take care of your mother and sister when I'm gone," my father would say every time we were alone. "I will, Papa," I always replied. He would look at me and smile. Things were different now. It was Adaku who took care of me, driving the car instead of my father.

My thoughts wandered so far that I didn't realize we had begun driving. In every house along the road, piles of firewood with *For Sale* slapped across them partially blocked the driveway.

"Firewood everywhere. They're destroying our forests," I said.

"They need to cook and eat," Adaku said without looking at me. Her eyes focused on the road, and her face appeared strained.

"What happened to gas cookers?" I asked. "That's what Mom used."

"Too expensive to buy gas cylinders. Our money is worthless."

"Nigeria has more natural gas than most other oil-producing countries. Why can't we harness that?"

"You people in America don't understand," Adaku said. "Nigeria is doomed. With corruption and unemployment, there is no future." It surprised me that she had joined those who referred to me as an American. Was I?

"It's not too late to turn things around," I said.

"You're home now. Show us how."

"I'm just a doctor, not an economist."

"We have no good hospitals, no electricity, crime is everywhere."

"What happened to Nigeria?" I asked.

"Corrupt politicians killed Nigeria."

"We can change things. Elect the right people."

"Who's we?"

"Everyone who loves Nigeria and Africa," I said.

"Don't get killed trying to change criminals," Adaku answered. "You're my only living relative."

"You forgot Elisha, Ikenna, and Obialu."

"Until I see them in Obodo, they're distant relatives."

"They're still your relatives, even if they live on Mars."

"What good is a relative who you don't see? In my opinion, there is no commitment without presence." Adaku blew her horn at a dog wandering close to the road and stopped her car. I looked around to see if there were cars behind us. The dog ignored the horn, and she drove on.

The police station was a one-story building in a remote area of town. Apart from the town hall across

145

the street, it was isolated. We walked on a sandy path that colored my shoes earthen red.

Inside the dusty waiting area, a stench filled the air. There was only enough space to stand. Men and women attired in worn African prints shuffled from one corner of the room to another. Occasionally, they wandered to a corner portioned off and forming an open holding cell with iron bars. Men clad in their underwear, mostly in their twenties, filled the holding cell. I wondered where the female prisoners were held. The men hollered for attention whenever someone walked closer to them.

Adaku kept close to me, her eyes wandering around the crowded room. Once she spotted an officer, she walked toward him. I followed her as if she was my mother. I couldn't blame her for taking control of my affairs because she understood the system better than me. I was just a returnee from America, uninformed and helpless in a complex legal system.

Adaku looked at me. Her silence pricked the hairs on my arms. After a few steps, while we were walking toward the police officer, a loud burst of gunfire echoed in the crowded room. It sounded as if it came from an open door at the back of the police station.

I froze. When I regained some of my depleted courage, I noticed the unperturbed crowd was carrying on with their activities as if nothing had happened.

"Who's shooting?" I asked Adaku, as if she could see beyond the walls.

"I don't know," she said without looking at me. She seemed more focused on her mission than my silly question or the gunshots.

"No one took cover or ran," I said. It was what we had done during the Nigerian Civil War.

"It's probably a prisoner escape," she said casually.

A man in ornamental African clothes with a long red hat stepped on my foot as he walked by. He turned around and said, "I'm sorry." After he walked away, he turned around again, walked closer to me, and looked at me. "I'm sorry, sir, I thought you were a friend I haven't seen in many years." The man's round face and protruding belly did not resemble anyone I could remember. He took three steps away from me and shook his head. Turning around to look at me again, he smiled. "You're Afam," he shouted in the crowded hall. He came to me and hugged me. I didn't hug him back. It was not my style to hug strangers.

"Ifeanyi, stop making noise. Are you drunk again?" Adaku asked.

"Because I love *palmie* doesn't mean I'm a drunk. I drink to be happy," Ifeanyi said. I smiled. It had been a long time since I'd heard the bar patrons' word for palm wine.

My sister looked away. I was surprised, but she walked away before I could ask any questions.

I studied the man's face, and the memories returned.

"Ifeanyi Muo!" I exclaimed. We shook hands and patted each other on the back.

"You look younger than me," Ifeanyi said with a smile as warm as the African sun.

"It's been so long," I said.

"You went to America and left us here to suffer."

"If you love palm wine, that's not suffering." We laughed.

Adaku came back for me. She pulled me by the hand and said, "We must go."

"I still remember your house. I'll come tonight," Ifeanyi said as we walked away, but I wondered why he wore an outlandish outfit on such a hot day.

"Did you register Papa's guns?" I asked.

"They want me to bring the guns to the police station for inspection before they'll register them," she replied.

"You know it's a ploy. They want to take the guns."

"It's as Dan said. He's friends with Ejike. Their plot is simple."

I said, "Remember how they tried that trick on Papa after the war? It was the military then, and now it's the police. Their uniforms may be different, but their motives are the same."

"We'll be smarter than them," Adaku said.

"Those guns are the only advantage we have to defend our property. I'll keep them at home."

"I agree," she said.

With that, we left the police station, a cloud of uncertainty darker than any storm hanging over us.

CHAPTER 16

The afternoon sun lured me out to the beautiful grasslands as it had when I was a child. When I immersed myself in its allure, it stung my exposed skin as the humid air warmed me to my core. The red soil did not fare better, baking in the hot sun and sizzling at the drops of my sweat. With no wind to fan my burning skin, the sting from the sun felt more painful than before, and it erased the beautiful memory of its gentle bites from earlier in the day.

I flung my father's loaded rifle over my shoulder the way he used to when the two of us walked the grasslands. Only death would separate me from the guns that had been in my family for decades. Registered or not, they belonged to me.

Every time I heard a ruffling sound around me, I reached for the sheathed machete fastened to my belt. When a long black snake slithered across my path, shaking the tall grasses as it tried to escape, I ignored it. After a short distance, the snake stopped running, raised its forebody with a spread hood, and hissed. I stopped. Only a fool would step close to a deadly snake ready to strike. Innate things could not be forgotten.

For a few seconds, the black cobra and I looked at each other. I wondered what the snake saw when it looked at me. When it moved at me, I lowered my rifle, aimed at its head, and pulled the trigger. The gunshot echoed, and the bullet tore through the snake's hood. The raised forebody dropped to the ground. I walked by the dead snake with a swagger, leaving the carcass to the birds of prey, emboldened by my perfect shot. It was the first time I had shot a gun in more than forty years, and I didn't regret it. I remembered what my father had said: "If you have to, kill to survive."

Walking the ancient paths created by my forebearers, I used my machete to subdue the stubborn thatched grasses. After covering most of the grasslands, I returned to the tallest anthill closest to the long driveway that led to my house. I pulled out my machete, circled around the anthill, and chose a spot to thrust in the blade. After I attacked from multiple spots, what remained was a heap of dirt no higher than an inch.

The thrill of leveling the anthill blinded me. However, when I heard a cough, I turned around with the raised machete. Three women and two men stood at a short distance, looking at me. The two men wore black suits and wiped sweat off their faces with white handkerchiefs. Two of the women wore oversized dresses, and the third wore a blue skirt; her white blouse had makeup stains on the left shoulder. I sheathed my knife when I looked at their terrified faces.

"Can I help you?" I asked. One of the men approached me, while the others stayed on the road, absorbing the hot sun.

"We're here to collect your tax," the sweating man said.

"Who the hell are you?"

"I'm sorry, sir. We're from the local government. I'm a revenue officer, John Eze."

"You're collecting whose tax?"

The remaining four walked closer while wiping their faces, as if moving away from the road would stop the hot sun.

"Come on, *oga*, it's your tax. I don't need to explain it to you, do I?" John said with a smile. Everything about him was condescending, and it annoyed me.

"I live in America, John. I pay my taxes there."

"You know you live here too, sir," John said. The woman in the skirt walked closer.

"I'm Clara, sir. I assist Mr. Eze."

"Clara, I believe John was doing a decent job of belittling me. I don't need two of you for that."

"Sir, Mr. Eze joined us a month ago. I'm trying to help you understand," Clara said. The rest of the group surrounded me. Did they want to help me understand or force me to comply?

"Hmm," I said. It felt like they were blocking the air.

"One of the councilmen asked us to collect your tax," John said.

"I've earned no money in Nigeria. Tell me why I should pay a local tax?"

"You own all these lands and the big house," Clara answered. I watched the rest of them smile as she spoke. Their smirks made me angrier.

"Rural properties are not taxed. They have no commercial value. Tell me, how many people in Obodo pay property taxes?" I asked.

"*Oga*, you're not fair to your people. You've made money in America and money here in Obodo. We'll collect your tax," Clara said. It was her intransigence that made my heart race and made me lower my rifle to point at them. I wasn't going to shoot Clara, but I wanted her to see my anger. The group moved three steps away. Watching the fear in their eyes, I smiled to defuse the situation. Still, it felt good watching the tax collectors squirm.

"If you show me anyone who pays property tax in Obodo, I'll pay mine," I said.

"Your case is different, *oga*. Your people want you to pay. We're here to collect your tax, or we'll take your land," Clara said with an air of audacity.

She walked closer to me with a stupid grin on her face. She muttered under her breath as if taunting me. I wanted to pick her up by the neck and throw her against the remaining anthill. Was it the sun that was getting to me or the unwelcoming behavior from Ejike since I'd returned home? I shuddered when I thought about what I was becoming, and when I remembered the open holding cell at the police station, the anger in me evaporated as fast as a drop of sweat on hot African sand.

One thing Clara had said stood out: "Your people want you to pay." It became clear to me then. The police and the tax collectors were agents for someone: a cousin using other people to carry out his nefarious acts. I worried about how far Ejike would go to achieve his goals, but I worried even more about how quickly anger and resolve to fight back had built up inside me. I worried about my anger resulting in bloodshed.

"We're done here," I said to the tax people, who were looking at me in silence. Perhaps they'd exhausted all their words. I could pay a tax, but only death could take the land of my ancestors from me.

Walking away, I turned around after three steps and saw them whispering to one another. Their gossiping stopped. They stood where I'd left them and looked in all directions, as if they were stranded.

CHAPTER 17

Early mornings and evening were the best times to stroll in our vast grasslands because the equatorial sun had no bite then. There were no fears of surrendering to the sun from exhaustion and dehydration.

Returning from my evening walk, I watched as the setting sun released cascades of oranges and reds, filling the sky until it descended below rows of tall palm trees. When I reached the house, I sat alone on the roofed balcony with my feet elevated on a table, watching the slow approach of nightfall. I remained there until the darkness effaced the last colors from the sky.

Time passed as I sat under the night sky, listening to an owl hoot. For the first time since I had come home, I heard the buzz and soon felt the bite of mosquitoes. The annoying sounds of mosquitoes, which only grew in number, made it seem like the insects had invaded my house. When I stood to walk inside, I saw lights from two cars driving down the road. I dashed inside and locked the door leading to the balcony.

Standing at the landing, I couldn't decide if I needed my father's revolver or rifle. It didn't take long before I heard a loud knock on the front door. I was still contemplating what to do. My hesitancy whittled away the time I should have been taking to fetch a gun. I vowed to be more resolute in the future when making decisions that my life may depend on. When I saw Adaku walking to the family room, I went to answer the door and hoped for the best. I turned off all the lights in the family room and approached the front door unarmed.

When I turned the outside lights on, I stood by the left side of the door and yelled, "Who is it?" To say that my heart wasn't racing would be a lie.

"Ifeanyi Muo, my brother." His answer was rapid and reassuring. The thought of facing a foe unarmed worried me, and his voice was a welcome relief. I reached for the switch in the family room and turned the lights on.

Ifeanyi wore blue shorts and a red jersey, so different from his elaborate outfit at the police station. The six men who were with him wore shorts and polo shirts. There was nothing menacing about them, but they were unknown to me, and their faces were as bland as plain white wallpaper.

Ifeanyi carried a brown calabash jar in his left hand. In Obodo, the calabash jar kept the sun away from choice palm wines. When I saw the foam

156

bubbling out of the three-gallon jar, I knew it was fresh. Ifeanyi introduced the other men without much fanfare: Okoli, Anicheta, Ibeziako, Ububa, Chinwe, and Ilozue. Even without hearing their surnames, I suddenly recalled them all from grade school. Who could blame me for forgetting faces I hadn't watched change from childhood to adulthood?

"We're here to welcome our brother home," Ifeanyi said as he handed the brown calabash to me. He cleared his throat and added, "We brought palm wine to celebrate your return."

"Thank you. Wow! What a surprise. Your visit means a lot to me. Finally, a friendly visit. Come inside," I said. I held the calabash of palm wine as we walked inside the family room. I looked around for Adaku to show her the gift but couldn't find her.

"You deserve the best palm wine. You're a worthy son of Obodo," Ifeanyi said.

"How long are you with us?" Chinwe asked.

"Stop asking silly questions. He's here with us today. Let's celebrate," Okoli said.

All the men responded with, "Yes oh!" The excitement in them was so strong that it pounded through me like a hammer. That feeling of happiness was transcendent.

I left the men to find Adaku. Upon reaching the kitchen, I retrieved eight glasses from the cabinet and placed them on a tray. On my way back, Adaku stopped me in the hallway.

"Be careful with those men," she whispered to me. Another warning from my sister when I thought my guests were harmless. I wondered if she was naturally distrusting.

"Is there anyone in this town who I shouldn't worry about?" I asked.

"Don't drink their wine," Adaku said, ignoring my question.

"You know I don't drink."

"How would I know?"

"You're my sister. You should know that."

"You've been gone for so long, I can't really say I know you well."

"So, I'm a stranger to you?"

"You came home alone. What am I supposed to think?"

"It wasn't my choice. Elisha didn't want to come with me." We sighed at the same time.

"I'll eventually find out from her what you did," Adaku said.

"I've done nothing. I try to be a good husband," I replied.

"Men are different from women. She'll tell me what you did when I call her."

"Whatever, sis."

She shook her head and walked toward her room. I continued to the family room. After I had placed the tray on a table, I turned all the lights on. My father's eyes looked at me from the framed photographs on the wall as I took his chair. From time to time I looked up at him and smiled. I knew he must be watching my steps ... and there had been too many missteps so far.

"We're in your house. You must pour the libation," Ifeanyi said.

Anicheta stood, lifted the brown calabash, and placed it close to where my feet rested. After choosing a glass, he gave it to me before returning to his chair. I lifted the palm wine and poured a small amount.

Lifting the glass above my head as my father used to do, I said, "A son watching his elders will do as his elders did when he becomes a man. I've become the man in my father's house to continue with his legacy and not take away his glory. All glories are earned, not bestowed on us. My father was a wise man and well respected. To him, I owe all the good things life has given me. He joined his ancestors, as all of us will one day do. Since we're still living, we ask for wisdom to reach our potential. Determination, so that we can fulfill all the promises we've made to the living and the dead. To all of you, my guests, may you live long with good health."

"Yes oh! Yes oh! Yes oh!" they bellowed.

I walked to the front door, opened it, and poured the palm wine on the soil, a symbolic sharing of the wine with my ancestors buried in Obodo. Returning to the family room, I said, "May we live long enough to witness the success of our children and share our great culture with our grandchildren."

"You're truly your father's son. An Obodo son. An African son," Ifeanyi said, beaming.

"They said you forgot our culture in America. But I'll tell them that you're as good as your father," Ububa said. He stepped closer to me. "No one takes away your rights unless you let them." I thought about what he said and wondered why he'd said it.

"Thank you for the compliments. If you ever wonder about my commitment to this revered place, just know that this is my home, and it will remain so for eternity," I said. They clapped.

"My brother, here's my number, call me when you need palm wine," Ifeanyi said as he scribbled on a piece of paper with shaking hands. I wondered how many calabash jars of palm wine had surrendered to his stomach that day.

"Thank you for the offer," I said.

They stood from their chairs, picked up their glasses, and took turns pouring the palm wine. I hid my glass from their sight. Not a drop of the palm wine touched my lips. They were so busy talking about events in Obodo that they were unaware that I didn't partake.

As the evening progressed, their chatter filled the air in my living room until the palm wine was gone. When some of the men rose to find the bathroom, they staggered. That was when the singing and dancing started. It was a song of jubilation and a sign of reverence for the patriarch of the household, which was now me.

Close to midnight, the men left my house, and their singing followed them as they walked to the road. They left their parked vehicles in front of my house, and in their drunken state, I felt that was for the best. I returned to the balcony, where mosquitoes feasted on my skin, and listened to the song coming from the darkness. Ifeanyi's visit and his gift of palm wine had brought me immeasurable joy. I wished my family were with me to share the wonderful camaraderie with my grade school friends. A major contrast with my cousin Ejike.

When I left the feasting mosquitoes to return to the family room, I turned the lights off and sat in the darkness alone. I could not mitigate my elated state and sleep wisely kept its distance from me.

Around 12:30 a.m., I retreated to my parents' bedroom to read my father's notebook.

CHAPTER 18

Before sunrise, the sound of a mourning dove woke me from dreams about earlier events along the Charles River. It was the fourth night I had slept in my parents' bedroom, but the previous three nights had been uneventful.

As I turned over, my father's notebook fell from my chest where it rested. Raising my head, I heard bursts of beautiful sounds coming from the bedroom balcony. Apart from the heavy dark curtains hanging from the ceiling to the floor, only a pane of glass separated me from the bird singing outside.

As I laid in bed with my eyes closed, the bird's cooing sounds continued at a higher pitch, with shorter intervals between. I wondered if the bird was desperate or in a state of heightened alertness. I knew that if it sensed danger, it would have flown away, but it stayed. How does one assess a bird's anxiety? I could only guess, but though it sounded anxious, I heard something different. It seemed to be a rare solitary rendition of a song I'd heard in the past from a pair of mourning doves before I first left home for America.

Something my father had said to me when I was young came back: "Birds are spiritual."

If I was a believer, an instinctive African son who was mired in the tradition of my ancestors, then I would've seen the notebook as a foretelling of me becoming a shaman. As a believer, the mourning dove would be a mystical bird, alerting me to a crucial time in my transformation. A bird, instead of a metallic or wooden gong, alerted me to how urgent matters were.

When I thought about my father, I realized all he had done for me. His catalog of medicinal leaves and their use for treatment of different ailments, all recorded in his hardcover notebook, was meant for posterity. A shaman's medicinal book. Whether I ever used it or not, it would be available for future generations. I realized that part of my role would be as a preservationist of my culture.

Opening my eyes felt as difficult as pulling open a closed lead door.

As the bird continued to coo, I resolved to find out if it was all right. Sitting up on the bed, I felt cold chills descend through my naked body. Feeling chills in the hot season worried me, making me wonder if a flu had seeped into my bones. Reaching for the comforter, I felt the coldness of my cell phone on the bed. Something was happening to my body.

The mourning dove cooed with increased frequency. I walked to the balcony doors. Separating the curtains, I saw rays of the rising African sun on the horizon. It was later in the morning than I had thought. My phone rang, loud enough to startle me and the bird. As the mourning dove took off toward a patch of green pasture, I returned to the bed to pick up the phone.

The screen read "Elisha." It was 5:30 a.m. in Obodo and 12:30 a.m. in Boston. I was happy and nervous at the same time.

"Good morning, babe," I said, excited. It was the first phone call from Elisha since my arrival in Obodo. There was a protracted silence. "Good morning, babe," I repeated. I heard a loud sigh on the other end.

"Afam, just to let you know, I filed for a divorce."

I knew she wasn't happy with me turning down the CEO offer and coming home, but I thought she'd get over that once she started to miss me, that she might even join me. Divorce seemed too drastic now. Peering in the distance, my eyes settled on a patch of heavy green vegetation where I was sure the medicinal plants my father's notebook described could be found. I thought about the medicinal importance of each leaf. But none of them could cure a broken heart. There was no cure for me, not from here.

"You've created these problems. You gave up a dream job in America to run back to Africa, where you don't belong anymore. Sometimes I wonder if you remember all the promises you made to me. There isn't much left for me to dream about with

165

you. I don't have the moon you promised me. So, I'll remove the burden of marriage from you." She sounded as if she was reading from a prepared statement. I wouldn't be surprised if she was.

"Do you love me?" I asked. The shock from her announcement had taken away my ability to think. Why ask a woman who had filed for a divorce if she loved me? Yet the emptiness I felt was yearning for something to fill it.

"I'll put your things in storage until you return," she said.

I watched the golden African sun rise from the eastern front of my family property, but in the midst of the early morning beauty, my star was falling.

"Do I still have rights in America? I thought the house belonged to the two of us?" I asked, my voice quavering.

"I have rights too. Happiness is my right. Yes, I have the right to be happy," Elisha said. Her voice sounded as cold as the winter weather in New England. It chilled my body.

"Babe, all I want is your happiness."

"You haven't shown me love or devotion. I don't know why Africa is more important than me."

"Have you told our kids?"

"Stop calling them kids. They're grown adults. Everyone knows I'm unhappy except for you."

"Why not wait until I come back to Boston?" I wondered where that statement had come from. I had no desire to return.

"We can divide our assets through our attorneys."

"Our assets? I'm not worried about material things. I'm worried about us. I love and need you."

"You've made your choices. I need to look out for myself. It was over between us the day you left me," Elisha said. Her words felt like bullets going through my body, painfully ripping through my flesh and bones.

"I didn't leave you, babe. You knew I had to visit home," I said. When would I stop saying things I didn't mean. It was not a *visit* but a *return* ... unless something changed that I didn't know of. Was it desperation that put words in my mouth that I didn't mean?

"There, you said it. You call Africa your home. Boston is where you left a deceived American woman. Do you have another wife there?" Elisha asked. Each time she spoke, her voice sounded more caustic. At that point, there was nothing left in me for her to shred.

"Babe, take everything we own. Without you, I have no use for it," I said.

"I don't want your charity. I'll only take what's due to me."

"I have no lawyer. Yours can divide our assets. Give mine to our children."

"Find your own damn lawyer," she said and hung up.

I left my viewing area, the place where my father used to stand to watch his children play outside. My father was gone, and no one was watching over me. I was alone, and I was the one watching the events happening outside, the man in charge of the house.

No one could address my problems but me. No one could come to my rescue if I needed help.

Sitting on the bed, I wondered how many times my father sat there to sort out the things going wrong in his life.

The rays from the rising sun filtering into the room brightened the dark spots, except for my heart. That, it left in darkness. I picked up my phone several times to call my children but couldn't do it. Every time I picked it up, I worried about how late it was in Boston. Finally, I sent a text to Elisha: *I love you, babe. Never forget that*. It was a plea to reconsider her decision. I waited for her reply but was given nothing. When I thought about my text message to her, I felt foolish sending a love note to a woman who was throwing darts at my exposed heart.

I accepted that a new challenge had begun in my life in Africa.

# # #

Later that morning, while sitting in the family room mulling over what to do about Elisha's divorce petition, I heard a knock on the front door. I tucked my father's notebook under a cushion before answering. Ejike, doused with sweat, walked into the house with two men as soon as I'd opened the door. The two men were tall, with protruding eyeballs, and dressed in black suits. They stood close to the front door as Ejike sat in my father's chair. His audacious behavior angered me.

168

"Ejike, do you mind getting out of my father's chair? No, forget that. Get your ass off the chair," I said.

"It's my house too. I can sit anywhere I want," Ejike said. First it was my land that he'd wanted, and now he'd returned to claim my house. What else was left for him to claim?

Ejike was recalcitrant after my request. The two men wandered around the family room and into the living room without any introduction.

"You're not welcome in my house anymore," I said.

"Your house? This place belongs to me too."

"I'll ask you for the last time to get your ass off my chair."

"That's all you learned in America, boasting and threatening," Ejike said. He stood up and stepped closer to me, as if sizing me up.

"If you keep this up, you'll push me to kick your fat ass," I said.

"You've added insults now. That one I'll not forgive." The men with him were watching without intervening. They kept silent, as if deaf to the verbal combat.

Pointing his finger at me, Ejike said, "After you run back to America, everything will belong to me." Then he walked toward the door, still pointing his finger at me, and the two men followed him. I was confused about the purpose of his visit. Was he unraveling? If it was an attempt to intimidate me, he'd failed.

"Gentlemen, I didn't even get your names," I said. The men turned and then smiled for the first time.

One said, "Afunugo Okeke, sir. I'm the local government chairman. We were told you came home."

"I'm his security escort, sir," the other man said without giving his name.

"Why are you in my house?"

"Your brother came to us with some issues. We'll discuss that some other time. I'm here to meet you," Afunugo said.

"I'm ready to discuss it now," I said.

"We're leaving," Ejike told me.

"Hold on, Ejike. I've heard you and what you wanted to say. I want to hear what your men have to say," I said.

"We're not his men. Ejike is a good friend. He's the local chairman of my political party. A good man," Afunugo said.

"I wonder how you define a good man. He's shifty. Trying to cheat my family out of our lands that we've held for generations. That's not a good man."

Ejike rushed toward me. When I stood astride and raised my fist, he stopped. I remembered when I used to throw punches at him when we fought in grade school, but his fat belly was my target that day. He stood growling like an angry lion. I beckoned to him to come closer, my eagerness to fight growing. He trembled and stood where he was. I even thought about approaching him to attack.

For a moment, we acted like children fighting in a playground, but the situation was more dire than a mere fistfight.

"How dare you insult me in front of Afunugo? You've no power here. I'll show you real power. It's not the type from your money, education, American wife, land, and properties you don't need. It's who I know. I've got boys who'll do anything for me. I'll bury you here."

"We're not here to fight your brother," Afunugo said.

"He's my enemy. I'll fight him to the death," Ejike replied.

"You're threatening me in my house," I said. "I should've beaten some sense into you when we were kids."

"It's our house. I'll get my share."

"If you continue with this stupid behavior, I'll teach you proper manners, even if I have to beat them into you," I said.

Ejike left without looking back. I heard him mumbling before I closed the front door. The men with him stayed. I wondered what had happened to Ejike over the years to create this monster. As much as I pretended to be unperturbed by his comments, I was worried about my safety.

"I'm sorry about my exchange of words with Ejike," I told the men.

"I hope you work things out. I wish I had stayed out of it," Afunugo said.

"I'm not sure if that could happen. He seemed angry with me."

"You're angry with each other. It worries me," Afunugo said.

"We're cousins. It's not like we're trying to kill each other."

"I've seen brothers fight to the death over land in this town. Be careful."

"I promise we won't kill each other—if he stays away from here. Please, sit down and tell me about the developments in our local government."

"We're not staying long. I have too many appointments. When you visit me, I'll show you what we're doing to improve our communities," Afunugo said.

"I accept your invitation. What can I offer you to drink?" I asked.

The two men looked at each other. "Whatever you have, sir," Afunugo said.

I left the family room as the men looked at the photographs on the wall. When I reached the pantry, I found a boxed Remy Martin cognac. After retrieving two cognac glasses from the kitchen, I returned. In the tradition of Obodo, I left the bottle of cognac on a side table next to Afunugo, along with the two glasses.

"The cognac is for you," I said.

"It's too early in the day, sir. Can we take it with us?" Afunugo asked.

"I offered it to you."

The men rose from their chairs, and Afunugo took the cognac. When they reached the front door, Afunugo turned around, handed his business card to me, and said, "You're a good man. Welcome home, *oga*."

172

I was confused. Between the two of us, I wondered who was the *oga*. I shook his hand, but before I closed the door, he added, "Your brother Ejike is unhappy. Please settle matters with him."

The word *settle* meant *bribe* in Nigeria. Why should I bribe Ejike? Bribe him to spare my life? What would happen when he ran out of my bribe money? Would he not come back for more? Settling with Ejike would never happen in my lifetime, so I had to deal with the consequences, whatever they might be.

When I returned to my father's room, I retrieved the revolver from the rifle case and held it. After walking around the bedroom, I sat on the bed and held the notebook in one hand and the revolver in the other. If I had any fear in me before then, it escaped from my mind and body. At that moment, I resolved that my survival was paramount, and to achieve my goals in Obodo, I had to make the spiritual journey to the Iyiofolo River.

CHAPTER 19

Days passed without much drama in my life. Close to
midnight on the first full moon after my return to
Obodo, I prepared for my journey to the Iyiofolo
River. I wore a pair of baggy khaki shorts without
underwear. Flinging my loaded rifle over my left
shoulder, I held the long machete in my right hand.
Outside, a bright moon appeared suspended in the
air a short distance from where I stood. It looked so
close that I felt I could reach out and touch it, so
bright that I could see a pin dropped on the African
sand next to my feet.

I traveled on deserted roads accompanied by my
thoughts, a loaded rifle, a machete, and the moon.
Even the local noisy owl took leave when my journey
began, and its absence made the night tranquil.
Walking on the path chosen for me, I felt as if I was
the only one awake in the village. When I turned

onto a narrow path leading to the river, the moon was even closer to me.

I stopped near the river to look back at where my journey had started, and I recalled some of the major events in my life. Then I couldn't stop from dancing, and it liberated me to wonder how Elisha would perceive my journey: from scholar to a man steeped in traditional mysticism. Looking at the bright moon, I envisioned the remaining events of the night and my future as a shaman.

At the river, the reflection and dazzle of the moon on the water's surface captivated me; it looked as if the river was standing still.

I put down the machete close to the river's edge and placed my rifle next to it. When I looked up again at the moon for guidance, what it had to offer was beyond my grasp.

After I unzipped my baggy shorts, they slid down and left me naked to the night and the moon. I kicked the shorts to my left and faced the river. It was then that I noticed the slow flow of the Iyiofolo. I cupped my hands and scooped water from the river. Lifting them above me, I let the water drip from my head to my body. I repeated the same process four times. Each time I scooped water, I recited, "For *Eke, Oye, Afor, Nkwor*," the four market days in Obodo, before I looked up to the moon, my revealer. I wondered when my enlightenment would begin.

I sat by the river's edge with my feet in the water. As the water cleansed my feet, I washed my face four times. As my father had written, after my purification by the river I would see beyond the capabilities of my eyesight, and the collective wisdoms of my ancestors would become mine. I bowed my head in anticipation of what I would become.

Heavy clouds moved in and covered the moon, surrounding me with absolute darkness. I heard howling and the menacing cackling sounds of night predators. Trying to understand what was happening, I felt as if the weighty clouds had blocked the path to my spiritual mission, depriving me of the needed inner journey to the quintessence of my existence. As the cackling sounds grew louder, I found my gun and machete. Remembering my nakedness, I put my machete down and tugged my shorts back on before picking it up again.

Time passed, and the darkness persisted. I couldn't tell if I had become blind. Were the dense clouds responsible for the darkness I felt, or had my brain switched off my vision?

In my Africa, the center of belief in omens, I wondered if the darkness was a curse. Was it a price I had to pay for the things I had done wrong or the rightful things I hadn't done? In some circumstances, it could be considered a form of punishment for the things done by my forbearers. Some believed that there was always a price to pay for our actions or inactions. I couldn't remember my father's notebook mentioning blindness as something that would happen during the ritual.

In the darkness, my hands trembled and the machete fell. When I recovered it, I held it tighter. That was when my knees buckled and sent my body to the ground. Crawling with my hand outstretched,

I covered a good distance before I felt the roughness of tree bark, a stout trunk. Pondering if this was the end of my seeing all things beautiful, my eyes instinctively blinked and then closed. I opened them again, but nothing seemed to have changed. Darkness still prevailed.

Confused, I hugged the rough tree trunk. It felt as comforting as a hug from Elisha, the woman I had thought was the anchor in my life. The thought made me smile. But what was the purpose of my smile when I was alone and in the dark? Only the darkness, and I appreciated it.

For a few minutes by the tree, my heavy breathing was all I could hear. But when I settled down, I thought I heard footsteps close by. Warm sweat dripped down my face, and my palms became moist. I placed my gun across my legs and waited with my back against the tree trunk. As my heart pounded, the footsteps died down. Who had followed me to the river?

Above me the winds howled, and a whistling sound hung in the air, the type of melody that a beautiful African girl with big, puckered lips would make. As the song scattered and drifted away, I realized that I was hugging a pine tree and that the whistling came from the swaying of its branches. Frustrated, I set out in what I thought was the direction of my home. Something in me that I couldn't explain guided me, and a voice repeated, *Don't stop walking*.

Even in the darkness I knew when I'd reached the major road leading to my house. I heard drumbeats and metallic gongs resonating from a distance. The beats increased in tempo when wooden gongs joined in the melody. They were the type of wooden gongs Obodo bestowed on her revered men during their funerals. Could I be imagining all that was happening around me?

Under the influence of senses I couldn't understand, I knew when I'd reached the driveway to my house. The musical sounds grew louder. I was close enough now to hear ankle bells and thumping feet resonating, as if dancers surrounded me.

Afam! Afam! echoed around me in rhythm with the beats coming from the drums and gongs. I wondered who'd brought musicians to perform the death song of my ancestors in front of my property. I patted my body to confirm that I was truly there. Had I died, or was I dying? How did the musicians know my name?

Hidden in the darkness were not only musicians but also strangers singing about my demise, the death of an African son, a sojourner who had returned to his roots. What happened to the patriarch I thought I'd become? I had completed all the steps I needed to become a shaman, yet Africans are complex. They rejoiced with you one day and cast you away the next. I couldn't see the singers and didn't know how to stop them from singing.

"Stop the damn song," I yelled. No one responded to my demand. The singing continued.

I thrusted my machete into the soil as if I were possessed and shouted, "It's me, Afam. Death has not called me. Anyone who calls for my death dies first." Retrieving my machete, I walked unburdened toward my house. The musicians continued, but

179

instead of shouting, "Afam," they shouted, "Afam Igbaoyibo is gone." That was when I realized that it was not me they sang about but a different Afam. So I hadn't died or wouldn't die. Believing that their words were as meaningful as a prophesy, I felt relieved.

When I reached my house, I turned around to see if the dancers had followed me, but I saw only darkness. I unlocked the door with my trembling hands. Before I entered my house, the moon came out, illuminating the grasslands, trees, and soil. I heard the musicians shout in jubilation before taking up the ancient welcoming-home song of a revered warrior. Was their song for the moon or for me? I sighed with relief: death had not found me yet.

As the tempo of the song increased, I thrusted my machete into the soil again, this time as if I were a conqueror, pointed my rifle at the moon, and released four shots for the four market days. I leaned my rifle against the wall of the house and lifted my feet to the rhythm of the night, a song for a returned warrior. As I danced, everything in me felt reborn. Several times, my baggy shorts almost exposed my nakedness.

After I retreated to my bedroom, the musicians continued to play throughout the night. As I lay in bed, I understood all the things that had happened to me. The voice inside me revealed that my nakedness by the river was designed to lead me down the path to humility, the quintessence of dedicated community service, and my new role as the shaman patriarch: a traditional healer with the combined knowledge of all his ancestors.

CHAPTER 20

It was noon when I reached my grandfather's gazebo. After setting down my bottled water, I sat on the ground where my grandfather used to rest. The corrugated-iron roof shielded me from the sun as I thought about my life. I understood what my life would become in Africa. My worries tried to paralyze me, but I resisted. I reached for the water bottle with trembling hands.

As much as I worried, I knew that my past would always be the same. Dwelling on it would only waste time. To reach my goals, everything, past and present, had to be considered.

I searched for the wisdom to guide me as I renewed my commitment to Africa. The conflicts between Africa, Elisha, and me brought about this introspection, but it was my father's predilection for the gazebo during his own inner conflicts that attracted me to the place.

When rain fell, we used to complain about getting wet; and when the tropical sun shone on us, we would complain about the heat. Rain fell on me, and the sun roasted my body. My decision was to accept their roles in my life. Africa needed me, and so did Elisha. Elisha had told me when we met that I completed her. I believed her. My dilemma was how to resolve the conflict between the two beings who needed my love and attention.

In the tradition of my people, I needed to pour a libation of palm wine before conferring with my ancestors. Instead of palm wine, which I did not have, I lifted my bottle of water, stepped outside the gazebo, spilled a small amount of it on the soil, and said, "Grandfather, forgive me for the dishonor. Please accept my water today until I return with choice palm wine for you." I felt that there was grace in accepting my limitations.

The hot soil made a bubbling sound as it received the water. A small crater formed where my water met the ancient earth. I remained in a state of exhilaration as the scent emanating from the bubbling sand infiltrated my nostrils and galvanized me. Standing in the beautiful sun, I forgot all my worries.

Returning to the gazebo, I retrieved my phone, went down the list of my contacts, and dialed the first number of the three people I wanted to talk to. The phone rang for a long time without an answer. Disappointed, I thought that maybe it was not a good decision to disrupt my communion with my ancestors with a phone call.

I was about to hang up when I heard Ikenna ask, "Hello, Dad, how is Africa?" Yet it was all too serious. It was unlike him to sound so formal on the phone, calling me Dad instead of Pops.

"Things are going well, but I miss you guys," I said. His hesitation prompted me to ask, "Are you busy, son?"

"No, I'm not. Just having breakfast."

"You're not a breakfast man," I said jokingly.

"We're with Mom. We spent the night with her," Ikenna said.

"Who's we? You're seeing someone? I guess I'm missing everything happening in Boston."

"No, Dad, just Obialu and me. We're spending more time with Mom since you left."

"I didn't leave, son. I'm in my homeland, where we belong," I said with a raised voice. I waited a moment before saying, "Did your mom tell you she's leaving me? Did you ask her why?" I regretted the question even before I finished asking it.

"Dad, you left her. She's hurting," Ikenna said. I heard the anger in his voice.

"Stop, Ikenna," a voice said.

"No, Mom, I won't. Dad needs to know what he's done to you."

"Let me talk to Daddy." I waited until I heard Obialu's voice. She asked, "Daddy, when are you coming home?"

"I am home. This is where we belong. Your mother needs to be here with me, but she doesn't want me anymore."

"Dad, you know Mom. She loves you and misses you. She's too proud to tell you," Obialu said.

"I hate him. He messed up our beautiful life," Elisha said in the background.

"She filed for a divorce," I replied. "I don't want a divorce, but I can't force her to love me."

"Mom, Dad said you filed for a divorce. Is that true?" Obialu asked.

Elisha yelled, "That useless man left me for Africa. Can you believe he turned down the best job for us in Boston? He ruined my career and my life. I hate him."

"Remind your mother that the job offer was for me, not for us. I didn't want it," I said.

"I'll stay out of that one," Obialu answered.

"Let me talk to Dad," Ikenna said in the background.

"Call me sometimes. I miss all of you," I said.

"I love you, Daddy," Obialu replied.

"Old man, you better come home soon," said Ikenna. "Mom is lonesome."

"It's over between us. He can have his Africa. I'm done with him," Elisha said.

"In Obodo, it's said that a man seeks a wife, and the woman has the authority to accept or reject. Your mother has rejected me. A proud man would move on, not beg for love."

"Mom accepted your marriage proposal, so the stupid Obodo thing doesn't apply here," Ikenna said. His loud voice didn't hide his feelings.

"A wife always has the authority to reject a man, even after marriage," I said.

"You know what, Dad? Fine. Freaking fine! Don't you get that you left her? Can't you, just for once, own up to that?" Ikenna shouted.

"The way you're sounding, I don't know if I should ask you to visit home," I told him.

"Don't ask me then," Ikenna said. He hung up.

Standing in my grandfather's gazebo, I resolved to worry only about the things I could change in my life. Believing that I had lost my wife's and children's affection, I accepted my fate. I sat and stared at the grasslands as my ancestors had, all the while looking for a divine remedy. I wondered how the grasslands of home would solve such problems.

Nothing appeared to have changed for generations, but in reality nothing remained the same either. Everything depended on one's perception. The tranquil space needed me, the patriarch of the Nwaku family, to lord over it. With my life, I made a covenant in the presence of my ancestors to be the overseer of the part of my homeland entrusted to me. Before my birth, the sun rose every day; during my life, it continued to rise; and when I died, the sun would continue to shine on the footprints I left behind.

When I returned home, my sister was in the family room with her head down. I looked around. Nothing appeared to have changed since I'd left it. Adaku looked at me with tears in her eyes.

"What's wrong, sis?" I asked.

"Didn't you hear the noise?" she replied.

"What noise?"

"The police officers came looking for you. They searched the house and took our guns."

"I was at the gazebo. You should've yelled for me," I said.

"With their guns drawn, I thought they'd shoot me," Adaku said. I put my arm around her, and she did the same to me.

"Our local police?"

"The same men who came here."

"I'll go to the police station to reclaim the guns."

"It's not about guns anymore. They want to arrest you for threatening Ejike."

"I know it's about Ejike. He said he'll bury me."

"We have to come up with a survival plan before nightfall," she said. "I know how they behave. They'll come back to arrest you."

"As long as you're safe, I'm not worried. I've not broken any laws."

As much as I wanted to be courageous, my body failed me. My legs shook and my heart raced.

"I'll make something for you to eat, then we'll go to my house," Adaku said.

I walked around the family room, wondering when the wisdom of my ancestors would come to me. Even with the promise of seeing beyond my eyesight, I hadn't envisioned the police's visit to the house. The only thing that worried me was my vulnerability without my father's guns. I was so consumed by my experience by the river that I had left the guns at home when I visited the gazebo, thinking that I was indomitable. There I was in my family room, cloaked in vulnerability, without anything to defend my sister and my property. I was as naked as I had been by the river.

"Sis, go back to your house. You'll be safe there. I'll find a way to solve this problem alone."

"It's my problem too. I'll stay."

"There isn't much left for me to lose. Elisha is filing for a divorce, and my son doesn't care about me. Without you and Obialu, I have no one. If they spill my blood here, I'll be buried where I belong. What else could I ask for?"

"They will have to kill me too," Adaku said. When I looked in her eyes, the fear I had seen earlier was gone.

"That'll be a tragedy," I replied. "Whatever happens, one of us has to survive to report their atrocity to the state commissioner of police or to whoever will listen and do something."

"I'm staying here," Adaku said. "I'll cook for us."

"Why do you always cook when stressed?" I asked. She smiled. I was glad I'd asked the silly question.

"When I'm in the kitchen, I only worry about not burning the food. I tend to forget everything else."

When she walked away, I went to my bedroom. Inside, I looked around, searching for wisdom as if it was lying around or hidden from me in a dark space. When I retrieved the machete hidden under the mattress, I thought about the ways I could use it if what I dreaded ever happened. Unfortunately, the machete did not relieve my fear. My hand still trembled.

CHAPTER 21

For two days, I had fever, chills, headaches, and nausea. When I dozed off, I had nightmares that woke me. The smell of food made me sick to my stomach. It was when I couldn't stand on my feet without wobbling that I asked Adaku to take me to Specialist Hospital in Onitsha. The name attracted me, though it had been one of the major hospitals in Onitsha even before I left for America. How we left our house or arrived at the hospital, I couldn't remember. How long I was at the hospital, I couldn't tell. I slept and dreamed about all the horrific ways I would die. It was hard to remember how many times I died in my dreams. When I regained consciousness, I was alone in the hospital room.

Adaku returned to my room at 5:15 p.m. with two doctors in green scrubs: one woman and one man. The woman's eyelids could barely stay open. The man's thinning gray hair didn't diminish his calming appeal as he approached my bed with a beaming smile. He was agile compared with the woman. He extended his hand, which I inspected in the dimly lit room: bony digits with shaggy gray hairs. I reached out to shake it, imagining a grip that would feel like claws but was surprisingly soft.

"I'm Dr. Eyiuche. Your sister told me it's your first malaria since you came home." He rested his hand on my shoulder. "You'll bounce back in no time." I smiled as I remembered using the same line on my patients.

"I hope so. There are too many things going on, and I need my strength to face them," I said, adjusting myself in bed.

"Malaria is worse than people think," the woman told me. "It takes a while to feel one hundred percent." Looking at her tired eyes, I felt sorry for her. She needed a good rest.

"I didn't get your name," I said.

"Dr. Sister Mary Bridget."

"You're a nun? So the doctor goes first, before sister? I didn't know," I said. She ignored me, and I regretted my comment. How could I blame her, forced to listen to an American returnee with a brain poisoned by malaria.

"I'm glad your fever broke. You were yelling in your sleep," Adaku said. She sat next to me, the bed bowing under her weight, and felt my forehead with the back of her hand like our mom did when we were young.

"What medications am I getting?" I asked.

"We're taking good care of you," Dr. Eyiuche said. I wondered if he had hearing problems.

"I know you are, but I want to know. I checked CDC recommendations before I left America," I said. I wanted to say more, but looking at Sister Mary's lips move, I knew she was eager to reply.

"We're in Nigeria. We don't take orders from your CDC," she said, exhaling as if she'd expelled something building up inside her.

"No one is asking you to take orders, but I want to know what I'm getting. I need to see my medical charts." I shifted around in the bed.

"Afam, let them finish with you first," Adaku said.

"It's not finished. I need to know."

"Specialist Hospital is the best hospital in the east. Most of our doctors schooled outside Nigeria," Dr. Eyiuche said.

"Do you mean China and Russia? That would still be considered third-world medicine." I was joking, but they didn't smile.

"The arrogance of Americans is with you. We're doctors, not third-world doctors," Dr. Eyiuche said.

"Then act like one and tell me what you're giving me."

Dr. Eyiuche turned to Adaku and said, "It's probably best to take him home. He has improved and now wants to fight."

"Maybe one more day? He needs to regain his strength," Adaku said. She stood from the bed, stepped toward Dr. Eyiuche, and added, "Let me talk to you outside."

"Sis, it's my life. I need to know what's going on."

"One thing I don't like is the way you act sometimes," Adaku replied. "You always boss people around."

"I'm not bossing anyone around. It's my right to have full information about my treatment. Apparently, in Nigeria, patients have no rights."

"You can stay as your sister suggested. We'll see you tomorrow," Dr. Eyiuche said.

"Don't you want to examine me? Listen to my heart and lungs? The shit doctors do?" It was unusual for me to curse, but I didn't regret it.

"You're doing well. There's no need to do another exam," Sister Mary said.

"One other thing," I said. "Don't send people in here to give me intramuscular injections. Use intravenous medicine. That's what real hospitals do. Sis, take me home."

When I stood up, my legs wobbled. I held on to the bed railings. Dr. Eyiuche approached me. He watched me sit down on the edge of the bed.

A woman in a white dress and old-fashioned nurse's cap walked into the room and stood close to the door. Sister Mary looked at her with a frown. I wondered if Sister Mary was having a bad day.

"Let him walk around the room today before he's discharged—unless he wants to stay, as his sister suggested," Sister Mary said. She left the room without waiting for discussion.

Dr. Eyiuche shook my hand again and left.

When I remembered how mosquitoes had feasted on my body while I sat on the balcony of my house, I vowed never to expose myself to things that could hurt me. Going home occupied my mind for the rest of my stay at the hospital.

# # #

Dearest Elisha,

We met on a Saturday afternoon during a blizzard. I hope you still remember that I was sick, and you offered to drive me home. When I declined your offer, you followed me home. That was one of the nicest things anyone had ever done for me. We were only classmates at the time. You surprised me even more with a phone call. After I recovered, I offered to buy you lunch as a token of my gratitude. Instead of lunch, we had dinner. The romance between us blossomed into marriage.

It didn't surprise me that you were on my mind when I was hospitalized for malaria a few days ago. I'm home now and doing well. Just wanted to let you know.

I hope you still think about me.

Love always,
Afam

When I sent the email to Elisha, I was unsure if she would reply. I had barely put away my laptop in the bedroom when I heard a knock on our front door, followed by Adaku's raised voice. Although I was still weak from my hospitalization, I ran down the steps to face five police officers struggling to handcuff my sister. They released her once they saw me.

"*Oga*, we came for you. Your sister said you were in the hospital," one of the police officers said.

"I was, but I'm home now."

Two other officers approached me and cuffed my hands, which then hung useless in front of me. They didn't tell me what my offense was, and I didn't ask. I was no longer blind to their scheme.

"Leave my brother alone," Adaku yelled.

My sister kicked at the men. Her foot didn't strike anyone, but that didn't stop one of the officers from lifting his rifle and hitting her with the butt of it. I swung at him clumsily with both arms, and he punched my belly. When he pointed his rifle at me, another police officer held him back. He shifted his rifle to his shoulder and raised his fists to punch me again. I knew I couldn't win a fistfight with cuffed hands. "Welcome home to Nigeria," I muttered.

"What did you say?" a third officer asked. I ignored him.

"Throw him in the truck. He can answer our questions at the station," said an officer with a sergeant's insignia on his shirt.

Two officers pushed me out of the house. Adaku yelled at them and followed us during my forced walk to their vehicle. When they threw me into the back of their truck, I had scrapes all over my forearms and legs.

Three officers sat with me in the back. Looking at their name tags, I could see that none of them came from my area or spoke my language.

"Good-for-nothing police," I said. "All you can do is punch a handcuffed man. Take my handcuffs off, put your guns down, and let's see who wins this fight." I lifted my hands to one of them. "Go ahead, take my handcuffs off." It was their turn to ignore me as their vehicle went through patches of potholes, tossing me around as if I were a bouncing ball.

At the police station, they pushed me out of the truck. I tried to land on my feet, but I landed on my side instead, skidding across the sand. Three officers pushed me into the station, laughing. I kept silent.

I was not "booked" as I had seen in movies and on television shows. Instead, they opened the jail door and pushed me into a small space with twenty or so other men. When the officer locked the door, he uncuffed me through the iron bars. The smell of feces and urine hung in the air as if it too was locked in the cell. Even the thought of breathing made me sick.

After the officer left, one of the prisoners approached me and said, "You're the *oga* they talked about all night." I ignored him. When some of the prisoners stepped closer to me, I held my breath. For a moment I wondered if death would have been better than staying here for what might be days. For some strange reason, my heart didn't race, my hands didn't shake, and my legs didn't wobble. I felt as if I had no strength left in me to fight—a resignation to defeat. It was an awful feeling.

"Only dead people give up," my mother used to say, but I was already dead inside that stinky jail. When I thought about Adaku and what might be happening to her, my heart pounded like a drum

195

struck by mallets. I began to pace, one step forward and one step backward.

When I closed my eyes, in desperate need of a mental escape, my brain wouldn't let me forget my surroundings. I had no other choice than to hold the jail's metal bars, watching police officers play checkers.

Hours passed. My bladder was full, my stomach churned, and, though the stench fortunately didn't kill me, my lungs suffered. When the entrance to the police station opened, three men in black suits walked in, and a few seconds after, I saw Adaku. I checked her wrists. She wasn't handcuffed. I wanted to shake the metal bars out of excitement until I remembered that animals in zoos do the same. But was I not in a worse environment than those animals? What difference would it make? I was locked up.

When Adaku saw me, she walked to the metal bars and sobbed, reaching out to hold my hand. I had to remain strong; even shedding tears would have taken energy I didn't have.

"I brought our lawyer; and Afunugo, who you've already met; and our state representative to secure your release," Adaku said. I wondered why Afunugo would help me. Was he not Ejike's friend?

"I've not been charged with any crime," I replied.

The men in the black suits joined Adaku. One of them said, "Doc, I'm sorry for the disgraceful act by our police."

"My apologies for not introducing you," said Adaku. "Olisa Chiefo is our lawyer." The man wanted to shake my hand. I did not, feeling much too dirty.

"Honorable Patrick Obele," Adaku said. The honorable did not offer his hand to me. Afunugo stood away from the rest of the men to observe. He didn't speak. When I thought about politicians—well, dirty politicians—I smiled. We were the same at that moment: dirty. That was why they didn't want to shake my hand.

"I called the DPO before we came. He promised to facilitate your release," Patrick said.

"I'm grateful for your help," I answered.

"How about us? We need facilities too," one of the other prisoners said. Why he thought we were talking about toilets, I didn't know. When I considered the fog that polluted the jail's air and how it could seep into one's head, however, his confusion made sense to me.

"We'll get you home soon," Adaku said.

"I hope so," I replied. "If I stay here overnight, I may give up."

"I won't let anything happen to you," she said.

"I trust you, sis."

"Don't let anything happen to me either," a prisoner said, and some of the others laughed.

Adaku, our lawyer, Afunugo, and the honorable went into one of the station's back rooms. They were gone for half an hour, maybe more. I wondered if they'd been arrested, but then they came out with the DPO. After the DPO spoke to his men, I was released. I didn't look back when I left the police station.

When we reached Adaku's car, I opened the back door and got in as she sat in the driver's seat. She turned around to look at me, frowning, and said, "I'm not your chauffeur."

"I know you're not. But I feel dirty, and I don't want to sit next to you."

"You can drive, and I'll sit in the back."

I realized I was being overly sensitive and joined her as a passenger in the front seat. When she looked away, I lifted my arms to smell my clothes, and I checked my breath, wondering if the stench from the jail would come out of my lungs. I scooted my body to the edge of the seat, farther away from her.

When we returned home, I placed my clothes in the dustbin and soaked my body in the bathtub for more than an hour before I took a shower to rinse off whatever of the jail was left on my skin.

CHAPTER 22

Each night I wrapped myself in a light cotton comforter and sprawled across my parents' bed. I had many nightmares about the time I spent in jail. I would wake up drenched in sweat.

On one dark, moonless night, I laid in my bed with the curtains drawn and listened to a noisy owl's scream. At times it sounded as if the owl was in distress, but my worrying neither helped the owl nor me. Both of us stayed up, dealing with our problems unsuccessfully.

I couldn't make out the objects in my room. Sleep wouldn't come for me. It ignored all my pleas. After more than an hour of trying, I accepted that sleep had abandoned me. I unwrapped my body from the comforter and walked to the bedroom windows to open the curtains.

Peering out, I found the darkness like a malady. Not a single star dotted the sky, and it was as desolate as my aggrieved soul. The darkness made it look as if everything that existed beyond earth had vanished. Things looked so dire that even the owl had stopped hooting, as if it had succumbed to whatever ailed it. I knew that death would eventually come for me someday, but the eerie feeling inside me—queasy stomach, thumping heart, and sweaty brow—made me feel that it had arrived.

Returning to my bed, I closed my eyes. Instead of sleeping, however, my thoughts wandered to the night I'd spent with Elisha before I left Boston. Remembering our best times together was the only thing I could do since Elisha had filed for divorce. There was nothing left to look forward to in my marriage. That part of my life was over.

Luckily, drowsiness came along and set me free from all my troubles. It was so until I heard whispering voices. Initially, they came from the eastern side of the house, close to my bedroom, until someone kicked a bucket in the dark and cursed loudly.

When it became obvious that the voices outside had moved, as if circling my house many times, I left the bedroom to look for Adaku. I walked barefoot without turning on the lights and felt my way to her room. When I reached it, I knocked quietly on her door.

"What's going on outside?" Adaku asked with a whisper. I was surprised she'd heard the voices too.

"There are people outside whispering. It has me worried. Open your door quietly, reach for my hand,

and follow me," I said. It was not long before I felt my sister's hand. I led her through the dark corridor toward my room.

"They've destroyed Obodo. All we've left here are crooks and killers," Adaku whispered as we reached my bedroom. To my surprise, her hand didn't tremble, her voice didn't quaver.

"Sis, nobody will shed my blood without a fight," I said. In my anger, I forgot to keep my voice down. The whispers outside died down, as if they'd heard me.

Feeling my way through the bedroom, I retrieved the machete from under the mattress. I heard my heart thumping in my ears as my moist hands grasped the handle of my sheathed machete. It was slippery now, making me wonder how I could effectively use it. I was afraid to unsheathe it in case I dropped it from my shaking hands. Cutting my toes off accidentally would not help.

"I love you, baby brother. You're almost as nice as Papa. I want you to remember that." I felt my sister's body now shaking, her voice quavering. Was she aware that I was afraid?

"They heard me from this bedroom. Let's go to the kitchen to hide," I said.

"What are we going to do when they come into the kitchen?" Her voice was even quieter than before, and her hands trembled more.

"Let's find our way to the kitchen first. I'll think of something," I said. Adaku held my arm tight as we tiptoed down the steps. It was after we'd reached the kitchen that I realized that the door wouldn't lock from inside. Why would someone cooking inside the kitchen lock the door? I sat on the floor of the kitchen with Adaku and the machete next to me. I wished the sun would come out. Even a full moon wouldn't be enough to alleviate my fear.

"You're the only brother I have. I can't let them kill you," Adaku said. What could she do that I couldn't?

"It's probably some mischievous kids. I'm not dying tonight. Neither are you," I said.

When I heard what I thought were footsteps inside the house, I reached for the door handle, turned it gently, and slowly opened the door, sticking my head out and looking around in the dark. Nothing moved except for Adaku, who pulled me into the kitchen. I left her in the kitchen, went to the left corner of the front door, and peeped outside. I saw only darkness. When I returned to the kitchen, I sat next to Adaku and leaned against the wall.

Fifteen minutes of silence passed. Just when I thought they'd left, the whispering resumed.

"I'll light the bottle and throw it through the window," a voice said. I reached for the machete.

"*Oga*, you better pay us well after we kill your brother," another voice said. I knew which of my African brothers wanted me burned alive. The thought of such a heinous act was as dark as that night. I couldn't believe what was transpiring. I even began to wonder if it was a dream.

I wanted something to distract my invaders, but the night was so still that even the pine trees had lost their whistle and the screaming owl its courage. What was left was my anger, my fear, my sister with her love for me, a sharp machete, and whatever the invaders came with to carry out their nefarious act, if I let them do so.

"Light the damn thing," a voice yelled. I recognized it.

"It won't light. Shit. I think I poured kerosene instead of petrol," another voice said.

"I'll fuck you up if you fail me," Ejike said. His loud voice was unmistakable. I never thought about calling the police. The same police that put me in a stinky jail for no cause. If I survived this assault, they would arrest me again instead of their friend Ejike, the perpetrator.

While I wondered what to do, a burst of gunfire shattered the silence of the night as bullets shattered the beautiful glass windowpanes of my father's house. My sister and I laid flat on the kitchen floor, the way we used to during the Nigerian Civil War. The rapid gunfire sounded as if it had come from a machine gun. Our conflict had escalated to a war, with only one side armed: Ejike and his men.

I thought about the sacrifices I had made leaving Boston to return home. Listening to my sister sobbing, I wished there was something I could have done to prevent what she was going through.

"Bury me next to Mom," Adaku said, weeping uncontrollably. I put my arms around her and wiped her tears with my shirt sleeve.

We heard a loud pounding on the front door. Adaku stopped crying, and we both fell silent, holding our breath. I could feel her heartbeat.

"Kick the damn door down," Ejike said. After his command, there was another loud noise, as if something had knocked over a wall.

Then footsteps running into the house, up the steps to the bedrooms.

"*Oga*, be careful. They'll hurt you, and we won't collect our money," a man said.

"We took their guns away," Ejike replied.

"*Oga*, you're smart," said another man. I counted three voices. I closed my eyes but opened them soon after.

"They have guns. They'll shoot us and claim it was armed robbery," Adaku said.

"Sis, go inside the pantry. Let me watch the door alone." I tried to unsheathe the machete, but my hand was slippery.

"We'll search every room. When I find them, I'll put bullets in their heads," Ejike said.

After what felt like forever, I heard their footsteps outside the kitchen door. I stood, wiped my hands, and took out my machete. I took a deep breath and held it. My last breath.

"*Oga*, let me go in first," a man said.

"I'm going in. I'll put bullets all through Adaku for all the insults I've received from her. The one from America, I'll put holes in his ugly face," Ejike said. Scanning the kitchen, I worried that the lights from the appliances would reveal my location, but it was too late to unplug them.

My heart pounded. It was not out of fear but of anger. I wanted to open the kitchen door and kill Ejike with my machete, but remembering the sound of the machine-gun burst, I waited. When it came to a knife charge against an automatic rifle, I knew who would win.

I held up my machete and waited. I wanted him to come in so badly that I almost invited him. That would be a stupid thing to do, of course. When the kitchen door opened, I saw the muzzle of a gun. Once I saw the hand holding the gun, I slashed at it with all the strength I could muster. The gun and the severed hand dropped onto the floor. Ejike screamed and fell forward onto his gun and severed hand. The men with him ran. I turned all the kitchen lights on and held my knife to his throat.

As Ejike continued to scream on the ground, I put my foot on his fat belly to hold him down. When I remembered my awful experience at the jail, I wanted to cut off his head. Adaku came out of the pantry at the right time. She spit on his face.

Ejike remained on the floor, wailing. I looked away to avoid the sight of his blood and any feeling of sympathy for him. Why should I feel sorry for a man who'd decided that two people would die that night?

I had many issues to worry about as Ejike continued to wail. Where were his men? Were they coming back? When would the police arrive if they knew what had happened to their friend? Remembering that I had no front door to prevent anyone from coming into the house, I rolled the wailing man on the floor over and took control of his gun, an AK-47. An automatic rifle with an NPF number on the butt. How had Ejike obtained a Nigeria Police Force rifle?

"We're in worse trouble than I thought. He came with a police rifle to kill us," I said.

"If you let me go, I'll forgive you," Ejike said.

"Forgive me? I'm thinking about sending you to hell. If you talk again, I may shoot your ass."

"He has a police rifle. That's why he's making noise. They'll come for their gun," Adaku said.

"Maybe he stole it." I was trying to reassure myself that the police wouldn't come to our house. I wanted to go and look out our front door.

"Don't go out there." It was as if Adaku had read my mind.

I had only one choice at that moment. I took out my phone and dialed a number.

"Hello, my brother, you need *palmie*?" Ifeanyi asked.

"I need more than palm wine, my friend. I need your help badly. Ejike came with some men to kill us. I cut off his hand, and he's lying on my kitchen floor bleeding," I said. I heard Ifeanyi take a deep breath.

When Ejike tried to wriggle, I pushed my foot deeper into his belly. He moaned.

"Don't call the local police," Ifeanyi said. "I'll call my friend. He's the commander of the special police patrol unit. I'll come with them to your place."

"Who are you talking to?" Adaku asked.

"I called Ifeanyi. We need help, sis."

"You shouldn't have called Ifeanyi. I have friends I could've called. Afunugo promised to help us too," Adaku said.

"I didn't know. I thought Afunugo was Ejike's friend?"

"He's not. Ejike owes him lots of money."

Ejike started mumbling as if he was losing consciousness. I rolled my foot around his belly to keep him alert, but I couldn't avoid looking at the pool of his blood on the floor. He had bled more than I'd realized. I ripped his shirt and used it to compress his arteries and stop the bleeding somewhat. I avoided looking into his eyes. It was safer for me not to be remorseful about a tragedy he'd caused. To me, he was no longer my cousin Ejike. He was a man who'd attempted to kill me.

Time passed slowly as I waited for a return call from Ifeanyi. If he had reached his friend, the commander of the special police, he would have called me back. I worried about the local police coming to the house to finish what Ejike couldn't do. If they showed up first, I would kill them with the police gun in my possession. What if no bullets were left in the magazine? At that moment, I didn't have the courage to take out the magazine and check for bullets. That would be disarming myself.

I heard a siren wailing outside in the night, disturbing the quiet. The siren grew louder, muting the wailing from Ejike on the kitchen floor. It stopped outside my front door. I knew they had come for me, and I wondered how many men I would have to kill to survive the night. Unlocking the safety, I raised the AK-47.

"Afam, they're here for their friend," Adaku said. Her voice quavered.

"I'll use my remaining hand to kill you. I knew they'd come for me," Ejike said.

"So you haven't changed, Ejike? Do you know something? I'll shoot you first before I kill them. You deserve to die," I said.

I heard Ifeanyi's voice: "They really kicked the door down."

"We're in the kitchen," I yelled.

Four police officers in blue camouflage uniforms walked into the kitchen while Ifeanyi stood outside. No smiles or introductions. They saw Ejike wriggle. I handed the AK-47 to the police officer who I thought was the most senior.

"We'll take him to our station. He committed a serious offense. If found guilty, which I believe he will be, he'll never be free again," the senior officer said.

"I hope he gets what he deserves. They should hang him," I said.

"I'm the commander of the patrol unit. My boys will get a full report from you and your sister," the officer added.

I looked around. For a change, the police officers were there to help me, not conspire against me. No one was there to protect Ejike's criminal activity. I turned to Ifeanyi and shook his hand as the police officers carried Ejike to their vehicle. Their commander stayed with us.

"He needs to see a doctor," I said. The police officer ignored me.

"You can't stay here tonight," Ifeanyi said. "I'm taking you to my house."

"I have a house," Adaku replied. "We don't need your help."

"I know you do, but my brother is staying with me," Ifeanyi said.

"He's my brother. Go home and drink your palm wine."

"What's wrong with you?" I asked. "Ifeanyi is trying to help." Adaku looked away.

"Your sister is a strong woman," Ifeanyi said. "I proposed to her when her husband died." The commander left us abruptly to join his men, as if he was tired of listening to the verbal exchange. I wondered if I was the only one who knew that he'd left.

"He was drunk and disrespectful," Adaku said. The siren came on as she spoke. Ifeanyi looked around and shook his head.

"I'm sorry, Adaku. Your beauty made me do it," Ifeanyi said.

"Sis, let's go with him. It's too late to drive to your house. If we stay here, who knows if it's only scorpions crawling into our house.

"I'll get my purse," Adaku said. She ran to her room as if something was chasing her.

"I didn't realize the commander left," Ifeanyi noted.

"You were too busy talking. Look around you sometimes, you'll see more and learn more that way," I said. Ifeanyi ignored me.

As we left the house, Ifeanyi dialed a number. He swung our broken front door around and shook his head. "I'll ask my boys to replace it for you in the morning."

"I know people who can do the job," Adaku said.

"Commander, I didn't realize you'd left," Ifeanyi said into the phone. "Remember to send your patrol team to guard my friend's house. Yes, I'm still at the Nwaku estate. We're leaving soon."

"The Nwaku estate" befitted the property. I had struggled with what to call it: my father's house, my house, our house, and so many other names. It was no longer my father's house, and I was now uncomfortable claiming it as my own. The estate belonged to Adaku, Elisha, Ikenna, Obialu, and me, the progenies of the Nwaku family and my American wife. Even after a divorce, I would still consider Elisha a part of the family, as her membership became permanent after she gave birth to our two children.

# # #

Loud snoring woke me after I had slept for barely ten minutes. When I looked around, my sister was still sitting next to me on the couch, staring at the wall of Ifeanyi's living room. He was reclined on a sofa, snoring like an old baboon. Inside that spacious living room, it felt as if the walls were closing in on me. When I remembered the jail, I felt grateful for where I was. And for being alive.

"Are we going to be okay?" Adaku asked. I rubbed her back and then put my arm around her. She placed her head on my shoulder.

"Sis, I'll do whatever it takes to protect you, even shedding my blood."

"They're after you, not me," Adaku said.

"I'll never leave again, sis. Get some sleep. I'll watch over you."

Although no one else knew that we were at Ifeanyi's house, my mind was not at ease. I worried about all the things that could go wrong before daylight, like the local police finding us or destroying our house.

When I closed my eyes again, I heard bursts of rapid gunfire. The sounds of automatic rifles and whistling bullets made my body shake. The awful time during the Nigerian Civil War, living close to a war zone, listening to the constant barrage of machine guns, the deafening sounds of exploding rockets, all flashed before me. It had been a war with no rules, and Ejike's assault on us that night had been equally anarchistic.

Soldiers had committed offenses against humanity during the war. They killed and maimed civilians. Raped and plundered properties. We children witnessed the traumatic deaths of innocents and vowed to be better people. Ejike too. He had broken all the promises we'd made to each other.

Each time I tried to fall asleep, awful dreams woke me. I wondered if I would ever recover. "You kill only if your life depends on it," my father once said. I had maimed to survive.

I thought I'd fully recovered from the trauma of the war after more than forty years in America. I wondered how long it would take for me to fully recover from Ejike's mini-war. There would be no America to escape to. I was home for good.

# # #

Before sunrise the following day, I left Adaku at Ifeanyi's house and drove to the capital city, Awka. I met with the state police commissioner and lodged a complaint against my local police department for complicity with Ejike's crime. As I was leaving the

211

commissioner's office, he said, "Hold on. I'll send officers with you."

"Retrieving my guns from the DPO is all I need," I said.

"You need my men's protection until my visit to your town tomorrow," the commissioner replied.

"I'm grateful, sir."

"I'll be there tomorrow."

I left his office and walked across the street to the state revenue commission, where I filed a formal complaint against my local tax collectors: I owed the state no legal taxes.

When I returned home with two heavily armed police officers, I saw that some men and women had gathered at the front of the house. They clapped when I got out of the car. Their applause confused me. So many things had changed since I went to America that I didn't understand some of the local behaviors anymore. The two police officers followed me closely, as if there were still dangerous people lurking around.

Two men hanging a new front door listened to Ifeanyi's instructions as my sister peeked out from a side window.

"I was terrified when I woke without seeing you," Ifeanyi said.

"I left a note for you."

"He was too drunk to see your note," Adaku said.

"Will you ever forgive me?" Ifeanyi asked.

"It could be love that she's afraid to express," I said.

"I'd rather be dead," Adaku said. Ifeanyi smiled.

My sister came out of the house and hugged me. I turned to address the crowd. My sister tugged my shirt and whispered, "Don't say anything. They're here for gossip, not because of love. They'll twist whatever you say for a juicy story."

"I understand, but I must say something." I cleared my throat and looked out over the people. "I'm grateful for your fellowship. Obodo is my home, now and forever. Let's love one another. That's the only way our town will progress. I'm here for all of you, and I hope you're with me, not only in words but in your deeds. Thank you."

They clapped again, and as they dispersed, I walked into the house to confer with my sister and Ifeanyi about retrieving my guns from the local police department.

# # #

Close to noon, I entered the local police station accompanied by the two armed escorts from the commissioner's office. I avoided looking in the direction of the jail where I'd been held. It was balmy inside the station and sweat poured down from my brow. I wiped my face with my shirt sleeve while the officer seated at a reception desk, a young man in his thirties, dabbed his own face with a hand towel. I thought about how hot the two men with me must be, in their tactical gear. I would have suffocated if I was dressed that way.

Three police officers walked in with a shirtless man. Watching their dangling rifles and handcuffs, I wondered if they were among the men working for

Ejike. They looked at us and retreated to one of the station's inner rooms with their prisoner. I approached the officer at the reception desk, my two armed men behind me.

"Good morning, officer," I said. He looked up while dabbing his face.

"Take a seat," he said. He looked twice, as if he recognized me.

"The commissioner sent us," one of my escorts said. The police stood from his chair, looked at the men with me, and saluted. It was then that I saw the partially hidden sergeant insignias on their shirts.

"I'm sorry, sir, I was writing a report," the officer said before he sat down.

"I'm here to pick up my guns," I said. The officer looked at me again. The men with me approached his desk. He stood up as if he was about to salute them again. He didn't.

"Which guns?" the officer asked.

"The ones you took from my house. Your DPO is the one I should talk to," I said.

"*Oga* is with someone," replied the officer.

"Tell him to hurry. We have to report to the commissioner soon," one of my escorts said.

The officer left and knocked on one of the closed doors. "DPO, some men are here to see you."

"I'm with someone. Tell them to wait. Don't disturb me again," a voice said from behind the closed door.

"Yes, sir. I'm sorry, sir." The officer returned to his desk.

"You should tell him we can't wait," one of my men said. He pulled a phone out of his pocket, dialed a number, and spoke to someone on the line: "We're at the police station. Yes, sir. No, sir. He's safe, sir. I don't know, sir. The DPO is busy, sir. I will, sir. Thank you, sir."

"Who's in charge here?" I asked. "You have custody of my guns, and I want them back."

Two police officers came out of the back room, looked us over, and saluted the men with me. One of them asked, "Are you here to turn him over to us?" I looked at the officer who asked the question.

"We're from Awka. Your DPO better hurry before the commissioner calls back," one of my escorts said.

The DPO came out of his room with a young woman in a bright pink dress. She barely looked at anyone before bouncing away on her six-inch high heels.

The DPO looked at me and the men with me. He looked at me again and said, "You've caused a lot of trouble."

"You sent Ejike with a police gun to kill me. Policing is supposed to be for protection of citizens. Not here, though. Instead of protection, you helped a crook attempt to kill me."

"I don't know what happened, but I received a report that you cut off his hand. You should've called us to arrest him," the DPO said.

"Really? You sent him to kill me, so I should call you when he failed? You're too much. Give me my damn guns, DPO."

"You need proper registrations for them first," the DPO said.

"That's why we're here," said one of my escorts as he pulled out an envelope from his pocket and handed it to the DPO. "The commissioner wants you to return his guns. Here is the note from him."

The DPO read the note quickly and walked into one of the back rooms. We stood at reception waiting and sweating for more than five minutes until he returned with two police officers I recognized from their early visit to the house. They looked me over and returned to the back room with the DPO. After another five minutes of waiting, they came back with my two gun cases. My two escorts took possession of the cases, opened them, inspected the guns, and returned them to the cases.

"Where's my revolver?" I said. "You better have it."

"It's inside this case," one of my escorts said.

"I'm a DPO and should be respected."

"You should be respected if you uphold the law," I replied.

"Obodo isn't America. Things are complicated in this country," said the DPO.

"Change for good should start from law enforcement people like you. Renounce corruption. Set good examples for us to follow, not trading your guns for favors."

"You're going too far with that accusation," the DPO said.

"I'm stating what happened to me."

"Insulting a police officer is a crime in Nigeria," the DPO said. His hands were shaking, his angry face hardly able to look at me.

"Giving a criminal a gun to use for killing is a capital offense in Nigeria," I said.

"Enough from you. You better leave before I shoot you," said the DPO. He touched his sidearm but didn't draw it.

My escorts pointed their guns at him. "DPO, the commissioner gave us permission to shoot to kill," one of them said.

"Let's go," I said. "There's no need for bloodshed. Let them hang the DPO if that's what he deserves." The DPO walked toward the room he had come out of, muttering curse words.

As we walked away, the DPO turned around, followed us to the door, stood there, and watched us leave. I wondered if he would shoot me in the back as I walked to my car.

CHAPTER 23

After the local police had been restrained by their state commissioner, for a few days I was able to sleep through the night without interruption. It was calm until a pack of dogs came to our property. They barked and howled all night, as if they were fighting. There was nothing on our estate to attract them, but that didn't stop them from hanging around. I wondered who'd sent them to claim our land, but then I laughed at my paranoia. Their barking stopped after what seemed an eternity, and I finally fell asleep. It was not until the morning sun invaded my bedroom that I sat up. A spasm of coughing blew out the stale air filtering into my lungs.

After days of trying to forget the unsavory things that had happened to me in Obodo, I prepared for my journey to the source of my grandfather's medicinal leaves. I left the bedroom clutching my father's notebook close to my chest, as if I was holding on to my own life. I believed that if the treatise in the notebook was accurate, I was carrying a compendium of forgotten medicinal plants. Scientific elucidation of the leaves' chemical content and their clinical benefit could help my hometown, both medically and financially. Passing such information down to future generations was one of the responsibilities of a shaman and patriarch, the ascribed landowner.

I attached my sheathed machete, now clean of Ejike's blood, to my belt instead of carrying the rifle. To save time, I skipped breakfast. My preference for a machete didn't surprise me because it had saved my life. I also decided that, if my return to Obodo was to help the people, I needed a different approach to settling misunderstandings. Killing with a gun wouldn't aid my position in the community.

Walking beyond the boundaries of the tended lands, I entered an area of grasslands. It was densely populated by stubborn thatched grass, rodents, and snakes. Each time I met an opponent, I retrieved my machete, subdued the grass or snake, and created a passable route.

Deeper into the grasslands, when I lifted the sharp machete to create a path, rodents and snakes scampered to hide. Their haste made me wonder if they'd heard about my encounter with the cobra, perhaps even about Ejike's fate. The faster they ran, the more convinced I became that they'd heard it all. There was nothing hidden because the winds and trees spoke loudly in Obodo.

Beyond the grasslands, at a considerable distance from the house, I approached an area where tall primordial trees reached into the blue sky. The ground closest to the trees was wet and had abundant green shrubs that appeared cultivated and pruned. Their bright red, yellow, purple, and white flowers astounded me. Some of the flowers closed their petals when I blew on their pollen as if protecting them from my intrusion. Peering deeper into the wooded area, I saw a small creek and small trees in a semicircular arrangement with ellipsoidal shaped violet colored flowers. The mere beauty and complexity of the place captivated me. I watched the splendor of nature and for a moment forgot why I had come there.

When a gentle breeze passed through, some of the flowers swayed, releasing their pollen to float in the air. I took my phone out of my pocket, pointed the camera at the individual plants, and snapped their pictures. I placed a mark on the corresponding page on the notebook for each one I photographed. When I went close to the shrubs with red flowers, a swarm of bees buzzed around my hands and face. One bee hung around my ear and would not fly away. In every facet of life, there was always one out of the many who would defy the rules. I slapped it dead to my cheek, and the buzzing stopped.

"There's a stranger in our land," a man's voice said behind me.

Forgetting my beautiful flowers, I turned around to see two men with curious-looking faces and sharp machetes. One was older and wiry, with a stoop. Thin streams of sweat collected in the valleys

221

created by his wrinkles. He looked more ancient than the primordial trees in the forest. Another peculiar thing was his eyes. I wondered how he could see through his mud-colored eyeballs.

The younger man had weak-looking hands and the same facial features as the older man, except for the lack of white hair and wrinkles.

"My father and grandfather owned this land. It now belongs to me," I said as I approached the men, machete in hand. I was determined to state my claim, forcefully if necessary. Their machetes couldn't stop me. But when the men retreated, I realized how combative I was being. I lowered my blade and placed it in its sheath as I stepped closer. They stopped.

"Afamefuna Onochie Nwaku," the older man shouted and dropped his machete. A labored smile added more wrinkles to his face. He shook my hand, hugged me, patted my hair, and knelt. While kneeling, he placed the palms of his hands on the soil and added, "My ancestors, our son is home." He should be talking to my ancestors, not his. It was my land. I ignored his mistake.

"I don't remember you," I said. The older man stood up.

"You don't remember my father?" the younger man asked.

"Forgive me. People age and look different," I said.

"Your grandfather and my father were the only reputable medicine men in Obodo," said the older man. "The leaves around here answered their calls. They were the most powerful medicine men." He shook his head after he spoke. "My age mates called me Uzoechi Dibia. They're all dead now." He walked to his left, then to his right. He turned to me and added, "I tended the medicine plants for you. Now I can die peacefully knowing that you're home."

"I'm grateful for all you've done to keep the plants alive," I said. I looked at the blooms again. "Continue to care for the plants. They need you."

Uzoechi danced around me and kicked up the soil with his feet. When he stopped, he placed his hand on my head and closed his eyes. His son's eyes turned to the color of blood, as if he was bleeding into them, before looking away.

"Old man, you're giving him the power you deprived me of. Am I not a worthy son?" the younger man said.

"You're not worthy, my son. I'll never share my secrets with you. Here's Afamefuna, the one we chose. He's our medicine man," Uzoechi said.

"Are you a shaman?" I asked. The old man looked at me and smiled.

"Do you ask if a river flows? It's as dangerous as asking if fire burns. From today, never ask a question you know the answer to. Only then can the leaves answer your call," Uzoechi said. He released a long, deep sigh as if expelling every burden inside him. Looking at the beautiful plants he'd nurtured on that small piece of land, I wished that death would spare him for a long time. Unlike Ejike, he did not claim ownership, only tended.

"I'm sorry for the question I shouldn't have asked," I said. Uzoechi placed his hand on my head again and mumbled to himself. His muffled words rhymed, as if he was reciting an incantation. He looked deep into my puzzled eyes before he stopped. He rubbed his muddy eyes.

"Never apologize when you're right," Uzoechi said. He was determined to challenge whatever I said.

It was his son's turn to sigh, an exhalation that bordered on frustration and disgust. As the son walked away and flicked his hand at us, the old man feigned a mocking laugh. I wondered if the son was named after his father. How little must he have achieved to be shamed in such a way?

A short distance from us, the son said, "I'll show all of you." What would he show us? Was it just another threat from another disgruntled young man? Unfortunately for him, the fear of death had left me, and I was staying in my homeland for good.

"Don't wait too long to show me," I yelled at him as he started to run. Was he running from me or from himself?

Uzoechi picked up his machete and walked away. I noticed that he took a different path than his son had. After he covered a short distance, he turned around and waved.

My encounter with Uzoechi felt like a dream. I waited until he'd disappeared into a tall grass field before I returned to collect fresh leaves and flowers from the medicinal plants. Placing each leaf on the corresponding page on my father's notebook, I started my own collection as the new patriarch of the Nwaku family.

On my way back to the house, I stopped at my grandfather's gazebo to confer with my ancestors, those who'd made everything that I was possible. As I sat on my grandfather's platform, reclining on a dais, I fell asleep. That was when the voice inside me spoke again: *We live in you, and you'll always be a part of this land for eternity. So will your son, Ikenna.* I wondered if it could really be referring to the same Ikenna I knew—the one from Boston, the American. I laughed.

With sleep barely cleared from my eyes, I saw a man walking toward the gazebo. I recognized his distinct staggering walk. I couldn't understand why a grown man would let palm wine push him around all the time. Walking side to side at times and forward with poor coordination, he finally reached me. I stood up to shake his hand.

"Thank you again for the other night. Risking your life to help us," I said.

"We want you home. Our town needs all her sons," Ifeanyi said. He sat and leaned against one of the pillars.

Apart from the grasshoppers flying around, the air was still. Not even a bird's song in the vast grasslands.

"I wonder if there's anything I can do for you to show my appreciation," I said.

"What I did was for us. I know you would do the same for me. You helped me when we were in school. Remember what you did for me after my father died? You gave me your pair of shoes when my mother couldn't afford a pair for me," Ifeanyi said. His voice was clear, his memory sharp.

"I had more shoes than I needed. That wasn't much of a sacrifice," I said.

"I didn't ask for help, but you offered your shoes. That's a man with character," Ifeanyi said. He looked around the gazebo, rubbing his head. He pointed at the pieces of earthen pottery strewn around and added, "Broken palm wine pots."

"They were my grandfather's. I never thought they were old relics for palm wine, though."

Ifeanyi walked to a spot with many scattered pieces and lifted one up, studying it closely. "Someone took out their anger on these," he said. "They were smashed with a sharp object. Look at the markings on them."

"They broke after I left for America. I'm not sure when it happened."

I joined Ifeanyi to pick up all the shards. We piled them inside the gazebo.

"Next time I visit, I'll bring a pot of *palmie* for your ancestors," Ifeanyi said.

"Isn't that too much for libation?" I asked.

Ifeanyi laughed. He shook his head and sat down. "The wine is for us. Just a drop for your ancestors."

Four pheasants landed close to the gazebo. Ifeanyi stood and threw a piece of broken pot at them. When they flew off, he laughed again. How much had he had to drink already?

"You know that too much palm wine isn't good for you," I said.

"My situation makes me drink. I can't stop wanting *palmie* every day."

"What's your situation? Are you sick?"

"They killed my wife. She was so young," Ifeanyi said. Tears started to roll down his eyes.

"An accident?" I asked. He looked at me as if I had asked the wrong question.

"The clinic in Obodo couldn't help her when she reacted to the medication she was given. She died at St. Brigid. They said her kidneys failed, her liver too. I was ashamed when her body couldn't fit in a casket from the swelling."

"I didn't know. I'm sorry about your loss." I walked around, rubbing my forehead. I couldn't remain composed watching Ifeanyi sob.

"That clinic we have is a disgrace. People go there to die. I'm glad you're home. You'll change things for the better." Ifeanyi wiped away his tears.

"Why didn't St. Brigid help your wife?"

"Who knows?" He stood and stretched. "But I must go. I'll come by tomorrow if your sister won't mind."

"I'll see you later," I said. As Ifeanyi walked away, I added, "I'll find help for your alcohol problem." Where would I get such help in Obodo? I felt bad saying something that would be so difficult to accomplish. However, he would benefit from whatever I could do for him.

After Ifeanyi left, I couldn't find the courage to return to the house. I looked at the broken pieces of earthen pots and wondered why I hadn't considered sabotage until Ifeanyi had pointed it out. There were so many new things to learn, and I had to change my views to conform with local norms. My life had been good until Ejike almost ended it, so I must endeavor to appreciate what I had.

CHAPTER 24

A kiss from Elisha was always as sweet as the candies my mother hid from me as a child: toffees rolled in aluminum foil and placed inside a jar with a tight lid. When I was around, my mother stowed the container away on a top shelf I couldn't reach.

On a Thursday morning a few days after my run-in with Ejike, I walked into the kitchen and felt a sudden desire to taste those candies. But when I opened the cabinet, I found none.

The most shameful thing that happened to me that morning was my yearning for my mother and the tears in my eyes when I searched for my mother's treats. When I thought about it, I realized that I was trying to forget the trauma of cutting off Ejike's hand. I knew that I wasn't a hapless boy, but the longing for my mother persisted. I wanted to return to moral goodness, a childlike state, if that was possible. Had it been immoral to defend myself violently?

How could I be a shaman when I wailed with the desires of a child? When I opened a kitchen window to let in fresh air, I also let in the daytime serenade of an energetic bird. Leaning toward the window to look around, I saw a great reed warbler perched on a small tree branch, its head pointed to the sky, the posture of pride. Opening its beak as wide as it could, it fluffed its brown neck feathers and let out a beautiful song that pierced the calm morning air.

Of all the things that enhanced the natural beauty of the land, this European bird appeared out of place, and its lovely mating call, so off-season, made me consider its purpose. As I thought about why it had traveled to Africa, I became aware that I'd wasted valuable time since returning to Obodo. Its song complete, the warbler flew away, searching for whatever had attracted it to Africa in the first place.

When Adaku joined me in the kitchen, I wanted to tell her about my fascination with our mother's candies and the warbler but couldn't. I would sound like a child telling silly tales.

Adaku had also been quiet since our traumatic night, and I wasn't sure if she could relate to my state of mind. Comparing the two of us, I accepted that we handled tragedies differently. Her serious look worried me, but I couldn't fault her. I wondered if she needed to talk to someone. A shrink, a counselor, or whoever they had locally. I wasn't the right person for her to share her deepest, darkest emotions. I couldn't be objective when I was going through my own internal turmoil. When she finally smiled, I saw an opportunity to talk.

"Good morning, sis. I hope you slept well."

"I'm tired. I hope it's not malaria," Adaku said.

"I hope not. I know what I went through with it."

"I'm stronger than you. All the hamburgers you ate in America didn't help."

"If I'm not strong enough for malaria, then you're not. We share the same genes."

"One of us enjoyed the comforts of America for almost a lifetime, and the other withstood the heat of Africa. Guess which one will do better with malaria?" Adaku asked.

"Let's stop all the silliness," I said. "We must make time to talk about the trauma we went through together. In America, they offer counseling for post-traumatic stress disorder. We may have that, and I believe we need help."

"We're Africans, not Americans. We don't need hugs and kisses to feel good about ourselves."

"We're humans too. Our hearts break the same as Americans'. There isn't anything about our genes that gives us immunity from that."

"You're going too deep with this conversation," Adaku said. "I promise to hug you every day. It'll keep you immune from heartbreak. If you bring your wife home, she'll do more by giving you kisses." We laughed. I had needed her humor badly this morning.

As she opened the refrigerator door, a knock came on our new front door. It was a gentle sound compared with what we'd heard in the past. Then, Adaku would've told me to be careful. Now, she didn't. I wondered if it was her way of expressing trust in my judgment. Or was it just apathy—had she seen too much and become numb to it?

When I opened the door, I found a frowning obese middle-aged woman wearing a long floral dress and gaudy pink necklaces. Her feet were in open-toed sandals stained with the local dust.

"May I help you?" I said. My greeting sounded more formal and American than I would have liked, but I couldn't take it back.

She screamed at me: "You're evil! What did my husband ever do to you?"

"Ma'am, do I know you?"

"Stop your evil American pretenses! You cut off my husband's hand. They said you're a doctor. I don't believe it. You're a witch." I heard Adaku breathing behind me. I didn't turn around.

"If that low-life Ejike is your husband, I'm sorry for your bad choice of spouse," I said. I wanted to say more hurtful things, but something held me back.

"You came back here to cause trouble. Go back to America," she said.

"You've no shame, coming to our house after what your criminal husband did," Adaku said. She stepped outside and stood close to the woman. Adaku pushed her and raised her hand to slap her face. Ejike's wife stepped back. I reached out and pulled Adaku back.

"Never set foot on this property again. I'll let you leave this time," I said.

"You'll regret hurting my husband. My children will come for you. They said so."

"That was how your husband started. Threats first, before he came to kill us. I'm here to stay. Tell your children that this land belongs to me, and if they set foot on my property, I'll buy caskets for their bodies." My heart pounded in my ears. If I wasn't a physician, I would've feared that it would explode.

"You went to America to learn how to kill. God will punish you," she said.

"Your husband deserved death, not losing his hand. He had a death wish. If he ever returns to Obodo, I may grant his wish." My heart raced all the more, and my body boiled.

"I suggest you leave now," said Adaku. She approached the festooned, overfed woman and shoved her.

"Push me again and I'll kill you," said Ejike's wife.

"Not if I kill you first," Adaku replied, raising her fist to punch the woman in the face. I grabbed her hand.

"Ignore her stupidity. Get back in the house," I said.

"You're calling us stupid," said the woman. "I know we don't have your American education or your money, but we're proud people."

"Twisting my words and denying what your husband is—a crook and a killer—won't solve your problems. If he could do what he did to me, I wonder how many people he has killed."

"He's not a killer. You lured him to your house and cut his hand off. That's what happened. How is he going to support us with one hand?"

"Support you? Looking at you, I don't think you need any support," I said. She squinted at me. I continued, "Lady ... no, excuse me, you're not a lady. Whatever you are, get out of here now, before you get hurt."

"My kids will come for you. They'll cut off your testicles."

"Now I know what to cut off when they come. Tell them I'm waiting." I stepped closer to her and shook my clenched fist at her face. "Leave now, if you know what's good for you."

She walked away without looking back. We returned to the living room and sat. Her threat concerned me, but I wasn't afraid. My hands shook with rage.

CHAPTER 25

On a Monday morning, I dressed for my visit to the medical clinic in Obodo. Ifeanyi's account about his wife's treatment had bothered me for days. I hoped that finding out more about what happened to her could help him resolve his alcoholism.

I felt that I'd achieved all the goals my father had wanted for me. With his design for my future realized, I wondered how my own goals fit into the life I had lived in Obodo since returning home.

# # #

The medical clinic occupied an acre of land along a major road. Although it was fenced and gated, it was unlocked for easy access. The main building rose above the height of the fence. Behind the clinic, a densely wooded land extended as far as my eyes could see.

Tall mango trees lined the spaces between the clinic building and the fence. Even on a sunny day, bountiful shadows from the trees protected the clinic from direct sun exposure.

Faded tan wall paint studded with red dust made the building look as old as the red earth it stood on. Dust covered the steps. Agama lizards wove around as if they owned the place. In Obodo, there is always something or someone trying to claim a space that doesn't belong to them. The lizards scampered as I approached the steps.

Inside the empty waiting room, the cracks and small shallow craters on the floor distracted me. Two doors leading into private rooms were also cracked in several places. The building needed a thorough cleaning and repainting, at the very least.

As much as the red dusting of the room's floor and walls upset me, the chairs in the waiting room had collected even more dust. A young woman in a yellow print dress and a wig sat behind a desk stacked with notebooks. She watched me silently while I inspected the clinic. The notebooks, with their stained covers, appeared to have been folded and unfolded several times.

When I approached, the woman returned to gazing at an open notebook. I was curious about her age; her face had the features of fading beauty.

"Good morning," I said after clearing my throat to get her attention. She looked at me with a frown. I imagined a smile on her face, which I felt would have enhanced her beauty. There were many

236

interesting features about her, but her full lips reminded me of the women in America with Botox injections. In Obodo, I assumed her lips were natural.

"May I help you?" the woman asked. I wanted her to smile so badly that I smiled as wide as my face would allow. She didn't respond, her face remaining expressionless. A woman wearing a pair of blue jeans came out of one of the waiting rooms.

"What's your name, miss?" I asked the woman at the desk.

"Angelica, *oga*," she said. She didn't stand for her introduction.

"I'm Dr. Nwaku, visiting from the States. Excuse me. I mean, I just came home from the U.S." The thought of introducing myself as a visitor in my hometown repulsed me.

"I'm Clara," said the woman who'd come from the other room. The women looked at each other. I glanced at Clara's blue jeans and wondered when Obodo women had adopted this attire.

"Clara? Since when?" Angelica asked.

"*Oga*, they call me Ebele," Clara said. Why had she introduced herself with a Western name first? Had she used her Western name first to impress me? "I'll tell everyone the big *oga* from America came to our clinic," Angelica said. She finally shared a beautiful smile as she spoke.

"Don't you have patients to see?" I asked.

"They'll come, *oga*," Clara said.

"How long do you stay open?"

"We open at 8 a.m. and close at 5 p.m.," Clara replied. She looked around the room and asked, "Can we get you a chair?"

"I'm okay." I turned to Angelica. "How many patients do you see a day?"

Clara answered for Angelica: "Six to eight."

"That's all?" That was more than an hour for each patient. I wondered how the clinic could justify that type of overhead.

"Our doc comes on Thursdays," Clara said.

"Who takes care of your patients when you don't have a doctor?"

Angelica looked at Clara, as if she needed help with my question. Clara walked over to Angelica, leaned toward her, and whispered in her ear. I heard Angelica sigh.

"*Oga*, we have a clinic director and board members. We're employees," Clara said.

"Are you nurses?" I asked.

"We're not. We can't answer your questions anymore," Clara said. If they weren't nurses, how would they care for patients without a doctor? Things looked worse than I'd expected.

"Show me around. I want to see your patient exam rooms," I said.

"Okay, *oga*, I'll give you a tour," replied Clara.

She walked toward one of the closed doors, and I followed. She opened the squeaky door and held it open. An agama lizard ran across the floor and climbed a wall. Clara didn't flinch. She stood there as if nothing had happened that was out of place for a medical clinic.

This room was a duplicate of the waiting area, but something more disturbing waited there. Six metal beds with no mattresses occupied the space. One bed had a white sheet stained with blood. The room held no hidden nursing staff, as I'd hoped. The owner of the place, the agama lizard, watched us from his wall.

"What the hell's going on here?" I yelled so loud that the lizard bolted, abandoning his territory. "Even a dead body would run away from your clinic. First thing you need to do is clean this place. I can see how my friend's wife lost her life here."

"Who's your friend?" Clara asked.

"Does it matter to you? She's gone. Clean this place."

"We don't have money to buy soap," Angelica said from her desk. It didn't surprise me that she was listening to our conversation. There was nothing else for her to do.

"I have to see your director. This is too much for me to ignore," I said. I tried to contain my anger, but my body temperature rose. Who was to be blamed for the sorry state of the facility? I had to find out so I could fix the problem.

"I'll call her phone," Angelica said. She dialed a number and after a short wait said, "Hello, Mrs. Okaro, a Dr. Nwaku wants to see you. Yes, ma'am. He's here now." Angelica handed the phone to me.

"Hello," I said.

"Dr. Nwaku, I'm sick. I'll see you after I recover," Mrs. Okaro said.

"I'm sure you got sick from your dirty clinic." My statement was unsympathetic, but I had no regrets.

"Doc, I heard about you. When have you ever come home to help us?"

"I'm here now to stop you from killing more patients. Tell your workers to clean the clinic."

"We didn't kill anyone. As for cleaning, I'll ask the board for more money."

"I need the names and contact numbers of your board members."

"Give Angelica your email address. I'll forward them to you," Mrs. Okaro said.

"You use computers? I don't see any here. Does your lizard use a computer too?" I asked. There was a brief silence.

"I have a computer at home. I don't have time for your insults. Goodbye." She hung up.

Angelica and Clara's concerned looks worried me. "Are you okay?" I asked.

"She'll be mad at us for letting you in," Clara said, her hand-wringing so eloquently conveying her state of mind.

"I need to call your doctor. My mind won't rest until he tells me how he works in such a filthy clinic," I said.

"We don't have his number," Angelica and Clara said at the same time, both in raised voices.

"Do me a favor then. Here's my email address. I need the names of your board members and their contact info. I need your doctor's phone number too." I scanned the room again, shaking my head in disgust. Clara looked at me and frowned. She and Angelica whispered to each other. I said, "You don't need to get upset. I'll pay you to clean the mess in here."

"*Oga*, we've got nothing to clean with. No detergent. No mop," Clara said.

Her expression was as transparent as an angry bull's. The thought of Clara unleashing her anger on me made me want to taunt her, but I resisted. I needed their help to reach the people who could make a difference in the quality of care available to the town.

"I'll buy cleaning supplies today," I said.

"Thank you, *oga*," Angelica said.

Walking out of the clinic, I couldn't dispel my anger. It clung to me, followed me out. Frustrated, I turned around to look at the filthy place. Clara and Angelica stood by the door. They seemed dejected but managed to wave at me. Things were so bad in the clinic that I didn't know where to start.

I sat in the car for more than fifteen minutes, my thoughts swirling. A woman carrying a young child walked into the clinic. Although I wanted to go inside to find out the reason for their visit, I knew it would be an ethical violation for me to do so. I waited, helpless, until they eventually left the clinic seemingly alive and well. Clara and Angelica stood by the door looking at me. They shook their heads before closing the clinic's door and windows.

As I drove away, I accepted my failure to mitigate some of the limitations of Obodo, at least in its healthcare delivery. Ideas of what I could do to help my hometown replaced my guilt as my rearview mirror lost its hold on the clinic's reflection.

CHAPTER 26

Hello, Udeaja,

I requested the yearly funding and expenditure of the health clinic in Obodo. So far, I have not received this information. I have a meeting scheduled with the state and local governments to request increased funding for the health clinic, but I will only meet with them if the financial information I requested is provided to me.

Without the information, I'll decline to participate in any activity regarding the clinic and may establish a parallel healthcare center. I also need information on the management structure of the facility. As soon as I get all the information I have requested, I'll decide on how to fund some of the projects I proposed to your board earlier.

I am grateful for your assistance,
Dr. Afamefuna Onochie Nwaku

There was a saying in Obodo that "No one can hide a pregnant belly for nine months: it eventually shows." There was another saying: "People hide dreadful things about themselves but broadcast everything that elevates them." Such was the case with my request to the Obodo medical clinic board. No one was eager to furnish the information I'd requested.

Judging by its deplorable state, the clinic was inadequately funded. I drafted funding petitions to the local and state governments, but after waiting for days without hearing from the board, I drafted an email to the board president. I sent the email after reading over it several times. I felt relieved after I'd sent it.

Good morning, Udeaja,
Since I did not hear from you about the budget and expenditures of the medical clinic in Obodo, I assumed that management is not willing to share the information. Without the financial information, it would be inappropriate for me to petition the governmental agencies for increased funding for the medical clinic based on financial hardship. If the clinic is a private facility, forgive me for assuming that it was a public entity. I regret to

244

inform you that I have no interest in working with a private facility.

Thank you for all your help,
Afamefuna

Immediately after I sent the second email, I heard from the board president.

Hi, Afamefuna,

The clinic is NOT a private entity. It is a government-run health clinic. The information you requested is not easy to put together from the limited records we have. The clinic's financial record-keeping method is unlike what you want. It is unfortunate that I live 500 kilometers away in Abuja and could not help them prepare the documents to meet your request.

For your information, primary health clinics are government facilities in Nigeria. The clinical and support staff members are employed and paid by the government. The board only controls limited funds for the management of the facility.

I don't know when I'll be in Obodo, but I'll help them prepare a financial report for you when I return home. We need your expertise in medical facility management and would appreciate your involvement.

Have a great day,

245

Reading his email, I felt the lack of urgency in its tone. I went to visit Ifeanyi.

He was sitting in front of his house, watching passing cars, not that there were many cars passing on the dirt road. He didn't rise immediately to greet me as he had before.

"A beautiful day for relaxation," I said.

"I've never seen a day wearing a dress. That's the only beauty I know, a woman in a beautiful dress, like your sister," Ifeanyi said. He smiled.

Ignoring his comment about my sister, I said, "Sunshine and blue sky make the day beautiful," and shook his hand.

"I guess you heard the news. Is that why you're happy?" Ifeanyi asked. I shook my head. He continued, "They caught the four boys who came to your house with Ejike."

"There were two boys in the house with him."

"Two were outside. Ejike gave all their names. They made him talk," Ifeanyi said.

"You seem to know everything around here."

"You have to if you want to survive."

An older man walking with a limp turned into Ifeanyi's driveway. We watched him approach the house with measured steps. His shirt was unbuttoned, and his oversized pair of shorts was held with a rope.

"*Nwaneliaku*," Ifeanyi shouted as he stood to greet the stranger.

"Who's our guest?" the man asked.

"Our American doctor," Ifeanyi said. The man shook my hand and observed my face.

"Welcome to Obodo," he said.

Ifeanyi looked at the man, looked at me, and then smiled. He didn't correct the man's mistake about me.

"I came to apologize," the man said. "Give me two weeks to recover. I promise to deliver better palm wine when I'm able to climb again."

"Get out of here. I can't wait for two weeks to taste palm wine," Ifeanyi yelled.

The man tried to run, but his legs wouldn't let him.

"Stop running," I said. The man stopped. I turned to Ifeanyi. "The man can't walk. Try to be nice."

"It's not your business," Ifeanyi said.

"If he's the man who supplies your palm wine, I need to talk to him," I replied.

"Stay out of it," Ifeanyi said. The man looked at us and shook his head.

"Who do I listen to?" the man asked.

"Me," I said. "I don't want Ifeanyi drinking. It's not good for him."

Ifeanyi scratched his neck, pulled on his ear, looked at the palm wine man, and said, "I want my *palmie*. There isn't anything else left to live for."

I told him, "I was at the clinic. A terrible place. Hard to understand why you took your wife there." Ifeanyi looked at me and swallowed hard.

"You criticize me for drinking, and now it's my poor judgment. Is there anything good about me?"

"You're a good person with a drinking problem. I'm trying to help you."

"Go help your sister. She needs a good man, not his brother," Ifeanyi said. I didn't think before I grabbed him by his shirt collar.

"Go ahead, choke me to death. Has Ejike turned you into a killer?"

"That's him?" the palm wine man asked. Then he ran away without a limp. I released Ifeanyi's collar, and we laughed.

"Your father shouldn't have given the local government that land to build a clinic," Ifeanyi said. I looked at him, trying to decide if he was drunk.

"We didn't own that land. I would've known if we did," I said.

"Your father bought the land for you to build a hospital. He leased it to the local government to build a hospital, not a clinic. Who could blame him when you didn't come home?" I looked at Ifeanyi and wondered why he'd withheld this information from me.

"My sister never told me. Are you sure?"

"I was at your house as a witness when they signed the lease. Your sister was there too."

"Who else knows about the lease? Are you sure I'm their landlord?"

"Your father gave it to them for a token one naira a year. The local government chairman gave Ejike the contract to build the clinic."

"Wow! We've so much land already. Why would my father need more land? It doesn't make sense."

"Ejike's mom was selling their lands to survive, so your father bought them from the people she sold to. She even sold all the lands your father gave to her. It's complicated."

"I wondered why Ejike was angry with me. It's making some sense now," I said.

"You're wrong, my brother," Ifeanyi said and smiled. He looked at me, shook his head, and added, "It was Ejike's fault. He had gambling problems. He spent the contract money before he completed the clinic. His mother sold the lands to pay his debts."

"I need to talk to my sister about all my father's transactions."

"You should. There are so many lands you own. That's where Ejike's jealousy comes from," Ifeanyi said. The conversation made me uncomfortable. I didn't want Ifeanyi to look at me as a greedy landowner. I valued his friendship.

"I'm sorry we got distracted. We need to talk about your drinking problem," I said.

Ifeanyi shook his head. "No. Not today."

# # #

After gathering all the contacts I could, I sent out an email to the clinic's board members. I wondered how many of them were aware that my father had given the land to them. I decided to avoid using my position as their landowner as leverage. Unless they brought it up, I would not.

Dear Board Members,
  My intention was to ignore the last email from Udeaja, but I felt the need to reply. I was at the clinic in Obodo again

and took some pictures. Attached is photographic evidence of my concerns. Conditions at the clinic are shameful.

The issues I am trying to reconcile are the following:

1. Is the clinic's problem inadequate funding?
2. Or is it the mismanagement of available funds?
3. Are nonclinical workers treating patients?
4. How many patients have died after visiting the clinic?

It is difficult for me to determine the main problem at the clinic without knowing the facts about patient care and the funding by governmental agencies.

When I returned to the clinic for photographic documentation of my concerns, the staff asked me to forget about the finances of the clinic and "helping my hometown." I do not operate on sentiments but on reality. I can work with the management if there is transparency.

To Udeaja: I did not mean to deride you, if that was your impression from our communications. Since your medical staff suggested that I did, I tender my apology again.

I wish you would address my request favorably. Doing so could help in improving healthcare delivery in Obodo. I *left my contact phone number with the clinic staff. If you fail to provide the financial information today, I plan to meet with the state commissioner for health tomorrow in Awka to review the state's funding of the medical facility.*

Thank you for your assistance,
Afamefuna Nwaku, MD

There was another saying in Obodo: "You can only hide the scars on your legs from strangers." The people you live with know where the scars reside, and long pants can't erase them from their memories. I had not forgotten some of the common deceptive behaviors of my people.

Udeaja wanted to conceal, and as much as I wanted to believe his sincerity, I found it difficult to do so.

Forty-five minutes after I sent the last email to Udeaja, I was sitting with Adaku when a young man on a motorcycle pulled up to our home. He reached inside a shoulder bag and retrieved an envelope. Before he knocked, I met him at the door. After I signed the express mail delivery form, he gave me a large white envelope. I gave him a dirty one-thousand-naira tip.

"Thank you, *oga*. May God bless you," he said before mounting his motorcycle.

As I walked through the family room to rejoin Adaku, my phone rang.

"Hello," I answered.

"Hello, Doc, it's Udeaja."

"I sent an email to you and the board," I said.

He cleared his throat. "I read it, Doc, and then called our members. They agreed to meet with you."

"I'll be in Awka tomorrow to meet the health commissioner. When can I meet with your board?"

"The health commissioner can't help you. We have the information you need."

"I have an appointment already," I said. "Let's meet in two days."

"I'm in Abuja. You're meeting with the other board members," Udeaja said.

"You're the board president. I can't meet the others without you. Let me know when we can meet." I was about to hang up when I added, "I'll ask the commissioner to meet with us."

"I'll take a flight in the morning to Asaba," Udeaja said.

"Let's meet at the clinic when I get back from Awka." I hung up before he could answer.

# # #

By the time I decided to open the express mail envelope, my heart was racing. I was afraid to see what was inside.

I made sure that I was alone in the room. My hands shook as I opened the envelope, which had come from a law firm in Boston. Sweat trickled down my face and dripped on the letter enclosed with the other documents.

As I read the letter aloud, a line in it worried me. Several times I read it: "We hope you would agree to a dissolution of marriage instead of a trial." The word *dissolution* made it sound as if the marriage between Elisha and I would be erased.

Emptying the contents of the envelope, I disregarded a petition of "divorce by mutual consent." Elisha's attorney probably felt compelled to give me choices since I was in the middle of Africa, where I had no access to the cornucopia of Boston attorneys. Although I had no attorney, I didn't feel the need for one. Elisha should have whatever she wanted from our joint holdings since she had sacrificed her profession to care for our children.

After reading Elisha's divorce request, I retreated to the bedroom. Lying across the bed, I looked at the ceiling for wisdom. The white paint had no words written on it for me. I couldn't understand how I felt inside—empty, a feeling of a loss, what had overcome me after the death of my parents. My breathing quickened as if I wasn't getting enough air.

When I thought about the lone mourning dove that had visited my balcony days before, I appreciated the bird's state of mind during its song. The way my heart continued to pound made me worry about suffering from a broken heart, the same broken heart syndrome that the research in Boston had been trying to elucidate.

In the middle of Africa, my medical research had become personal, and a dilapidated medical facility in Obodo, situated on land I owned, had none of the advanced medical technologies I would need if I became the victim of the complications of losing a lover. What Elisha wanted was an unmitigated marital dissolution. Was there a formula to distribute our children's affection? Her attorney did not offer one. Luckily, I fell asleep while lying on the bed, and when I woke, my heart rate had slowed. What did my brain do to regulate my heart? I hoped it hadn't caused any damage when it reined me in.

CHAPTER 27

Early in the morning on the day of my meeting with the clinic's board, I watched the daylight dawn from my bedroom window. I was grateful to be alive, but Ifeanyi and his late wife occupied my mind. Was there a way for the clinic to offer Ifeanyi recompense? I knew it wouldn't bring her back, but it could change his destructive behavior.

Rain hadn't fallen in days, and the grasslands were changing from green to brown. My mind waded through several options for reducing the healthcare delivery problems in Obodo, but it also considered the personal matters weighing me down. Tall palm trees stood in the way of the rising sun, the rays from it casting orange and yellow hues across the scant white clouds on the eastern horizon.

Peering across the dry land, I heard bird songs that brought me serenity. Singing birds taking off and landing on nearby trees evoked pleasant memories of my childhood in Obodo. I began to feel better until I thought of love and loving. My understanding of love was as scant as the water in our river during the dry season. As the dry season progressed, it became a collection of puddles that evaporated in the stifling tropical sunshine.

Contemplation was a bitch that nagged at me often. That was how it felt when Elisha's avowed love for me had been extinguished. Despite my initiation as a shaman, I still had no magical power to preserve our love. My marriage to Elisha had been as vulnerable as a burning match in a tropical windstorm.

In the past, when my marriage had seemed infallible, Elisha told me that she loved me and couldn't live without me. On the days I was away from home for medical seminars, she couldn't sleep. She would stay on the phone with me until she nodded off. She told me that curling up to my back was the only sedative she needed. Unfortunately, the divorce papers didn't mention her physical and emotional need for me. The language her attorney used was as unfeeling as a rock.

After watching the sun come out of its hiding place behind the tall trees, I suppressed an overwhelming urge to call her. Maybe I needed Obodo more than it needed me. My desire to reconnect with something that had been missing from me, the site where my umbilical cord was buried at my birth, became stronger as I gazed across the grasslands. That journey, if I could complete it, would help me mend my tattered soul. Moreover, I needed the spiritual connection for my mental stability. To accept a physical rejoining with what I was missing would mean the end of everything that I was. Settling for a spiritual connection to my buried umbilicus was the epitome of courage compared with walking away from everything that I was or giving in to death when it confronted me.

Wearing a beautiful red chiffon dress, Adaku joined me. She leaned on the railing and peeked at me from the corner of her eye. It felt as if she didn't want to disrupt my meditation, if that was what I was truly going through. After a few minutes she said, "I left breakfast for you."

"I'm not hungry. I'll take a walk first."

"Don't go too far," Adaku said, expressionless.

"Are you okay?" I asked. She didn't look away as she would have done in the past when something weighed on her.

"I don't know. I feel out of sorts," she said.

"I can't read your mind. Tell me what's going on."

"I haven't been sleeping well since that night."

I knew what she meant. I had struggled with sleep too since then. "If Ejike was a stranger, it would've been easier for me. But we wore each other's clothes as kids. He grew up in our house. He ate Mama's cooking. Papa took us hunting together. He was like a brother I didn't have. Sis, my heart is broken."

She replied, "After you left for America, and once he came back from Lagos, he used to come to the house to console our parents. That's the image I have of him that makes everything senseless."

"I had some regret until his wife showed up to threaten me," I said. "The only thing that scares me now is me. My heart has hardened. I don't want to live that way."

"I don't want you to be that way," Adaku said, putting her arm around me.

"You know what? We just had our first therapy session. The only thing missing is the hug you promised me," I said. We laughed and hugged.

Her eyes were still on me when I left the house, barefoot. When I felt the sand between my toes, I wanted that feeling of joy with the earth pushing past my feet to last forever. Maybe it wasn't only joy that I felt but freedom too. I was not a director or a CEO, just a free man. But maybe, in my father's house, I was in charge.

"I'll leave the back door unlocked," Adaku said from the balcony.

"I'm not the house help." I laughed.

"The way you're dressed, even I wouldn't hire you."

"I'll work without pay."

"Silly you. Go away."

"Another therapy completed," I replied.

I knew my destination, but I wasn't sure if I would complete the trip. It was a simple journey to reconcile with the spot where my parents chose to tether me to the soil of Africa. Making it to that spot could change my life permanently. Only I knew where I needed to go.

It's not your time to join us. Return home, the voice in me said after I took more than twenty steps from the front door. It was clear to me whose voice I heard. I had guessed in the past when it spoke to me, but now I had no doubt.

It had been years since my father died. I needed his wisdom that morning, but I had to disobey his direct order. It had been his voice that taunted me in Boston and ordered my return home. My desire to gain his admiration, if that was possible after his death, had caused the strife in my marriage. It was difficult to please two people I loved at the same time.

"Father, if you can hear me, I'm making this journey. Not even you can stop me until I find my soul. I've known for a long time that I need to do this. I need it as badly as I need life. It's the only way to discover my essence." I waited for the voice to speak, but it kept silent.

Walking, I lowered my head out of respect for my father and for the shame I'd brought for disobeying him.

When I heard a cacophony of bird calls, I looked up and saw a giant iroko tree, its expansive shadow looming over a stretch of land covered by decaying foliage. Stepping under its shade, I appreciated its dark, raised, weathered bark. Some of the bark covering the mighty trunk was as sharp as blunted knives, as if the tree needed roughness for protection.

I was awestruck by its mightiness.

"Father, if you don't already know, I've found the tree of my life."

A group of birds flew away, but a few silent ones remained. They watched me as I searched for the stones where a part of me had returned to the earth on the day of my birth.

It did not take long for me to find the stones. Two rocks covered with algae marked the resting place of my umbilical cord. After sixty years of exposure to the tropical weather, the stones' resilience reminded me of a needed virtue in life: adaptability. It is a virtue I would need, as one of the major landowners, to survive here.

I cleared a dry area and sat next to the part of me that had returned to Mother Earth.

Something caused my eyes to close. That was when cold chills descended through my body. My hands shook. I was afraid that malaria was afflicting me again. I laid on the ground and curled up in the fetal position. I heard my loud breathing as air whistled through my nostrils.

The nasally whistle was as sedating as sleeping pills, making me lose awareness of my surroundings. When I opened my eyes, I couldn't see. It remained so until the bright images of five men festooned with ornamented African regalia appeared next to me. They stood in a circular formation, as if conferring with one another. I only heard indiscernible, murmured words.

One of the men walked closer to me and yelled, "Get up! Even a dead tree does not fall. It stays stubborn and erect until the wind pushes it down. You're my son. Get up! Find your wife and lie next to her, not your umbilical cord. Someday, you'll return to the earth, but not today. Get up!" When I awoke from my slumber, an hour had passed. I looked around me and saw no one. The air was still; it was not a day for a dead tree to fall.

I ran toward the house, humming every Obodo song I could remember, never looking back. It was not the day to join my ancestors and surrender my body to Mother Earth. The voice in me, appearing in a physical form, had asked me to lie next to my wife. It was my father, that omniscient voice in me. I wondered if he didn't know that Elisha had filed for a divorce. Even he wasn't perfect.

In my quest to connect with the physical aspect of my life buried in the soil of my hometown, I discovered that even the voice inside me didn't know everything. As the patriarch of my family, I accepted that I was fallible too. What would benefit everyone was the acceptance of imperfection and the willingness to change our views or actions when necessary. My journey had strengthened everything I was, every experience I had, and prepared me for my future in Obodo.

CHAPTER 28

There were two types of liars in Obodo. The ones who worried me the most looked into my eyes while they wove their webs. Those had no souls, and they even lied to themselves when necessary. The ones who looked at the ground and stammered were the ones trying to survive. Most of the time, they were harmless.

When I arrived at the clinic for my meeting with the board members, I found a locked gate. Standing outside, I looked in all directions but didn't see anyone. I leaned against the car and waited. Thirty minutes after the meeting was supposed to start, I left the facility. I cursed in frustration all the way back to the house. I slowed when I came to our driveway.

Three white Toyota Camrys with government license plates were parked in front of the house. I looked inside one of them and saw a large folder on the passenger seat labeled *Dr. Afamefuna Nwaku*. I became worried. For days my life had been peaceful, and I was afraid that this would change.

I walked into the family room with a racing heart. Three men in black suits and two women in floral dresses stood up. A fat-necked man with a pudgy body walked toward me.

"I'm Udeaja. You have a beautiful estate. Very expansive." He shook my hand, and it felt as if I was squeezing bread dough. His smile and amiable personality surprised me. I had expected more hostility based on the emails we'd exchanged. He turned to the rest of the board members, and they began introducing themselves.

"I'm Esther Ekodi, your cousin." The woman's face didn't look familiar, and I knew all my cousins. It was that African thing: my brother, my sister, my cousin, and all the other words used to claim kinship. At least Esther was modest enough not to claim that she was my sister. Adaku would have challenged her to prove it.

The rest of the group—Grace Uzonna, Raphael Olisa, and Gaius Aghalu—introduced themselves without fanfare. When I looked at them closely, they appeared better fed and dressed than most of the people I had met in Obodo. Their untanned skin looked as if it had avoided the tropical sun for many years.

"I was at the clinic, as we discussed," I said.

Udeaja continued to smile. "We visited the clinic this morning. You're right. It needs cleaning. Maybe painting too."

"We've got no money. That's our main problem," Grace said. Her statement annoyed me, but I feigned a smile.

"My father used to tell me that I need to know where I started and where I reached to know where I'm going," I said. They looked at one another quizzically.

Udeaja loosened his tie, wiped the sweat off his face, then said, "We have limited funds to run the clinic. I'd appreciate your assistance."

"I've asked before. How much money do you get from the government?" I realized that I'd raised my voice.

They whispered among themselves, their conversation dragging on and making me angry. I stood and went to the kitchen. When I returned with several bottles of water, I left them on the side tables and returned to my chair. Gaius took a bottle of water, but the rest looked at the bottles, unsure of what to do.

"We don't have accountants in Obodo. This isn't America," Raphael said.

"That's a stupid excuse," I replied. "We learned to add and subtract in primary school. Last I checked, one plus one is still two. You don't need accountants to tell me how much you get and spend."

Udeaja looked in my eyes as he spoke. "Government funding is complex. Different funds for different things." If my eyes could've told him what I thought of him, the meeting would've ended then.

"Stop!" I yelled. I stood over him and asked, "So, because you've got money in different banks, you don't know how much you have all together?"

"It depends on the type of money we're talking about," Udeaja said. He appeared unwavering.

"Money is money. You can add it, subtract it, multiply it, and, maybe in your case, divide it among yourselves," I said. Looking at their mouths agape, I thought I would need tape to keep them shut.

"You're calling us crooks," Udeaja said.

"How did you find out?" I answered. "I tried to hide my feelings the way you hid your financial statements. It didn't work for me. It only works for crooks."

"We can't work with you," Grace said.

They stood from their chairs and filed past me. No more words were exchanged as I followed them to the door. Although I was angry, I was happy that I'd expressed how I felt. I was tired of being polite.

Before they got in their cars, I said, "Our town needs a decent healthcare facility. That was what my father wanted when he gave you the land. I'll work on it."

"Your cousin Ejike stole the clinic money," Udeaja said.

"That was years ago, I heard. Who's stealing the money now?" I asked. No one answered.

They ignored me and drove off.

# # #

I was in Awka an hour before my scheduled meeting with the health minister. I parked the car in front of the ministry and leaned against it, watching school-aged street hawkers with dismay. I wondered if the minister worried about the plight of the children in front of his ministry.

My meeting didn't take place as scheduled. It took only a text message from the ministry saying *Meeting cancelled*, sent thirty minutes before the scheduled time, to end it. I didn't reply. There was no use in getting more upset.

As people in Obodo said, "There is no wisdom in looking at the headstone for the cause of death." As much as I wanted to be optimistic about my goals with the health clinic, I thought about the sudden cancellation of my meeting with despair. Had the clinic board members been involved in that decision? I wondered if the life of an average citizen in Obodo mattered to the people entrusted to run the healthcare facility. I had no proof to validate what I thought, but there was no other explanation for them withholding the funding data of a public healthcare facility.

On my way back to Obodo, I decided to visit a prominent hospital in the city of Onitsha. It was the hospital where Ifeanyi's wife had died. Although it had been reputable before I left Nigeria, I wanted to see how it had fared over the years and maybe find out if they were responsible for her death. About two miles outside Onitsha, I was faced with a horrible traffic jam. The hour it took to inch my way through gave me plenty of time to think, though. When I examined my idea to collaborate with any of the hospitals in Onitsha to operate a decent clinic in Obodo, I became apprehensive. Apart from the funding issues, why would a hospital from Onitsha come to Obodo to set up a clinic? As I considered proffering steady patient referrals to the hospitals and volunteering my time in exchange for their help, I approached my destination: St. Brigid Hospital. Driving up a hill lined with mango trees, I gasped at the sight of so many young street hawkers, barely clad children meandering under the scorching sun and running barefoot on the hot asphalt road, and rows of kiosks littering what would have been a beautiful landscape. Watching the school-aged hawkers chase speeding vehicles while balancing trays of wares on their heads was disheartening. Things had definitely worsened since I'd left home.

I was on a mission for better healthcare delivery in my hometown, but the plight of the child vendors was even more horrific than what was happening in Obodo. I knew where I was going but didn't know if I should abandon the journey. I remembered the dictum "Solve one problem at a time." But I was human. I worried, especially about the children.

The hospital was a brown three-story building with fading ornamental railings. Several flowerbeds of hibiscus ran along the walkway. Patients in wheelchairs were pushed along by their families, and some hospital workers walked about. The entrance had two large swinging glass doors held open by cement blocks. I wondered if the doors ever worked the way they were designed: to open automatically to visitors.

There were no security guards as I entered the reception hall, which was as big as an average living room in an American house. Several empty oak chairs leaned against the walls. A young man in khaki pants and a brown shirt sat behind a desk, his eyes trailing me until I came close to him.

"I'm looking for your CEO," I said. With everything weighing on my mind, I forgot the basic pleasantry common in Nigerian society. After I spoke, I read "Obi" on his name tag.

"Good day, *oga*," Obi said. His smile and politeness betrayed my deficiencies colorfully.

"I'm sorry, Obi. I hope you're doing well," I said. When I realized my folly—using an expression uncommon in eastern Nigeria—I quickly added, "*Kedu?*" which, in the Igbo-speaking eastern parts of Nigeria, was commonplace. Obi's smile became as wide as the Niger on hearing the local dialect.

"*Oga wetin* be CEO?" Obi asked. I was surprised that a receptionist at a hospital didn't know what the abbreviation stood for—the same title Elisha had wanted for me and was divorcing me for not accepting. It must be important; it had to be known by all; for it had been coveted by my wife, who yearned to be the spouse of a Boston CEO and the toast of local country clubs.

When I heard a shuffle of feet, I turned around to face four people lined up behind me.

"I'm looking for the big *oga* for the hospital," I said.

"Oh! That *oga*?" Obi stood from his chair and pointed his finger outside the reception hall. "That's him with visitors." Looking outside, I saw a man in a plaid suit standing with two women. I nodded my thanks to Obi.

As I approached the man, he smiled as if he knew me.

"I'm Dr. Afam Nwaku from the U.S." Adding "the U.S." in my introduction was a ploy, but I needed it. I wanted him to be favorable to my request.

"Nice to meet you," the man said. He left out his name and then shook my hand. The two women stared at me, faces uncracked. Their eyes traveled twice from my head to my dusty shoes. Their abdominal areas bulged in their tight-fitting white dresses, as if the clothing was made of elastic bands. I stood by my observation that many Nigerian women were indeed fed well.

"I didn't catch your name," I said.

"Oh! Anthony Chinwendu. I took over the hospital two weeks ago."

"You're new? I guess my problems can wait."

"No, no, no. What can I do for you?"

"I'm from Obodo. I need help with ..." I hesitated. At that moment, I wasn't certain what I needed from the new CEO of a hospital in Onitsha. He hadn't been here when Ifeanyi's wife died. Even if he had been, would he discuss it with me? I had to abandon that idea.

"We can talk privately if you want." He looked at the two women and added, "Let's meet again next Monday." The women walked away without saying goodbye. I wondered if they had read my thoughts about their weight.

"My issue is not a private matter. I found the health clinic in Obodo in a poor state. I need help to improve the facility." I hesitated and then added, "A friend's wife died here. I would like to come back with him someday to find out the details of what happened to her."

"We're a private hospital. You probably need to contact your local government. As for your friend's wife, you need to contact our medical director," Anthony said.

"Have you thought about setting up satellite clinics around Onitsha?" I asked.

"I'm new. We are still struggling with our deficient budget. A lot of people can't afford what we charge here in Onitsha. I wonder how the villagers in Obodo could afford a private clinic," Anthony said. When he noticed several people gathering around us, he added, "Let's go inside and talk."

Anthony walked toward the left side of the hospital. I followed, full of questions. When we reached a side door, I asked, "Do you get funding from the state government?"

"Only state hospitals and clinics do," Anthony said while holding the door open for me.

I didn't move. "Do you know how much clinics get?"

"It's published by the state budget office," Anthony said. He looked at me. "Be careful with our people. They can kill if they feel pressured."

"I've experienced that already," I said.

"So you know how bad our country has become. There's no respect for life anymore. They watch American shows and act them out."

"Why blame another country for our problems?" I asked.

"Guns and killings started in America. You should know that."

"Really? I didn't know. Americans showed our ancestors how to kill with rocks and spears?" I asked. He looked at me as if he didn't know what else to say. It would always be easier to blame others for our problems. Americans hadn't told Ejike to attempt to murder me. If Africans blamed Americans for their murderous behavior, who would the Americans blame for theirs?

When I turned to walk away, he said, "Give me a month to settle down and then come back."

"I'll see you in a month," I said.

After I left St. Brigid, I saw an impressive building with *International Bank* written on its side. Its flashy glass walls—a sharp contrast to the other banks, which were covered with dust—compelled me to drive into its fenced-in compound. Sitting in the parking lot for more than ten minutes, I called Adaku for her opinion about working with a bank. I needed to open a local bank account, but picking a bank based on how flashy it looked was not the best way to choose a reliable financial partner.

When Adaku answered the phone, I said, "I'll be home late. I'm opening an account with International Bank."

"We've family accounts with other banks. We can go together tomorrow," Adaku said.

"No. I need to open a trust account for the clinic in Obodo."

"You don't have to. We have Papa's money. Use that."

"I don't need the money. It's for you. You deserve it more than I do," I said.

"Come home, please. I don't want you in Onitsha after dark," Adaku replied.

"I'll see you soon, sis," I said and hung up.

Driving home without opening a local bank account, I reassessed my approach to solving the patient care issues in Obodo. I decided that a confrontational approach wouldn't work well with the board members. Their actions supported the idea that they were part of a corrupt system; and remembering what Anthony had said, I knew I was dealing with a dangerous group. Money was their interest, not the dismal state of the health clinic.

Determined not to walk away from what I felt was my obligation to the town, I accepted the risk involved.

CHAPTER 29

Many beautiful days had passed by the time I summoned the courage to write to Elisha about my feelings. She had ignored my emails and phone calls, and I refused to contact her attorney as she demanded. What I had with Elisha was not for attorneys to divide between us. Properties and investments didn't matter to me. How could such things matter without her love? There was nothing wrong with bequeathing my American holdings to her. From her behavior, I wondered if she wanted a legal battle with me, but I had no reason to indulge in such. I was still in love with her.

I wasted many days mired in contemplation as the lingering love affair with my wife pecked at my heart. On one Wednesday morning that started as a beautiful day with sunshine and a slight breeze, an ominous haze soon tainted the sky. Although the haze persisted and delayed my departure, it didn't curtail my plans for the day.

Ifeanyi hadn't spoken to me since the day we'd exchanged words in his house. Many times I had wanted to visit him, but I couldn't summon the courage to face him without significant information about his wife's tragedy at the local clinic.

When I heard a soft knock on our door that morning, I didn't hesitate to open it. Ifeanyi stood before me with an expression that was hard to read. Was it a smile or a frown?

"I knew today was going to be special," I said as I hugged one of the rare men who had been upright with me in Obodo.

"I wanted you to see me sober. No *palmie* for a week," Ifeanyi said.

"Good for your liver," Adaku said. I couldn't tell how long she'd been standing behind me. She had become my shadow.

We walked into the family room and sat, except for Adaku, who stood next to me.

"Be nice to me," said Ifeanyi. "I deserve it."

"I don't know why men choose to destroy themselves," Adaku said.

"Men?" he replied. "What do you know about us? You married a man; and when he died, you hid yourself from the world."

"Mourning takes longer than people realize," I said.

"Tell me about it. I'm afraid I will never get over my wife's death," Ifeanyi answered.

"My biggest problem was guilt," I said. "Not being home for my parents. Somehow I thought they would wait for me. Live forever. That was selfish."

"I was here, but I still feel that I didn't do enough for them," Adaku said.

"I worked every day," said Ifeanyi. "Didn't spend enough time with my wife. When she died, I regretted every night we didn't have dinner together."

"Look at us, blaming ourselves for our lives' imperfections," I said. "We can't go back to our yesterdays. They're gone for good. What we have is a support group for us. A group of three." We laughed.

"We're pathetic," Adaku said.

"We've been hurting," Ifeanyi replied.

"I'll make breakfast to pacify us," Adaku said. We laughed some more. It was good laughter. The healing kind.

"I feel better already," Ifeanyi said.

I told him, "I was at St. Brigid recently. I met a new guy in charge over there. I can't promise you much at this time, but I'm working on finding answers for you."

"It's your actions that console me. I'm glad you came home. I needed an honest friend," he said.

"Well, I'm glad I met you at the police station. I hope you don't mind me asking, but what happened to your beautiful outfit? You've dressed down since then."

He laughed. "You changed me. You wear simple shirts and shorts. Nothing fancy."

"It's too warm to wear more than that," I said. I looked at Ifeanyi in his khaki shorts and white polo shirt. He looked at me too. We pointed at our identical outfits and couldn't stop giggling.

"I need to be around someone like you, not all these men around here who live beyond their means," he said. "They resort to crime to measure up. Look at you: with all you have, you walk around barefoot."

"I love the freedom I have here. If it weren't for Ejike, I would've said I'm in paradise. Let me change that: I'm in paradise but surrounded by hell. That's better."

When Adaku returned with a tray of food, we retreated to the terrace. She set down covered serving dishes that belonged to our mother on the table. When I uncovered one of the dishes, an appetizing fragrance escaped. Even the beef stew and jollof rice she served looked like our mom's preparation.

As we ate, Adaku watched Ifeanyi closely. I waited for their combat to begin, but my sister was silent, glancing at me repeatedly. She wanted to say something; finally, she couldn't hold her words any longer. She walked from one side of the balcony to another.

"Since Ifeanyi is here, I'll tell you something you don't know," she said. We waited as she fidgeted and wrung her hands.

"What's wrong?" I asked.

"I know what's wrong. She doesn't want me here," Ifeanyi said.

"That's not true," I replied. "My sister watched me cut off our cousin's hand. That's what she's going through. We've not talked as much as we should about it."

Adaku said, "Every time Ifeanyi comes around here, I worry. Will he turn out to be like Ejike? A friend today and an enemy tomorrow? That's my fear."

"Sis, we can't live in fear of everyone. We have to trust good people."

"Adaku, if you want me to leave and never come back, I will," Ifeanyi said. He stood from his chair. Looking at me, he added, "I understand your sister's fear."

"Don't go, but promise not to change," Adaku said. She hugged Ifeanyi and cried. "Don't think I'm weak. If you ever harm my brother ..." She stopped talking, and we all laughed.

"I do need to go, though," Ifeanyi said at last. "There's a young woman who wants to meet me. I can't keep her waiting."

"There's one benefit of being sober," I said. I watched my sister frown and wondered if she was unhappy with Ifeanyi's announcement.

After he had left, I retreated to my bedroom. When I sat on the bed, I couldn't remember why I was there. When I heard a knock, I didn't need to answer.

Adaku came in and sat next to me. "Have you spoken to your wife lately?"

"I don't have much to tell her."

"I know you can't look in my eyes when you lie to me," she said and turned to me. I kept looking at the floor. "You talk about group therapy. How about family therapy?"

"What's family therapy?"

"What a family needs when they've got problems. I was angry with you for a long time, but when I saw you walk into our house after many years, the only thing I felt for you was love. You need your family here with you," Adaku said.

"Sis, things are complicated. No matter how angry you got with me, I'll always be your brother. Marriage is different. It can end. Maybe the right word is *dissolved*."

"You're not making sense. Did you leave your wife?" Adaku asked as she stood to look at me.

"Elisha filed for a divorce, not me."

She shook her head. "I'll call her to get the truth."

"I've got papers to show you if you don't believe me."

"Your papers won't tell me what happened in Boston between the two of you."

"Nothing happened between us. She wanted something that I didn't. Maybe it was a need. I don't know."

"That's the issue with a lot of men. You don't make enough effort to understand your partner."

"They offered me a job I didn't want. It would've stopped me from coming home," I said.

"I'm glad you didn't accept. You belong here."

She left the room without asking any more questions. I was relieved that she'd left me to solve my own problems, but what she'd said lingered with me.

# # #

When I arrived at the river later that day, the shallow water was barely flowing, almost as if it had lost its strength. I marveled at the beautiful rows of studded raffia palm trees on both banks. I wondered how I could have missed their magnificence on the night I needed cleansing, but soon I remembered the debilitating anxiety that had accompanied me to the river.

After finding a piece of rock big enough to serve as a seat, I lifted it to search for scorpions before I sat down. Some habits were difficult to forget. As I spent more time in Obodo, I began to realize that the African in me had only remained dormant while I sojourned; it had never left. It became clear that this was also part of my marital problem. My acceptance that abandoning Africa would be equal to forgetting my name was a healing process I needed.

I sat on the rock, stood up, and sat again several times. What propelled me to rise was a restlessness, like a lion in a cage. At times I walked passable lengths of dry land by the riverbanks. If I had found myself, then what was I searching for? If I was a shaman with a forest of medicinal plants, what else did I need to be a healer?

Birds and squirrels watched me from the trees. My legs didn't wear out, and my determination never floundered.

Many birds were perched as I walked by the banks, but none of them sang for me. They watched me parade around as if I were an African prince waiting for recognition. Maybe I was waiting for a coronation, if I deemed myself a king.

Love and happiness were the nutrients needed for my soul. That thing in me compelled me again to stand and search deeper inside. My yearning was for love, and there was only one person who held that love.

I opened my tablet to write a note that would lay bare my soul to Elisha. I had to remind her about that special part of me that needed her love to achieve happiness, the vulnerable part of me that a divorce would destroy.

The river flowed with tears from the soul of Africa. I held on to my own tears because they wouldn't change anything. Instead, I let my soul weep.

When I looked at the tablet, all I could see was a blinding light. I rubbed my eyes, but the bright African sun continued to efface the screen. A tear landed on the glass. I accepted that it was a teardrop from the African sky. How could I weep for a love that no longer belonged to me? Why did I search for a soul that no longer searched for my own? We were no longer mates.

I started to type:

Dearest Elie,

I came to the banks of the Iyiofolo River to find the courage to reveal my soul and longing for you. An interesting thing happened to me when I started. Instead of finding the courage to plead for your love, I realized that your happiness should matter more to me. It's hard for me to accept that the river cleansed my soul, but it did. The love you gave me will always be with me. I've accepted that I don't need anything more than what you're willing to give me. Painfully, I accept all the conditions you have stipulated in your divorce filing.

You may give away my personal belongings to charitable organizations. Place my documents in a box and ship them to me.

I hope you'll continue to be a part of me in ways that you're comfortable with. I'll need all the support you can give me as I adjust to our new status. When you remember me, try not to dwell on my failures. Remember that my love for you is eternal and that my gratitude for your love is immense.

I'll sign the divorce papers and return them to your attorney. Take care of our children.

I'll always love you,
Afam

It wasn't what I had come to the river to write, but my soul had a mind of its own. It guided me in relating to Elisha's needs. After reading my note several times, I felt that it was the embodiment of loving my wife without losing my soul.

As I was about to send my email, I heard someone say, "I thought you were an illusion. Forgive me, I had too much to drink before I saw you." I thought it was Ifeanyi until I turned around.

Standing close to me was a man wearing tattered shorts. His hand clutched a piece of rope that was wrapped around the narrow neck of a large brown calabash jar, as if he was holding a puller tie around a horse's neck. I became worried about how I could get so distracted and put my safety in jeopardy. Even the birds looked around while feeding. I sighed.

"Who am I greeting?" I asked. It surprised me that I used the indirect form of asking a stranger his name. It was, though, a customary practice with elderly men in Obodo. I guessed that I qualified as one. It was the custom of men with wisdom. Maybe I had become wise.

"Okoye Iduka, a palm-wine tapper." He looked at me with a crinkled expression. "You're not from around here?"

"I'm a native son," I retorted. A patriarch belonged to the land and his people. That qualified me as one. My buried umbilical cord would bear witness to my status.

"Didn't mean to upset you. You just don't look like one of us," Okoye said.

"How do we look?" I asked with a smile.

"Look at me, a wine tapper. Look at you, a refined man."

"You're at work, and I'm here to look at the river. It's not how we look that matters but what's inside us."

"That's why you're not one of us. No man in Obodo comes here to look at the river," Okoye said with a smile.

"They're missing a lot. The river calms and motivates. It speaks to our souls and weeps for us so that we don't have to weep."

"The river doesn't provide food for the family."

"You can fish to feed the family, or find inspiration for what you need to do," I said.

"There's no fish in the river. See the sand that erosion brought." Okoye pointed to the shallow water. He looked around. "Do you see anyone around us?"

I inspected the river, its banks, for as far I could see. I saw bountiful rays of African sun and a desolate land divided by rows of raffia palm trees.

"Our people need to appreciate nature more," I said.

"You feed your family first, drink a little palm wine to forget your problems. And after, how does one fit the river in?" Okoye asked as he chuckled.

"It depends on how people allocate their time. It's good to make time for relaxation."

"That's what palm wine does. It relaxes you."

"That can become a problem if you drink too much," I said.

"Don't tell our people not to drink. I've got to make money," Okoye said. I thought about Ifeanyi, who gave up drinking, and his palm-wine supplier, who lost a customer. One gained improved health, and the other lost a source of revenue.

As he was walking away, Okoye turned around and asked, "Does the stranger have a name?"

"Afamefuna Onochie Nwaku, a native son," I said.

"Your father named you well. Here's my son who replaced me to keep my name alive forever," Okoye said.

"Remember, I'm a native son. I know the meaning of my name, I hear the wind whistle it," I said.

Okoye laughed as he ascended a small hill and disappeared. His laughter lingered on while I sent the email to Elisha. After wiping the sand off my pants, I left the river as I found it: desolate. Luckily, my soul had found redemption.

CHAPTER 30

Time passed as quickly as the wind before a tropical storm. By the time Adaku and I came back from Onitsha, it was dusk. Setting up funding schemes for the educational and medical foundation had taken longer than we expected. As we drove closer to our house, I saw a man leaning against one of the pillars. His faded red African-print dashiki was draped around his protruding belly.

I slowed the vehicle and directed the headlights at the stranger. He covered his eyes. When I stopped the car, I peered around in the twilight to determine the number of people around the house. The lone stranger approached our car before Adaku and I could get out. I left the headlights on until he reached the driver's side. Even before I opened the car door, I recognized the man's wobbling walk.

"You've returned for another crime?" I asked as I opened the car door. But it wasn't Ejike as I had thought.

"I'm here to punish you," the man said. "You'll pay for what you did to my father."

"Who's your father?" I asked. I knew who he was, though; genes don't lie.

"I'm your brother Ejike's son."

"Your father deserved what happened to him. What your father did was an abomination. It's forbidden in our culture. Even if they release him from jail, he'll never live among us in Obodo."

"I'll spare your life if you sign the papers against his execution. They'll spare his life if you do," the man said. "That's the only way I'll let you live."

"If your father succeeded in killing me that night, where would I be today?"

"But you're alive. He would've killed you if he wanted to."

"I'll let the court system determine his fate. I'm done talking about it unless you're here for me," I said.

"You Americans are heartless. I should've known the type of man you are."

"You called me your brother, but now I'm an American. Is that what your father called me before he set out to kill me?" I asked. There was no sorrow left in my heart for Ejike.

"My mom told me not to talk to you. I should've listened to her," the man said. I looked him over, and his resemblance to his father repulsed me. I was afraid that my heart would never forgive and that only my death would let me forget what Ejike had tried to do to me.

"I've kept quiet for too long," Adaku said. "Where was your mother when your father left his house in the middle of the night? Did she ask him where he was going? I bet your mother was a part of his criminal activity." My shadow had returned. Though, truly, Adaku was always a part of me.

"Rot in hell. My mother didn't do anything to you," the man said.

I replied, "That's where your father is heading. I'll watch them hang him."

"I gave up on your family. You're a disgusting piece of crap like your father," Adaku said. She walked to the house and left the two of us by the car.

The man walked closer to me. I took two steps back while watching his hand. I needed a safe distance between us. I sized him up and knew where I would hit him. I would kick his balls in. I didn't have a knife to cut them off as I'd promised his mother I would.

"We're no longer family," I said. "I'll never accept you or your father as my cousins again. Think about it: he wanted to kill us in the middle of the night. An evil scheme to claim land that doesn't belong to him."

"It was the devil that made him do it," the man said. He moved closer to me again, and I retreated to my left for an easier attack, if needed. I even imagined him wailing like his father when wounded.

I walked toward the house, but he followed.

"Stop following me," I shouted at him. He stopped.

289

"They'll hang my father if you don't sign the petition. Please, *oga*, tell the police you're not charging my father."

"That's why you're here? Afraid they'll hang him by his neck? If they give me the rope, I'll do it for them."

My anger had swelled so much that I was afraid I would explode. When I turned to face him and his massive belly, I knew I had to walk away. I saw Ejike, not his son. I needed to avoid hurting him for his father's crimes against me.

When I entered our house, Adaku was standing at the door, holding a revolver. I wondered what she would have done if the young man became belligerent. Time and events had changed all of us, including my sister, who was now a gun-toting angry woman.

CHAPTER 31

The magistrate court was situated at the border of Obodo and Ezilu. It was a British colonial era one-story building with peeling whitewash paint trimmed with black oil paint. The ground wore the look of a traditional home in Obodo, thick with an abundance of loose brown sand but lacking the normally ubiquitous palm trees.

Visitors to the courthouse approached or left the building like flies swarming around a carcass: there was no set path for pedestrians, and the footprints the visitors left littered the sandy ground. Drivers randomly parked their cars on patches of brown grass.

Looking at the building, it evoked no discernible style, just a mere square structure. One could easily infer that nothing had changed in Obodo for more than forty years. It reminded me of the dire situation at the medical clinic. As much as the clinic worried me, I left those thoughts behind when I entered the courtroom.

Inside, two sections were separated by a guardrail. Apart from the framed photographs of the Nigerian president and the governor of the state, the walls were barren. A magistrate sat behind a big desk on a dais. Although the courtroom had open windows, warm, musty air pervaded the space. It felt as if the legal authority had locked out fresh air.

Sitting higher than everyone, the bespectacled magistrate focused on her desk. Looking at her from where I stood, it was hard for me to guess her age, but one thing stood out: as she read the documents on her desk, profuse sweat escaping from the sides of her judge's wig dripped onto her black robe. She didn't seem to care, wiping away her sweat with the back of her hand.

With stern faces, lawyers and their clients sitting close to the guardrail whispered among themselves. Occasionally they looked at the magistrate, as if they were tired of waiting for the proceedings to begin.

Armed police officers brought four men in handcuffs and shackles into the courtroom. The men wore dirty shorts and stained polo shirts. They were barefoot. The police officers stood next to their prisoners as the bailiff, an elderly man in oversized khaki pants and a white shirt, said, "The magistrate court is now in session. Her Worship, Magistrate Christina Ozoka, is presiding."

I scanned the courtroom for Ejike but couldn't find him. While searching, I missed the introduction of my case and the identification of the prisoners.

"You have no representation?" the magistrate asked as she looked at the four men. When no one spoke, she added, "How do you plead?"

"Guilty, Your Worship," the four men said. After a few seconds, one of the men said, "Your Worship, Ejike paid us to do it." A mumble erupted from every corner of the courtroom.

"Order, order!" the bailiff shouted. The courtroom noise died down.

"Where's Ejike?" the magistrate asked.

I waited for the police officers to inform the court about Ejike. After none of them spoke, I approached the guardrail. The bailiff used his hand to signal for me to halt. I stopped. The magistrate had ignored my approach until the bailiff stopped me. It was then that she looked at me.

"Your Honor, Ejike is my cousin," I said. Turning to point at the four handcuffed men, I said, "He brought these men to my house to kill my sister and me. They came with an automatic rifle. Five men should stand before you, not four."

"Enough. You're in *my* courtroom," the magistrate said.

"I want Ejike to pay for his crime, Your Honor."

"You disrespect this court. Address me appropriately, mister," she said, her voice raised.

"I'm sorry, Your Honor. Damn! I can't stop screwing up. Forgive me, Your Worship." I looked at the magistrate's crinkled face. Steam exuded out of her pores instead of sweat. Her sharp gaze felt as if it was cutting through my body.

"You traveled to your damn America and came home to insult everyone. I'm dropping all the charges. Bailiff, next case." The magistrate hit the table with her gavel so hard that it broke. How did she know that I had returned from America? I didn't want to guess, but I could smell the odor of rotten justice.

"You can't dismiss the fucking case. Are you paid off too?" I asked.

"One more word, I'll have you arrested," the magistrate said.

"You're a disgrace to the court. Go ahead, arrest me. I've been inside your fucking jail. Shot at by your friend," I shouted.

"Arrest him," the magistrate yelled. I looked at the police officers, but they looked away. No one obeyed her order.

"I'm going home, Your Dishonorable," I said. She pounded on her table as she shouted curse words at me.

While walking out of the courtroom, I felt my body temperature rise. My hands shook so hard and my legs wobbled so much that I was afraid to drive.

When loud noises erupted behind me, I turned. The four barefoot men I saw earlier ran out of the building without handcuffs or shackles. Their jubilation infuriated me, and my thoughts went to my gun. Watching their smiling faces, I wanted revenge.

As the four men approached, I was prepared to receive their mockery. One of them walked up to me.

I held my breath when he said, "*Oga*, we're sorry. I'll never do bad things for money again. Please forgive us."

The rest added, "We're sorry, *oga*."

"We heard your brother is in Awka. The police officers there are hard," one said.

"Did you pay the magistrate to drop your case?" I asked.

"Ejike may have paid, but we didn't," another man said.

"Is that who bought your case dismissal in court today? I need to know." They looked at me for a while as if they didn't know what to say.

"*Oga*, we're sorry. Please forgive us," one of the men said. Begging appeared to be easier than telling the truth. I understood the ploy.

It took a while for me to exhale and let out all the hatred. Searching their faces for even a speck of honesty, I said, "Before you try to hurt anyone, ask yourself one question: what has the person done against you?"

"You're a wise man," one of the men said.

"What I told you has guided my life since childhood," I said. Their anxious-looking faces surprised me. "Never let your feet touch the grounds of my estate again."

"Unless we come to beg for money," one of the men said with a smile as they ran in different directions.

Ejike's absence and the failure of the local judicial system to indict him didn't diminish my life in any way. However, it raised my curiosity about how the police were handling serious crimes and about the court's indifference to the gravity of offenses. From my limited experience, courtroom protocol mattered more than the seriousness of the crime. A damning conclusion.

As I left the grounds of the court building, I called Ifeanyi, the man who had connections to the police. I needed to know where and when they would arraign Ejike for his crimes.

CHAPTER 32

I woke to a tranquil Thursday morning. There was normally nothing special about Thursday mornings in Obodo. However, this was the day when Ejike would be arraigned at the Anambra state high court in Awka, the capital city.

I paced around the bedroom in anticipation. As much as I wanted Ejike to be punished for his crime, I didn't want to see him in the courtroom.

My stomach ached all morning. I skipped breakfast. Instead of eating, I watched my sister play with her food. She was probably going through the same apprehension I felt but wouldn't admit it. Acting tough was her game.

After I showered and ironed my pants and shirt, I dressed. When I discovered I was wearing a wrinkled tie, I took it off and decided to go without one.

Adaku and I drove to Awka with Ifeanyi, who had become an integral part of our family since he came to our rescue the night we were attacked. Even Adaku now tolerated him.

My phone rang as we were entering the court building. I watched Adaku and Ifeanyi ascend the steps while I stayed outside to take the call.

"Hello. Hello," I said. I was impatient because of our late arrival. I didn't want to miss the court proceedings.

"I'm trying to reach Dr. Nwaku," a female voice said.

"I'm Afam Nwaku."

"Good. This is Prophetess Ofuluzo. I want you at my temple by noon for prayers. I saw a vision in my sleep. You've been mean to your people. God is giving you a chance to repent. If you don't change your ways, you'll die." I wondered how she knew my phone number.

"Madam prophetess, I need to be in court. Have a good day." I hung up. The phone rang again.

"What now?" I asked, irritated.

"God has ordered you to withdraw the case against your brother," she said.

"I have no brother. Goodbye."

"I'm warning you. You'll die at midnight if you fail God."

"Tell God I'm sorry. I'll be in bed at that time."

"That's blasphemy. You'll die tonight."

"If you're one of Ejike's messengers, a killer prophetess, kiss my ass. I'll watch him hang." I hung up.

I walked into a full courtroom to join Adaku and Ifeanyi. When I thought about the silly phone call I had received, I smiled, and Adaku looked at me curiously.

Two prosecutors for the state sat behind a table, and the defendant's lawyers' table was empty. Two police officers brought Ejike into the courtroom in shackles, his stump covered with a tight wrap. He looked around the courtroom as he approached a chair, avoiding direct eye contact with me.

Ejike's wife, his sister Ifeaku with a wooden cross around her neck, and five men walked into the courtroom and sat together. His wife looked around the courtroom and when our eyes met, she looked away. Ifeaku hung her head. It was after Ejike's wife sat down that I thought about the voice of the prophetess. It struck me then. That voice. I remembered it from the day she came to my house to plead her husband's case. I looked in her direction and smiled. She frowned.

It didn't take long before the bailiff entered the courtroom. He stood close to the side entrance door until he approached the judge's bench and said, "All rise. His Lordship Orakwue Ikpe is presiding." The judge motioned for the proceedings to begin.

"My Lord, we have a case of attempted murder using a firearm by one Mister Ejike Otigbuaku from Obodo. He attacked the home of his cousin in the middle of the night with a police-issued automatic rifle. He had four accomplices charged in a separate court. His cousin chopped off his hand to save himself and his sister from his murderous intent."

The judge interrupted the lead lawyer. "Enough. I've heard enough. This is an arraignment. How does the defendant plead?" Ejike rose to his feet and stammered. His legs wobbled, and he held his chair. "How does the defendant plead?" The judge waited for an answer, his hand touching everything on his desk. "Do you have a lawyer, mister?"

"No, sir," Ejike said. He looked at his wife, as if he needed clarification, before he added, "I don't have money for a lawyer."

"We'll enter no plea until you get legal representation," the judge said.

Police officers pulled Ejike up from his chair as he struggled to wipe away his tears.

"I plead guilty. Please spare my life," Ejike shouted.

"So you plead guilty to all the charges against you?" the judge asked.

"Yes, My Lord. Please spare my life."

"Hang him," I shouted, walking away. Adaku and Ifeanyi followed me.

Ejike's son, who was walking into the courtroom, lunged at me with a red pocketknife. I ducked. His knife scraped my forearm before it fell on the floor. Adaku dove for the knife. When Ejike's son tried to wrestle the knife from her, she stabbed his hand. He threw two punches at her with his bloodied hand before I kicked his legs hard. His knees buckled, and he landed on his face. Blood gushed from his wound as he laid on the floor screaming obscenities. When I saw blood dripping from my forearm, I took the pocketknife from Adaku and lifted my hand to stab Ejike's son. Ifeanyi held my hand.

"You're a fucking bitch. I'll stab you to death," Ejike's son yelled. I raised my foot to kick his face but stopped when I remembered I was in a courtroom with witnesses.

Police officers rushed to where we stood. Adaku raised her hands. I couldn't lift my arms as my hands trembled with rage. They ignored Adaku and me.

Another narrow escape, I thought, as police officers restrained and handcuffed Ejike's son.

"We'll not arrest you. It was self-defense," one of the police officers said to Adaku. She didn't respond to their comment. She hugged me and held on.

"I'll kill all of you. You're dead," Ejike's son shouted as they led him away from the courtroom, bleeding. Adaku inspected my arm and shook her head. I saw tears in her eyes.

"You're a lucky man," Ifeanyi said.

"I hope it's the last time someone will test my luck," I replied.

Looking around the courtroom, I saw two men restraining Ejike's wife and Ifeaku as they screamed obscenities at me.

"Kill me. I have nothing left to live for," Ejike's wife sobbed.

Ejike lowered his head and used his only hand to wipe his tears. When he raised his head, his slanted eyes were fixed on me, his lips pressed tightly together. With his crinkled face, Ejike looked as if he was in physical pain.

The judge ignored what was happening. He didn't move from his chair or comment about it. He carried on as if nothing had happened.

Instead of running away from the violence, most of the people in the courtroom had gathered to watch. I was shocked. What had happened to my country?

"You still need legal representation for your sentencing," the judge said after Ejike's son was led out of the courtroom and everyone returned to their seats. Ejike nodded. The judge gaveled to end the session and walked out of the courtroom.

What worried me as I stepped out of the courtroom, which had no metal detector, was my anger toward Ejike and his family. I felt no sympathy for my first cousin, who had occasionally shared my bed with me when we were young. I wanted him and his family dead.

Adaku, Ifeanyi, and I sat in the car for a long time with my torn shirt tied around my wound before we left the court premises. We didn't look at each other or speak. I knew what was going through my mind, and it was frightening enough. I wanted revenge. I didn't want to know what Adaku was thinking.

CHAPTER 33

For two days I was alone in the house. Adaku had gone to her home to clean the dust. That was what she said. I had volunteered to help her, but she refused my offer. The first day I was alone, the house was quiet and I slept well.

A loud crashing noise woke me on the second night. For the rest of the night I stayed awake with the revolver under my pillow and the rifle next to me. Although I pointed the gun barrel away from me, when I rolled around in bed, I found the rifle was pointed at me. My heart raced faster than an airplane taking off from a runway when I saw my own loaded gun pointing at me. But my fear from the loaded gun was quickly overtaken by something else.

The noise coming from the ceiling sounded as if something was strolling from one end of the roof to another. At times it sounded like something was tumbling around in the attic. What could be putting on a gymnastics show up there? I checked all the rooms on the second floor of the house. None of them had been breached. I even went outside with my loaded gun and a flashlight through a side door to look around. I found nothing on the roof. Could it be the ghosts of my parents taunting me?

On the first Friday of December, the sun rose to caress the stifling early morning air. Walking around the house wearing only my briefs, sweat trickled down from my head and face. I placed a towel around my shoulders, but it didn't offer my warm body any relief.

When I opened all the curtains and windows in the house, the sun revealed the small specks of dust resting on the dark surfaces of the rooms. I inspected all the rooms in the house, including the closets. In the kitchen, I opened all the cabinet doors and looked in all the drawers. Small, oblong objects on the floor inside the pantry attracted my attention. I turned the ceiling lights on and found a tablespoonful of discolored rice. From how discolored it was, I guessed that it dated back to when my parents had lived in the house.

After inspecting all the rooms without finding the source of the noise, I became worried. I took a walk outside to look at the roof again, now in the daylight, from all sides. From my limited view, I couldn't find any unsecured roofing material. Wondering if the noises were new, I remembered that I had attributed every noise I'd heard in the house before to Adaku. Could it be that the noises hadn't come from her?

I took a longer walk to the major road leading to our property; the same road that had welcomed me home. Men and women walking along the roadside looked at me curiously. I heard their murmurs as they passed. Unfortunately, none spoke to me, except for one old man who hobbled by, stooped and low. His gray facial hair had a tinge of brown, and his eyeglasses had only one lens. I wondered how he could see through that smudged lens and how he'd lost the other.

After the old man passed, he turned around and approached me.

"You're still living? I heard you had died," he said.

"I'm alive. You can touch me," I said. I wondered if he'd heard that Ejike had killed me.

"You look younger. Unless my eyes and palm wine deceive me," the old man said.

"What's your name, sir?" I asked, trying hard not to chuckle at him.

"I'm Ikuku Obikwelu, the wind that no man can trap."

"Really?" I tried to say more but couldn't hold in my laughter.

The old man walked on as if he had taken offense. I ran after him.

"My apologies, sir. I didn't mean to offend you," I said.

"You changed. I remember your kindness to me years ago," Ikuku said.

"You've mistaken me for my father."

He came closer to me, looked at my face intently, touched it, and shook his head.

305

"You look the same to me."

"I look like my father," I said.

"If you look like him, act like him," Ikuku said.

"I don't know what you mean."

Several people walking by slowed to listen to us. I looked at the most curious ones and smiled.

"Your father was the nicest man I knew. Kind to a fault, sometimes. I need to go, my stomach is sending me notices," Ikuku said. I wondered how the people in Obodo became so colorful with their words.

"Fix your eyeglasses. It'll help you see better," I said.

"Now an insult. Ikuku doesn't take orders." He walked on.

"It would help you see better," I repeated.

"I see better than you. I hear better than you. Advice for you: Know everybody in Obodo if you're the man in charge of the Nwaku palace. When you're in that big house, you won't know what the villagers know or see what they see. They'll see evil first, before you do."

"I'm grateful for your advice. What has Ikuku seen and what has he heard?"

"I warned a young man not to cast stones at your house and urinate on your land, a sacred ground. He abused me with his tongue. He didn't know your land is sacred," Ikuku said.

"What's sacred about it? My father never told me," I said.

"Your ancestors consecrated the land to *Olisaebuluwa*, the mightiest of the gods. That's why the land was never farmed."

"But grasslands are not farmed in Obodo."

"Who made them grasslands? The spirits that own the land. My son, you're the caretaker for the gods," Ikuku said and stroked his beard. He laughed as he left me.

I returned to the house, looked around the massive grasslands surrounding it, and thought of the burgeoning responsibilities entrusted to me.

# # #

Close to noon, after another thorough search of the house without finding a bogeyman, I left to visit the medical clinic. I thought about taking Ifeanyi with me but decided against it out of concern for the effect the visit could have on him. Although I had stayed away from the clinic for a while, I had been communicating with Udeaja by email frequently. From our communications, I had learned more about the clinic board's activities than he realized.

On reaching the clinic, I found a locked gate. I discovered a small side entrance that would lead me in. Four white Toyota Camrys were parked at a hidden corner and resembled the ones that had come to my house. I ascended the steps to the reception room. It was empty, but I heard voices coming from one of the inner rooms. I knocked on the door and waited for a response. The voices inside went silent. Instead of knocking again, I opened the door. I knew I was an uninvited guest, but I was in my hometown, the land belonged to me, and the clinic belonged to all of us.

In addition to all the clinic board members I had met in my house, the room contained a middle-aged man with graying hair who sat apart from the rest. His gray plaid blazer, made with a heavy worsted wool material, appeared bigger than his shoulders. Judging from his profuse sweating, the hot, humid air must have been slowly cooking him.

"Doc, are we expecting you?" Udeaja asked as he looked at the other board members. No one spoke or smiled. From their tensed lower eyelids, some of which were wrinkled, and the slanted eyebrows on others, I could see they were angry.

"No, you're not. I was just passing by. Sorry to interrupt your meeting." I walked toward the middle-aged man sitting away from the rest and extended my hand. "We haven't met. I'm Dr. Nwaku."

"Dr. Ikedioro." He shook my hand reluctantly.

"You're the once-a-week man?" I asked with a smile.

"That's what the clinic could afford," Udeaja said. Dr. Ikedioro looked on.

The rest of the board members glanced at one another and then at me. As I engaged each one, holding their gazes, I let my smile linger.

"This clinic needs a doctor every day," I said. "Patients don't choose a convenient day to get sick. A friend lost his wife after her visit to your clinic. Maybe it was a day your doctor didn't work."

"There's no money to pay him," Udeaja said, standing.

"We don't have the money to pay him," Esther repeated. "You're a troublemaker. Leave us alone."

308

Her statement made me chuckle. It made no sense. Walking closer to Udeaja, who appeared unsure of what to say or do, I said, "I'll pay for his services." When I thought about what I had said, I regretted it. I hadn't asked how much his salary was.

Dr. Ikedioro's face lit up. He stood and shook my hand more firmly than before. He tried to walk back to his chair but returned to shake my hand again. A firmer handshake each time, as if his confidence was gradually improving.

"When do I start?" Dr. Ikedioro asked.

"We've not accepted the offer," Udeaja said. He looked at the rest of the board members as if he needed their opinion. None of them spoke.

Approaching each member, I asked, "Do you accept my offer?" None of them answered until I went to Esther.

"It's a government facility. We need approval from the state," Esther said.

"Get it. Tell them I'm cleaning and remodeling too," I said.

"What changed your mind?" Udeaja asked.

"Finding out how incompetent care killed my friend's wife and left him a broken man helped move me."

"It's people like you who should help this town," Udeaja said.

"My father gave you the land. Do you want my blood? Well, let's start by putting together your yearly budget. I'll forget about the past."

"Thank you," Esther said. For the first time I saw a smile from her.

As I was walking toward the door, Udeaja said, "You can stay."

With my back turned to them, I said, "It's not important to me. The only thing I need is the cost of everything I promised." I took more steps toward the exit before I added, "I need a full report on what happened to Ifeanyi Muo's wife. She visited your clinic, received treatment, and died. Someone has to be held accountable for what happened to her."

"We'll put the budget together, my brother, but I'm not a doctor. Our doctor will address your concern," Udeaja said. I guessed he'd remembered that I was his African brother. Dr. Ikedioro didn't respond to my request.

"Dr. Ikedioro, when should I expect your report?" I asked.

"I don't answer to you. Your big estate doesn't impress me. Ask your friend to come to us with a request," Dr. Ikedioro said. It was the same Nigerian doctor's arrogance about patients' medical records. The same treatment meted out to me at the Specialist Hospital.

"Unless you're hiding something, I need that report," I said.

"Your American training is going to your head. You order people around, abuse them, parade yourself around. It stops with me," he replied.

"We'll find the information you need. I'll ask our clinical director to help," Udeaja said.

"If you do so, I'll quit," Dr. Ikedioro said, approaching me. "I'll not accept any money from you. Fuck you and your money."

"We'll accept anything you offer to the clinic," Udeaja said.

"You should employ another doctor. Dr. Ikedioro is not a good fit for our town," I said.

"That's why they tried to kill you," said Dr. Ikedioro. "I wish they'd succeeded."

"We don't feel the same way," Esther said.

I watched as Dr Ikedioro frowned and his breathing quickened. As he sat back down in his chair fidgeting and stewing, I smiled at him.

CHAPTER 34

On a beautiful sunny day, Adaku and I sat on the balcony, looking at our food instead of eating it. Splayed on the breakfast table were my favorites: a plate of roasted plantain, a bowl of thick custard, and a vegetable omelet. Several times I tried to dish out my food, but my appetite had deserted me.

Something troubled my mind, but I couldn't name it. Disturbingly, it felt as if something bad was about to happen. Adaku and I sat without eating or talking. It appeared as if whatever troubled me was also troubling her.

A white Toyota van drove to the front of our house. Seeing the van Adaku left in a hurry, as if she was expecting it. She didn't excuse herself or give me time to ask questions.

When she reached the van, her whisper to the driver raised my suspicion. So many terrible things had happened when we had guests that I couldn't help but shift in my seat.

When Adaku left, the driver, a young man probably in his late twenties, leaned against his vehicle. I wondered if his white dashiki would pick up the red dust.

When she rejoined me, I held on to my glass of water and waited to hear about our guest. She looked at me and smiled, making no attempt to share any information.

That elusive concern I had lingered on, but watching my sister hurriedly finish her breakfast I felt confused.

"You're leaving?" I asked.

"I don't know what you mean," she said.

Her eyes focused on the road leading to our house. Instead of talking, she shuffled her feet, and her trembling hands dropped her fork. As her fidgeting worsened, I became concerned. I wondered if someone had threatened her life.

"What's going on?" I asked, smiling to mask my fear.

"I'm going to Enugu," Adaku said.

"That must be it. You're scared of Enugu. I'll go with you."

"That'll mess up everything."

What could I mess up? I looked at the white van for a clue about her trip and saw only the driver pacing around. Even if I wanted to travel with Adaku, I doubted if the driver would wait for me to get ready.

"Your driver is as restless as you," I said. Adaku looked at me and smiled.

"I'm doing it for you," she said as she stood.

"You're doing what for me?"

"You'll find out eventually," she said as she left the terrace.

Looking at our breakfast table after Adaku left in the white van, I realized that we hadn't eaten much. After cleaning up the terrace, I returned to the bedroom. Sitting at my father's table, I turned on my laptop. My mind wandered to what Adaku had said: "I'm doing it for you."

When my fingers finally found the keyboard, I typed, *Returning to Africa: My Permanent Home.* I sat for another five minutes, trying to decide what I should write for the first line of my memoir. Resting my fingers on the keyboard, my mind wandered to Elisha and my children.

With several thoughts swirling, a sudden chill traveled through me. As hard as I tried to shake it off, it felt as if a heavy blanket of loneliness was draped over my body. My eyes couldn't focus enough to read the words I had typed.

A few minutes passed. In that solemn mood, a loud crashing noise from the attic stirred me. With my heart racing, I ran to the corner and picked up my rifle. After closing the bedroom door, I turned around and ran to the bed. Lifting the mattress, I retrieved the machete hidden under it. The machete that had saved my life. With gun and knife, I braced myself for what waited outside the bedroom.

When I reached the end of the hallway, I looked up and found that the small attic door was locked. From the paint at the corners of the door, it looked like it hadn't been opened for a long time. As much as I dreaded going in, I wouldn't be able to sleep without knowing what lived there.

I found an aluminum ladder, which was the easiest part of my adventure. It was finding the courage to climb into the dark attic that took some time.

When I opened the small attic door, it squeaked and frightened me. A gush of balmy air escaped and bathed my body. It felt like I had stepped into a hot oven. After summoning my courage, I flashed my cell-phone light into the dark spaces inside the attic. When I found nothing out of place, my hand steadied.

I became more confident that the attic was uninhabited, and I was about to end my search when I heard a hissing. When I pointed the flashlight at the rafters, I saw a pair of eyes looking at me. I was vulnerable up here, confronting something that probably had better vision in the dark than me. I pulled my machete out of its sheath and retreated to the attic opening, my legs and hands shaking. I descended slowly, afraid of falling, eyes focused on the opening.

In my haste, I'd left the attic door open. Standing in the hallway, I thought about how to close it. The house guest peeked its head through the opening and descended the ladder. Its tan-colored, six-foot body adorned with black diamond-shaped markings slid down the ladder with ease. Seeing that it was a boa constrictor, I hurried to the ground floor to open all the doors leading out of the house.

I had difficulty deciding where to hide while still being able to see the snake. I had an eerie feeling that

I could be wrong about the type of snake it was. I watched it slide down the steps and leave through the front door in no particular rush.

How had it gotten into the attic? Were there more? I had so many questions that I didn't know the answers to. After closing all the doors leading into the house, I closed the attic door. Leaning on the balcony rail, I watched the snake slither into the dry grasslands. As nature had designed it, the snake blended in with its environment. When I thought about where the boa constrictor had come from, I remembered the night Ejike had broken the front door down. The snake had probably crawled into the house from the front entrance while it was missing a door. I felt relieved that the last vestige of Ejike's invasion of my house was gone, or so I hoped.

# # #

Quiet returned to my house. While I was in my bedroom, I could hear the churning of the refrigerator in the kitchen, a noise that came at regular intervals. After a while, the refrigerator noise became as annoying as a car with a clanking engine. My mind fixated on the sound until I fell into a deep sleep on that beautiful afternoon.

I wasn't sure how long I'd slept when the loud voices woke me. In my sleepy state, I heard multiple voices in the house. It felt as if I was dreaming. Worse yet, I was too weak to react. My heart began to race. When I heard, "Daddy, we're here," I knew it was a dream. I felt that my eyes were open, so I closed them tighter to dive back into that dream. It

317

was only there that I could hear my daughter's voice again and feel her hug.

Not long after I'd closed my eyes, a hand shook my body. One of the people who had threatened me must have gained access to my bedroom. They wanted me to watch as they killed me. Why kill a man in his sleep? That wouldn't be much fun.

When I opened my eyes, I saw Obialu sitting on the bed next to me. The sight of her beautiful smile and the feel of her hand resting on me made my heart race faster. In seconds, tears flowed from my eyes as if they were water spigots. I looked at the faces standing close to my bed, and more tears flowed.

The faces of Ikenna, Obialu, Elisha, and Adaku had a surprising effect on me. I could see the faces of my mother and father behind them. At that moment, my family was complete, as my father had always wanted. The Nwaku clan, on our consecrated ground in Obodo, with me as the patriarch to oversee the undisputed land of my ancestors. There was nothing left for the voice in me to say. From that moment, all the decisions and pronouncements belonged to me.

"Welcome home. Welcome home to Obodo. Welcome home to our Africa," I said to my family.

Everyone sat on the bed. As the five of us hugged, I smiled. When I looked at my sister's face, I found my mother's smile, and when I looked at my son's face, I saw my father's happiness. We were complete in that bedroom. All of us, the ones who were alive, the ones who refused to die, and the dead. We had different experiences in our lives, but we would always share one experience in common: love.

Elisha looked at me intently. She kissed my lips and cried as we held each other.

My son ruffled my thinning hair the way I used to ruffle his when he was little and said, "We love you, Daddy." He had not called me that in more than twenty years, and it felt good being the patriarch of the Nwaku family.

CHAPTER 35

Elisha and I sat on the loveseat in the family room, holding hands. She leaned her head on my shoulder as we watched our children walk from one corner of the family room to another, looking at the photographs with my sister. I heard chuckles from time to time as they critiqued the outfits of yesteryear. In Obodo, some would say that happiness is as elusive as a ghost, but I found it that day with my family. Sitting with my wife, I could feel the happiness with my quiet heart and tears of elation.

It was love that had made us strong, and it was the same love that had betrayed us. When I looked at the beautiful woman who rested her head on my shoulder, I saw my happiness. It was not the birds' songs that tickled my heart but the feeling inside me that Elisha still loved me. It was not the beauty of the rising sun that made me feel warm inside; it was the love burning in me. I resigned myself to love.

Elisha said, "I couldn't love you without your soul, and Africa had your soul. To love you, I knew I had to love Africa to be one with your soul. Here, I'm with you in Africa, our paradise. Guess what? You belong to me, and I belong to you and Africa."

"Well, I should give myself credit for all the phone calls I made to Elisha and the begging," Adaku said. "I couldn't imagine my brother's happiness without his family."

"Sis, it has always been you who deserves everything our parents left for us."

"You mean everything they left for you," Adaku said.

"I still believe that Afam should've accepted the CEO job," said Elisha. "I wanted to be respected, to be among the top in Boston."

"Happiness and big titles don't always go together. I'm happy here," I said.

"It's hard to know where I belong, but I know that my soul will always be with yours. We belong together. I might have made mistakes when I was angry, but I believe that you'll forgive me," Elisha said.

"There is nothing to forgive. I'll cherish each day you're with me."

"We're bound together by providence, and we share love by our desires," Adaku said.

There was nothing to add to her statement, which was draped in the wisdom of my people.

"Are we obligated to Africa too?" Ikenna asked. He looked at Obialu with a smile.

"We share the same destiny." I said.

# # #

Elisha and I were two happy souls playing in the field of contentment. That was where we started when we left the house that afternoon. We held hands and wandered into the grasslands of our estate with no destination. We left it to our love to lead us. Love has its own sensibilities. There is no direction in the journey of love and no compass to guide you.

We skipped and wrestled in the grasslands. We kissed and fondled in the African sun. We laughed and cried in our paradise. Words were not needed, just our souls with their secret messages.

When Elisha and I reached the entrance to our estate, we leaned on the fence to watch people and cars go by. They turned to look at us, mumbled, and waved as they left the two happy souls to be.

An old man walked by. He rubbed his eyes twice before he spoke to us.

"Eya! Eya! That's the sight of a happy man. Mama *oyibo*, thank you, thank you. Our brother has found happiness." I wondered if the old man knew me.

"What did he say?" Elisha asked.

I turned to the old man and said, "She's an Obodo mother, not a foreign mother." The three of us laughed.

"I need to learn your language," Elisha said.

"The only language that matters is the one my heart understands, and that's your love," I told her.

323

The way Elisha kissed me made the old man blush. He left us when he realized that the only thing we needed was each other. And Africa.

CHAPTER 36

A few minutes before midnight, with a full moon hanging in the sky, my mind was inundated with contemplation. I knocked on Adaku's door to wake her. She responded immediately, as if she'd been waiting for me.

"Afam, you can't sleep either?" she asked.

"I have a reason to be awake," I said.

"I know that Elisha and the kids surprised you."

"It was good for me. You can't imagine how happy you made me."

Adaku came closer and looked at me as if she was looking at a stranger. "What's going on, Afam? You've got a gun and a knife. I thought our problems were over."

"We're going out."

"Who's going with you? Not me. I'm tired of trying to stay alive." She looked at me more closely.

"You're going with me," I said.

"I'm tired. I'm sorry, I can't."

We must have made enough noise to wake the whole house. Elisha, Obialu, and Ikenna joined us.

"Afam, why do you have a gun?" Elisha asked as she rubbed my head.

"It looks like Daddy is going out to hunt for our meal," Obialu said. We laughed.

"We're going to the river. Adaku has to understand her value to the family," I said.

"I can't go with you. It's late, and I'm afraid," Adaku said.

"You be careful out there," Elisha said.

"Who said I'm going?" Adaku asked.

"Please stop, sis. If our father wanted me to be like him, he would've kept me at home, not sent me to America. Our father was a wise man who wanted the best for his children and his hometown."

"Why are you talking about this in the middle of the night?" Adaku asked.

"We need some sleep," Ikenna said.

"Sis, there is nothing I am that you're not or even better. It has always been you who deserves what I was given. I'm returning what belongs to you. The Nwaku estate belongs to us, not me. You've been its caretaker for decades. No one should deprive you of that right because you're a woman."

"Do you have malaria? Is something wrong with you? You're the patriarch of our family," Adaku said. I shook my head. My family had wide eyes when listening to me.

"I've returned home the way our father envisioned. A changed man. My role is to help

326

elevate healthcare delivery in Obodo. That's what Papa wanted for me."

We looked at each other in silence, but we knew what the other was thinking.

When I began my sojourn, I knew I wasn't perfect but I sought perfection. When I succeeded professionally, I knew it came from the strength my ancestors bestowed on me genetically and by their wisdom. Where I failed, I knew it was my fault. On that night I was cleansed, I saw darkness by the river, but I couldn't understand its significance. Through inherent wisdom, I finally realized that it wasn't me who had the gift in the family to be a shaman but my sister, Adaku.

# # #

Adaku finally agreed with my request, and we left for the river. I traveled with her as her guide and protector.

We sat at the edge of the Iyiofolo River, Adaku and me. Harmattan haze dimmed the moonlight, and the cool air dried our lips. When we dipped our feet in the water, a sudden chill traveled through my body. Leaning forward, I filled my cupped hands with water and splashed it on Adaku's face. Her body shivered, but her chattering teeth didn't stop her recitation. I repeated the steps stipulated in the book as my cooled hands trembled. When the ritual was over, the wind subsided, the haze dissipated, and, as if a light switch was turned on, the moon brightened.

When Adaku stood up, my cold feet remained in the river and trembled. She held my hand and lifted me up. I stood by the banks of the Iyiofolo River with my sister, but no darkness befell us.

When Adaku led the way, the way she used to do when we were children, I did not follow. I pulled her back, and we walked side by side. We were equals in every aspect of our lives, and that was the way it was supposed to be. Forever.

THE END

ABOUT THE AUTHOR

Fidelis O. Mkparu is a Nigerian immigrant to the US, and in this novel, he sets out to speak to his experiences and those of his fellow immigrants. He is a professor of Medicine at Northeast Ohio Medical University and a senior attending cardiologist at Aultman Hospital and Mercy Medical Center in Canton, Ohio. Previously, he was a Spaulding fellow at Massachusetts General Hospital at Harvard Medical School. His preceding novels *include Love's Affliction* and *Tears Before Exaltation* (CIPA EVVY Awards Winner, Literary & Contemporary Fiction 2018).

Lansford Guy
THE GUARDIANS

Wayne E. & Sean P. Haley
AN APOLOGY TO LUCIFER

David Kruh
INSEPARABLE

Shawn Mackey
THIS WORLD OF LOVE AND STRIFE

Jeanne Matthews
DEVIL BY THE TAIL

C.K. McDonough
STOKING HOPE

Phillip Otts
A STORM BEFORE THE WAR
THE SOUL OF A STRANGER
THE PRICE OF BETRAYAL

Erika Rummel
THE INQUISITOR'S NIECE
THE ROAD TO GESUALDO
EVITA AND ME

Vanessa Ryan
THE TROUBLE WITH MURDER

Larry F. Sommers
PRICE OF PASSAGE

J. M. Stephen
NOD
INTO THE FAIRY FOREST
RISE OF THE HIDDEN PRINCE
SILENCE AND RUPTURED WATERS
THE RISE OF RUNES AND SHIELDS

Jessica Stilling
THE WEARY GOD OF ANCIENT TRAVELERS
BETWEEN BEFORE AND AFTER
AFTER THE BARRICADES (*May 2023*)

Claryn Vaile
GHOST TOUR

Felicia Watson
WHERE THE ALLEGHENY MEETS THE MONONGAHELA
WE HAVE MET THE ENEMY
SPOOKY ACTION AT A DISTANCE
THE RISKS OF DEAD RECKONING
WHERE NO ONE WILL SEE (*Apr 2023*)

Daniel A. Willis
IMMORTAL BETRAYAL
IMMORTAL DUPLICITY
IMMORTAL REVELATION
PROPHECY OF THE AWAKENING
FARHI AND THE CRYSTAL DOME
VICTORIA II
THE CHILDREN OF VICTORIA II

Joyce Yarrow
SANDSTORM